ALSO BY ED MCBAIN

THE 87TH PRECINCT NOVELS

Cop Hater • The Mugger • The Pusher (1956)

The Con Man • Killer's Choice (1957)

Killer's Payoff • Killer's Wedge •
    Lady Killer (1958)

'Til Death • King's Ransom (1959)

Give the Boys a Great Big Hand • The Heckler •
    See Them Die (1960)

Lady, Lady, I Did It! (1961)

The Empty Hours • Like Love (1962)

Ten Plus One (1963)

Ax (1964)

He Who Hesitates • Doll (1965)

Eighty Million Eyes (1966)

Fuzz (1968)

Shotgun (1969)

Jigsaw (1970)

Hail, Hail, the Gang's All Here (1971)

Sadie When She Died • Let's Hear It for
    the Deaf Man (1972)

Hail to the Chief (1973)

Bread (1974)

Blood Relatives (1975)

So Long As You Both Shall Live (1976)

Long Time No See (1977)

Calypso (1979)

Ghosts (1980)

Heat (1981)

Ice (1983)

Lightning (1984)

Eight Black Horses (1985)

Poison • Tricks (1987)

Lullaby (1989)

Vespers (1990)

Widows (1991)
Kiss (1992)
Mischief (1993)
And All Through the House (1994)
Romance (1995)
Nocturne (1997)
The Big Bad City (1999)
The Last Dance (2000)

THE MATTHEW HOPE NOVELS

Goldilocks (1978)
Rumpelstiltskin (1981)
Beauty and the Beast (1982)
Jack and the Beanstalk (1984)
Snow White and Rose Red (1985)
Cinderella (1986)
Puss in Boots (1987)
The House That Jack Built (1988)
Three Blind Mice (1990)
Mary, Mary (1993)
There Was a Little Girl (1994)
Gladly the Cross-Eyed Bear (1996)
The Last Best Hope (1998)

OTHER NOVELS

The Sentries (1965)
Where There's Smoke • Doors (1975)
Guns (1976)
Another Part of the City (1986)
Downtown (1991)
Driving Lessons (2000)
Candyland (2001)

Money, Money, Money

A NOVEL OF THE 87TH PRECINCT

Ed McBain

Simon & Schuster
New York   London   Toronto
Sydney   Singapore

SIMON & SCHUSTER
Rockefeller Center
1230 Avenue of the Americas
New York, NY 10020

SIMON & SCHUSTER and colophon are registered trademarks of
Simon & Schuster, Inc.
For information about special discounts for bulk purchases,
please contact Simon & Schuster Special Sales:
1-800-456-6798 or business@simonandschuster.com
Book design by Ellen R. Sasahara
Manufactured in the United States of America
1 3 5 7 9 10 8 6 4 2
Library of Congress Cataloging-in-Publication Data
McBain, Ed.
Money, money, money : a novel of the 87th Precinct /
Ed McBain.
p.   cm.
1. 87th Precinct (Imaginary place)—Fiction.
2. Police—United States—Fiction.   I. Title.
PS3515.U585 M6 2001
813'.54—dc21   2001041162

ISBN 0-7432-2406-X

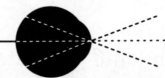

**This Large Print Book carries the
Seal of Approval of N.A.V.H.**

This—as always and forever—is for my wife,
Dragica Dimitrijević-Hunter

The city in these pages is imaginary.
The people, the places are all fictitious.
Only the police routine is based on
established investigatory technique.

Money,
Money,
Money

1.

The two men on the narrow dirt strip were both wearing white cotton pants and shirts. They stood beside the Piper Warrior III in broad daylight, waiting for Cass to hand over the locked aluminum suitcase. She gave it to the larger of the two men, and watched as they walked to a dark blue Mercedes-Benz glistening in the sun alongside the cornfield. The doors on either side slammed shut into the stillness, and then there was only the sound of insects racketing in the scraggly woods nearby.

Today was Pearl Harbor Day, the seventh of December, though it didn't much feel like it here in Guenerando, Mexico. Cass stood beside the airplane, sweating in the afternoon heat. She assumed there was money in the aluminum suitcase. She further assumed they were counting it over there in the Benz. She guessed that the cargo they'd be turning over in exchange for the money would be dope—either heroin or cocaine. She didn't care much either way. She stood in the shade of a spindly eucalyptus for almost forty minutes. At last, the two men came out of the Benz and handed the aluminum suitcase back to her. The one with the mustache was grinning. He handed her a long white business envelope with a rubber band around it. The other one watched solemnly, expectantly.

"Open it, *por favor*," the one with the mustache said.

She slipped the rubber band over her wrist, opened the envelope. There was a whole bunch of hundred-dollar bills in it.

"Count them," the serious one said.

She counted them.

There seemed to be ten thousand dollars in that envelope.

"For me?" she asked.

"*Para ti*," the one with the mustache said.

Damn if they weren't tipping her!

"Well thanks," she said. "*Muchas gracias.*"

"*Muchas gracias*," the one with the mustache said, grinning.

"*Muchas gracias*," the other one said. He was grinning now, too.

She couldn't help grinning herself.

The Baboquivari Mountains stretched northward to Kitt Peak. She flew low behind them. There was an anti-drug radar blimp in the sky over Fort Huachuca, but she had talked to other pilots who'd made the identical run dozens of times and who knew there was a so-called radar deficiency within plus-or-minus four degrees of the Kitt Peak Observatory. If she flew northward through "Gringo Pass," as the security gap was called, she could avoid detection. Besides, she'd be on the ground again near Avra Valley in eighteen minutes, so even in the unlikely event that she did show up on radar, there wouldn't be enough time for Customs planes to take off and chase her.

She didn't even know the last name of the man who was paying her $200,000 to do this little job for him, a quarter of it already in a bank account back East, where she'd rented an apartment within ten minutes of laying her hands on all that cash. She'd first met him in Eagle Branch, Texas, after one of her whistle-stop hops. What she did was fly light machinery, chickens in crates, melons, computer parts, sandals, what have you, all over Mexico in single-engine planes that were new when Zapata was still a boy. She'd occasionally been dating a Texas Ranger named Randolph Biggs, who made frequent trips to the Rio Grande where he helped the border patrol dissuade wetbacks from entering the sacred shores Cass had gone to the Persian Gulf to preserve and protect. In a bar one night, he'd introduced her to this guy named Frank. Kind of cute, but no last name. Just Frank. Frank's enough, he'd told her. She wondered now how much Randy had got for introducing him to a good pilot willing to take risks.

Instruments on the Warrior—such a mighty name for a single-engine light aircraft—were kin-

dergarten compared to the Chinook helicopter Cass
had flown during the Gulf War. Way they played it
on television back home, everything was a surgical
strike and nobody but the enemy suffered any casu-
alties, which of course was a crock. More hardware
up there in the Iraqi skies than she'd care to fly
through ever again in her lifetime. Little different
here in Arizona. Better pay, too.

She could see the lights of some quiet little desert
town down below in the near distance. What's a bad
girl like you doing in a nice place like this? she
wondered. Don't ask, don't tell. Man says fly four
shipments for me from Texas to Mexico, I'll give
you fifty grand a trip, two hundred total, you tell
him Mister, you've got a deal. This was the last of
the four trips. Rented the Warrior in San Antone,
nice little rig that handled like a dream. She'd
drop the plane off at the Phoenix airport later
tonight, as pre-arranged, hop a commercial liner
back East, be snug in her own apartment long before Christmas.

There.

Just below.

The signal light.

She flashed her own wing lights, dipped in lower
for a better look. When you came in low over Baghdad, it was to drop a smart bomb down Saddam
Hussein's chimney. Only trouble was they'd never
got to him, ended the war too damn soon. Well,
some you win, some you lose. She guessed.

She made a pass over the site, and then swung

around for her actual approach into the wind. A car's headlights came on, illuminating the strand of sand more fully. It was long and narrow. She watched the altimeter, pulled back on the flaps, leveled the pedals, glanced at the speedometer, this would be a piece of cake, douse your lights, boys, who needs them?

The strip here was level and flat, she felt the wheels touching, hit the brakes, lowered the flaps, and rolled along the beach to a full stop some twenty yards from where she'd seen the headlights. She cut the engine. The night was still. Immediately, she took the forty-five from the flap pocket of her jump suit.

She waited inside the cockpit, in the dark.

Kept waiting.

In the Gulf, she'd packed a forty-five automatic in a holster at her waist, case she got shot down, a distinct possibility. Lots of unfriendly people down there, waiting to get their hands on an American pilot, well, who could blame them? A female pilot, no less. Cassandra Jean Ridley, Lieutenant, U.S. Army, 714-56-32, that's all she was obliged to tell them. Didn't even have to say she was with the 101st Airborne. Here, she didn't know *who'd* be waiting for her. But she knew she had a hundred and fifty thousand coming for delivering this last suitcase. Money like that, a girl couldn't be too careful.

The rap on the window startled her.

She slid it back, right hand tight around the walnut grip of the Browning in her lap. She had to pee.

First thing you did when you got back to base was rush to barracks to pee. The male pilots just unzipped and pissed right where they'd landed.

"Welcome to Arizona," someone said.

Cheerful voice, the speaker nothing more than a blur in the dark. Two other men with him. She did not loosen her grip on the automatic. She was waiting for the single word that would tell her these were the people expecting the shipment. Buried any which way in whatever sentence they chose to use. But until she heard it, she sat right where she was with the gun in her hand and her finger inside the trigger guard.

"Nice night," one of the men said.

Try again, sweetheart.

"Hasn't been much rain."

Rain.

Bingo.

"Who's got my money?" she asked.

"Where's the suitcase?"

She released the door lever, climbed out onto the wing, and dropped to the ground, the gun dangling lazily, familiarly at her side.

"You won't need that," one of the men said.

"Gee, I hope not," she answered.

The desert air was a bit chilly. She wished she had on her flight jacket. One of the men was carrying a small leather case the size of a laptop. He placed it on the rim of the door, snapped it open. Another man turned on a penlight. She was looking at a lot of U.S. currency.

"A hundred and fifty thousand," one of the men said. "Final payment. As agreed."

"Where's the suitcase?" another man said.

"Mind if I count it first?" Cass said.

"Why don't we all just sit out here in the open till Customs spots us?" the third man said.

"Count it out for me," Cass said.

"Count it out for her," the first man said.

He was the one with the cheerful voice. He sounded a trifle impatient now, but she didn't give a damn *how* he sounded. One thing she'd learned in the Army was you didn't back off. Not on the ground, not in the air. So far all the risk these guys had taken was to sit here in Shit Wallow, Arizona, waiting for her. She was the one carrying the cargo, she was the one who *still* had the cargo sitting in a plane *she'd* rented. So go right ahead, she thought, *get* impatient. That's *my* money you're treating so casually there.

The one who'd mentioned Customs slipped the thick rubber band from one of the packets and looped it over his wrist. There was a small tattoo on the back of his left hand. Some kind of bird, looked like a hawk, wings spread wide, claws gripping a fish. He spread the bills to show her there weren't any pieces of newspaper cut to size in the bundle. Then he began counting them out loud, one by one, ". . . five, six, seven," Cass holding the gun, watching, listening, "eight, nine, ten, a thousand. One, two, three, four . . ."

On and on. There were fifty bills in the packet, all

of them hundred-dollar bills. When he counted out
the last bill, he rubber-banded the stack again, and
dropped it back into the leather case. There were
thirty packets of bills in all, each of them about
three-quarters of an inch thick. It took the man less
than fifteen minutes to count them all out. He
snapped the lid on the case shut, and handed it to the
first man, who folded his arms across it and held it
against his chest like a schoolgirl carrying books.
She suddenly thought of Fall River, Massachusetts,
where Lizzie Borden had got away with killing her
father and her stepmother and where, coinciden-
tally, Cassandra Jean Ridley had spent the first fifteen years of her life, my how the time did fly. What
am I doing *here?* she wondered.

"The suitcase," he said.

Cass climbed back into the plane and pulled out
the suitcase from where she'd stowed it. She carried
it out again in her left hand, the gun in her right, still
hanging loose. She was thinking they could shoot
her dead the minute she dropped to the ground
again, grab the suitcase full of dope, she was sure it
was, ride off into the night with the dope *and* the
money they'd so patiently counted out for her.

It didn't happen.

She revved up the engine again, the little leather
case with $150,000 sitting on the seat beside her,
another ten grand in the flap pocket of her jump
suit. Tonight I'll be back in the big bad city, she
thought. Her heart was pounding as fiercely as it
had over the sands of Iraq.

Hanukkah would start at sundown today, the twenty-first day of December. Will didn't much care. He wasn't even Jewish.

This was always the most dangerous time, going in. Well, coming *out* was no picnic, either, but then you could march right through the front door, say you'd been there to fix the toilet or the sink, nice day, ain't it? Somebody saw you going in, though, that was another story. Specially when you were going in through a window on a fire escape, now *that* was a little difficult to explain.

He'd been watching the apartment from the roof across the way for the better part of a week now, knew when the lady came and went, even had an opportunity once to see her in the altogether, though inadvertently, he wasn't no damn Peeping Tom. Redheaded as a cardinal, she was, carpet matching the drapes, a fair sight to behold and a rarity in this day and age. He always so-called cased a joint, he hated criminal jargon, for at least a week before he went in, sometimes two or three, because the one yearning he did not have was to spend any more time behind bars.

Lady was putting on a short red fox jacket now, which meant maybe there were more furs in there than he'd figured. Thing that had first attracted him to her when he was scoping *all* the apartments across the way was a sable coat came down to the floor, had to be worth fifty large at least. You could always tell a woman with a new fur coat, she pranced in front of the mirror with it all day long. He decided that going into the apartment for just the sable alone might be worth it, plus whatever other little goodies he might find in there. The building was on South Ealey Street in a section of Isola called Silvermine. It was a doorman building, which usually meant any other kind of security was lacking. The lady was heading for the front door now—

"There we go," Will said out loud.

He still spoke with a Texas twang he should've lost after thirty-seven years on this planet, especially since he'd left the state when he was eighteen and never did go back except for his mother's funeral. He was still a sophomore at UCLA when she died. He guessed maybe her death had something to do with him flunking out the very next year. Her dying so young and all. He sometimes wondered if his life might've turned out different if she hadn't died and he hadn't flunked out of college. He wondered if he'd've become a burglar, anyway. He guessed maybe he would've.

Will gave her ten minutes to get clear.

Then he jumped the airshaft to the roof of her building, and came down the fire escape to the ninth floor. He wasn't expecting any kind of burglar alarm, and there wasn't any. He jimmied the turn-bolt lock on the window, and was inside the apartment in ten seconds flat. No need for a flashlight here in the living room at ten in the morning. Anyway, there was nothing to steal in this room but a TV set and a stereo and he wasn't any junkie burglar, thank you. He went into the bedroom, went to the windows first to pull down the shades so nobody would look in and see a guy six feet tall at a buck-ninety roaming a bedroom where a lady lived alone. Only when the shades were down did he go to the wall switch and snap on the overhead lights. Bed nicely made, he surely did appreciate neat people. He yanked back the cover, stripped both pillows of their pillow cases, and then went to the closet. The door was closed. He opened it and found—well, oh my stars—not only the long sable coat but a mink stole as well, the lady really *had* been on a shopping spree. Both were too bulky to fit inside the pillow cases, he tossed them on the bed for now, and went to the dresser.

Everything neatly laid out here, too, rolled nylons and pantyhose in one drawer, tank tops and cotton panties in another, T-shirts and sweaters, all precisely put away as if they were color-coded or something, he figured all at once that either the lady was a nurse or else she'd been in the military. In the top drawer, there was a jewelry box. He opened it. Nothing in it but a bunch of cheap costume jewelry and a long white business envelope with a rubber band around it. He slid the rubber band off, opened the envelope. What he was looking at was a whole big bunch of U.S. currency. He fished in his jacket pocket for his eyeglass case, slipped the glasses out of it, hung them on his nose and his ears, and looked into the envelope again.

The money in there was hundred-dollar bills.

He didn't stop to count them till he was safe at home again in his apartment on South Twelfth Street, just off Stemmler Avenue. This was now close to twelve noon, and it had begun snowing outside. He sat in an easy chair under a lamp with a lamp shade that somehow had ketchup stains on it, and took the white envelope out of his jacket pocket, and then took the rubber band off the envelope again, and took out the bills and began counting them.

What it turned out to be was $8,500 in hundred-dollar bills.

Will hadn't expected such a big haul, and the very idea of sitting alone here four days before Christmas, in an apartment even he admitted was dingy, seemed illogical for a suddenly wealthy individual. He took $500 from the stack of hundreds, put on his coat, and went out whistling.

It was snowing quite heavily by the time Cass got back to the apartment at two-thirty that afternoon. She went into the living room, tossed the red fox jacket over the arm of the sofa, turned on the Christmas tree lights, and then poured herself a Courvoisier on the rocks. Sitting alone in a chair by the window, she sipped the cognac and basked in the winking glow of the Christmas tree, thinking how lucky she was to have a nice apartment like this one in this wonderful city at this very special time of the year. She wondered what she might like to buy next. Or should she wait till after Christmas, when she could get everything on sale? Today was the twenty-first. Christmas wasn't too far off.

She eased out of her pumps, $400 at Bruno Magli, stretched her legs, and suddenly realized just how tired she was. Rising, carrying the shoes in one hand and the brandy snifter in the other, she walked into the bedroom, snapped on the light switch, and almost spilled cognac all over her brand-new dress, $2,100 at Romeo Gigli. The closet door was open. She saw in a single eye swipe that the sable and the mink were gone. All the dresser drawers were open, too. Her envelope with what was left of the Mexican tip money was gone. She felt an immediate sense of violation, someone had been in here, someone had taken her things, gone through her private possessions, taken her goddamn *things!* She felt as angry as she had when some twerps in Basic pissed in her footlocker, felt like rushing to the still-open window and screaming at the top of her lungs, "You goddamn *thief!,*" a lot of good that would do. Calming herself slightly, but only slightly, she checked the closet and the dresser more closely, trying to ascertain if he'd taken anything more than the obvious. It seemed that was it. Hadn't bothered with the Angela Cummings bracelet she'd bought last week, all shiny and bright in its aqua blue box. Hadn't been lured by the Hermès scarf, or the cashmere sweater, or the pre-Hellenic winged Eros pendant from an antiques shop on Jefferson, had satisfied himself merely— *merely!*—with the sable and the mink and what was $8,500 in cash the last time she'd counted it, the son of a bitch!

She actually pounded the dresser top in anger, pounded it again and again with her closed fist, screaming, "You mother-fucking son of a bitch bastard!," obscenities she hadn't used since the war, and then calmed down just a little bit and went to the phone and dialed 911.

Will was telling the blonde that he'd been born and raised in San Antonio, Texas, but that he hadn't been back there in quite a while.

"What's the Will for?" she asked. "William?"

"No, Wilbur," he said.

"Wilbur Struthers?"

"Wilbur Struthers is what it is, ma'am."

She almost burst out laughing. She didn't. She even managed to keep herself from smiling, which he certainly appreciated. They were sitting in a booth in a bar called Flanagan's, on Twenty-first and Culver. Will had first ordered a bottle of Veuve Cliquot, which the waiter didn't know what it was, or care to know, it was that kind of bar. So he had asked Jasmine—that was her name—what she might prefer instead, and she had ordered a Harvey Wallbanger, and he had ordered a bourbon and water for himself, and they were now on their third drink each, with their knees touching under the table, and their heads very close together above the table. He figured if he played this one correctly, she would soon be in his bed back at the apartment.

He told her how he'd booked onto a tramp steamer after he quit college, headed for the Pacific Rim, found himself in Cambodia just about when the Khmer Rouge were rampaging there, got himself taken prisoner, and spent two years waiting for them to blow his brains out before he attempted a daring escape that landed him first in Manila and next in Singapore. Jasmine figured he was full of shit, but he had the tall rugged look of a cowboy, wearing a dark blue turtleneck that complemented the lighter blue of his eyes. Gray sports jacket, darker gray slacks. His hair a sort of sunwashed brown, rather than truly blond. Good strong face, good strong hands. Southern accent—or whatever it was—that didn't hurt the Home-on-the-Range image. Too bad he's a trick, she thought, although he hadn't yet asked her how much this would cost him, or anything so crass as that, which she considered the sign of a true gent. She figured he'd get around to it sooner or later, but meanwhile she enjoyed listening to him tell her about the time a

Khmer Rouge soldier put the barrel of a pistol in his mouth, which only happened to her every night of the week, more or less.

When it got time to pay for the drinks, Will handed the waiter a hundred-dollar bill, and then asked her if she'd made any other plans for the night. If she hadn't, did she think she might enjoy accompanying him back to his place? Perhaps they could find a liquor store that sold Veuve Cliquot, a truly astonishing champagne, he told her, which they could drink while watching a movie on HBO. She still figured he was full of shit, but she thought this might be a good time to mention that she got five bills for the night, Around-the-World under-stood, of course.

Will blinked.

"I'm a working girl," she said. "I thought you knew."

"I'm sorry, ma'am, I surely didn't."

"So what do you think?"

"I never paid for a lady's favors in my life," Will said.

"Always a first time, cowboy. Teach you things you never dreamt of."

"I dreamt most everything," he said.

"Does that mean yes or no?"

"I guess it means no," he said. "I'm sorry."

"No sorrier'n I am," Jasmine said, and picked up her handbag and said, "Have a nice Christmas," and threw her coat over her shoulders and went swivel-ing toward the front door, passing within a few feet of where the waiter was handing Will's hundred-dollar bill to the cashier.

The cashier, a woman named Savina Girasole, held up the bill to the light to check the otherwise invisible polyester strip. The embedded security tape revealed itself at once, the upside down *USA 100 USA 100 USA 100* repeating itself over and over again down the left-hand side of the bill. So it's genuine, Savina thought. But there was something about the feel of it—well, not exactly the *feel,* the paper certainly *felt* as reliable as any other U.S. bill. But . . .

Well . . . the *look* of it.

The funny writing in ink across Franklin's face, for one thing. The *smell* of it, too. It had a sort of sweet smell. Savina didn't normally go around sniffing money that came in, but this bill really did have an odd aroma. Not like marijuana, nothing like that. More like some kind of cheap perfume. As if it had been between the breasts of some girl who bought her brassieres off downtown pushcarts.

The guy whose bill it was sat in the booth all alone now, nursing his drink as sad as could be. He looked like an all-American back yard barbecue champ, which didn't mean he was above passing a phony hundred-dollar bill, which if it ended up in her cash register would cause Mr. O'Brien to fire her. Ronnie O'Brien was the owner of the place and not anybody named Flanagan, no matter what it said on the sign outside. Savina didn't want to lose her job. So she picked up the phone resting alongside the credit card machine, and called the number she had Scotch-taped to the side of the cash register.

"So as I understand this," one of the detectives was telling Cass, "all this guy took is two expensive furs, is that it?"

"Yes, that's it," Cass said.

She hadn't mentioned the missing cash, and she didn't intend to.

"One of them a full-length sable coat . . ."

"Yes, from Revillon."

"How much would you say it's worth, Miss?"

"Forty-five thousand dollars," she said.

"And the mink stole? How much was *that* worth?"

"Six thousand."

"Insured?"

"No."

"You should insure things, Miss."

"I intended to."

"Your initials in either of them?"

"Both of them."

"And what would those initials be?"

"CJR."

"For?"

"Cassandra Jean Ridley."

"Could you please spell Ridley for us?"

"R-I-D-L-E-Y," she said. "What are the chances of getting them back?"

One of the detectives was redheaded. With a white streak in his hair. The other was short. She figured the chances were nil.

"We have a very good recovery record, don't we, Hal?" the redheaded one said.

"Well, so-so," the short one said, and smiled.

Which confirmed Cass's doubts.

"We'll let you know if we come up with anything," the redheaded one said. "Here's my card, I'll write my beeper number on the back in case you think of anything else." The card said he was Detective/Second Grade Cotton Hawes of the Eighty-seventh Detective Squad.

"Thank you," Cass said, though she couldn't imagine what else she might think of to call them about.

"We know just how you feel," the short one said.

"Oops!" the redheaded one said, and stopped dead in his tracks and bent to pick up a black eyeglass case on the floor near the dresser. "Almost stepped on them," he said.

Cass did not wear eyeglasses.

"Thank you," she said at once, and took the case.

"Have a nice Christmas," the short one said.

"You, too," Cass said.

She led them to the door, and locked it behind them. The minute they were gone, she looked at the name and address imprinted on the case in barely legible gold letters:

Eyewear Fashions, Inc.
1137 Stemmler Avenue
(corner of 22nd Street)

Cass went to the closet for her red fox jacket.

The knock on the door came at a little past four that afternoon. Will went to the door and said, "Yes?"

"Secret Service," a voice said. "Mind opening the door for us?"

Secret *what?* Will thought.

"Say again?" he said.

"Special Agent David A. Horne," the voice said. "Few questions I'd like to ask you, sir. Routine matter."

Which to Will meant he ought to go out the window this very minute. Trouble was, there was no fire escape outside the window.

"Just a minute, let me put something on," he said, even though he was fully clothed. In the next thirty seconds, he debated whether he should go hide the stolen hundred-dollar bills in the toilet tank or the freezer compartment of the fridge, both of which places would be searched at once if this was related to the burglary he'd committed on South Ealey. He decided to play it cool.

"Just a minute," he said again, and went to the door and opened it.

The man standing there was tall and thin and blue-jowled, wearing a neon blue parka and a woolen hat with ear flaps. "Special Agent David A. Horne," he said again, "with an 'e,' " and opened a little leather case to show a gold star that looked like the ones the Texas Rangers carried back home. Will tried to think if there were any outstanding warrants on him back home. He couldn't think of a single one.

"Good evening," he said. "What can I do for you?"

"It's still afternoon," Horne corrected. "Is your name Wilbur Struthers?"

"It is."

"Ask me in," Horne said, and smiled.

"Sure, come on in," Will said.

He was somewhat frightened now, but he spoke calmly and politely because it was always best to be polite to policemen. Even back home in Texas, Will spoke politely to policemen, whose long suit was definitely not courtesy. But Horne was a Secret Service agent with considerably more sophistication, he hoped. He stepped into the room now, looking around as if there might be an accomplice or two lurking about.

"You were in Flanagan's earlier today," Horne said. It was not a question.

"That's right," Will said.

The hooker, he thought at once. Something happened to the hooker, so now the Secret Service is here to question me about her. He hoped it was nothing serious. He hoped nobody had killed her or raped her.

"You had some drinks there," Horne said.

"I did."

Had she been poisoned?

"You paid for them with a hundred-dollar bill," Horne said. *"This* bill," he said, and removed from the inside pocket of the bulky blue parka a narrow folder that looked like the kind you put money in for a Christmas gift to your mailman or your doorman, except that it had a gold star embossed on the front of it. Horne opened the folder and took a hundred-dollar bill from it. "Recognize it?" he asked, and handed it to Will.

"All hundred-dollar bills look alike to me," he said.

"Where'd you get *this* hundred-dollar bill?" Horne asked.

"I won it in a crap game," Will said.

"Won a hundred dollars in a crap game."

"Yes, I did."

"Where? What crap game?"

"Pickup game on Laramie," he said.

"Where on Laramie?"

"Don't recall the address," he said.

Two different agendas here, he was thinking. Man here wants to know all about this hundred-dollar bill, I want to make sure he don't find out I stole it.

"This all you won in the crap game?"

"Just the hundred, that's all."

"Went out to spend it, is that right?"

"That's right."

Listen, he thought, why the fuck are you asking all these questions?

But knew better than to say.

Two different agendas here.

"I talked to a girl named Jasmine before I came up here," Horne said.

"Oh?"

"Got your name from her."

"So?"

"Ran a computer check."

Will said nothing.

"Seems you ran into a little trouble here in this city, is that right, Wilbur?"

"It's Will, by the way."

"Sorry, I didn't know that, Will."

"That's okay," Will said.

He was thinking it still didn't take the curse off the oldest cop trick in the world, calling a suspected perp by his first name, which reduced him to the status of a menial. What this was here was *Will* and *Mr.* David Horne.

"Burglarized a gas station seven years ago, did time for the deed up at Castleview. That the only burglary you ever committed, Will?"

"The one and only," Will lied.

"That's commendable," Horne said. "But none-theless, on the basis of this hundred-dollar bill here, I was able to obtain a search warrant."

"A *what?*"

"I believe you heard me," Horne said, and handed Will a court order with a judge's signature and all on the bottom of it, authorizing a search of this very apartment for monies paid as ransom . . .

"Ransom?" Will said.

"Ransom in a kidnapping, is what it says. *Ransom* money, Will."

"That's not my bill," Will said at once. "I told you. I won it in a crap game."

"Well, that's good, Will, because the serial numbers on this bill match the serial numbers on one of the bills paid as ransom in a kidnapping case we're investigating. Do you understand the implications of that?"

"I'm not a kidnapper," Will said.

"That's good, too, Will, because I have a search warrant to look for any *other* bills that may have been part of the ransom payment," Horne said, and took off the blue parka to reveal a dark blue suit, a white shirt, and a red tie. The suit jacket was taut over bulging pectorals and broad shoulders. The man was a fitness freak. He took off the hat with the ear flaps, revealing a head of very black, very thick hair.

"Is it the President?" Will asked.

"Is what the President?"

"Who got kidnapped?"

"I have to warn you not to say anything that might prove incriminating," Horne said.

Oh, Jesus, it's the President, Will thought. Because if it *wasn't* the President, then what was the Secret Service doing in this? It was the *FBI* who investigated kidnappings, wasn't it? All the Secret

Service did was protect the President of the United States. And his family. So it had to be somebody in the White House who'd got kidnapped.

Horne was moving over to the closet now, where the bills sat in a shoe box on the shelf over the hanging sable coat and mink stole, both of which Will had also stolen. I can run right this minute, he thought, go visit my cousin Earl living in Fort Worth with a girl used to be Miss Texas in the Miss America contest, came within a curly blond crotch hair of winning it. Spend a few weeks down there till this whole kidnapping thing blew over, which he hadn't done anyway, *damn it!* All he'd done was burglarize a fucking apartment!

"Well, well, what have we here?" Horne said.

He was looking in at the sable coat and the mink stole.

"Your search warrant says you're supposed to look for money," Will said.

"These are in plain view," Horne said.

"In plain view" was an expression the police used when they appropriated something without benefit of a search warrant.

"They're my girlfriend's," Will said.

"What's her name?"

"Jasmine. Who you talked to."

"She told us you only just met," Horne said.

"Well, that's true."

"And she left her furs here?"

"She trusts me."

Horne gave him a look. But he didn't pursue the

matter of the furs any further, perhaps because his mind was on the President's kidnapping, who it had to be, or else someone in his family, otherwise why the Secret Service? I ought to run for it right this minute, Will thought. Horne was reaching for a shoe box on the shelf. Run for it or not? Will thought. Horne took down the box. Which? Horne took the lid off the box and looked into it. He reached in for a white envelope with a rubber band around it. He took the rubber band off the envelope. He opened the envelope.

"Well, well," he said again.

"That's not plain view," Will said.

"Now it is," Horne said, and fanned the bills. "Where'd you get *these* little mothers?"

"Same crap game," Will said.

Horne began counting.

"This is a lot of money here," he said.

"Yeah, it was a big crap game."

"Looks like five, six thousand dollars here."

"More like eight," Will said.

"You won eight thousand dollars in a crap game?"

"I got lucky."

"Who was in this game?"

"Bunch of guys I never saw in my life."

"So let me get this straight, Will," Horne said. "You're asking me to believe that one or more of the men in this crap game of yours *could* have been the kidnappers to whom these bills were paid as ransom, is that it?"

"I guess that's it," Will said.

He knew he was already in the toilet. He knew Horne would yank out a gun and a pair of handcuffs in the next minute. He'd be spending Christmas Day in jail for a goddamn kidnapping he didn't do.

"Listen," he said, "you really do have the wrong person here."

"Maybe so," Horne said, and gave him a long, hard look.

Will's hands were shaking. He put them in his pockets so Horne wouldn't see. He hated himself for being so goddamn scared here, but he couldn't help it. A kidnapping was serious stuff.

"Tell you what," Horne said.

Will waited.

"What I think I should do is confiscate this money here," Horne said. "Give you a receipt for it, check the serial numbers downtown, get back to you later today."

Sure, Will thought.

Secret Service or not, every cop in the world was identical to every other cop, and they were all fuckin crooks. Next thing you knew, eight thousand bucks would find its way into a fund for the widows of Secret Service men who had died in the line of duty. Only thing he didn't understand was why Horne was granting a possible kidnapper the opportunity to flee. He watched as the man meticulously copied the serial numbers on all the bills, signed the sheet of paper with the numbers on it, and handed it to Will. He looked for his parka, found it where he'd draped it over one of the chairs, and put it on.

"I don't have to warn you not to leave the city," he said.

"Not while you've got all my money," Will said.

"See you later," Horne said, and put on the hat with the ear flaps, and walked out of the apartment.

It was twenty minutes to five.

So what do I do now? Will wondered.

Hell, I'm an innocent man here!

Except for the burglary.

But Horne hadn't been interested in any burglary, Horne didn't even know any burglary had *happened*. Horne had been interested only in the hundred-dollar bills that had maybe or maybe not been paid as ransom in a kidnapping case he was investigating—but how come the Secret Service? Anyway, that was the entire scope of Special Agent David A. Horne's interest. The money. Check the serial numbers. If they match, come fetch old Wilbur here.

But let's say the serial numbers do *not* match. I mean, out of all the millions of apartments in New York City, what are the odds on my breaking into the only one that happens to be the apartment of a redhead who'd done a kidnapping and stashed the ransom money there? What are the odds on that kind of thing happening? I mean, *really*. A thousand to one? A million to one? I'll take odds like that on a horse any day of the week.

So the odds have got to be in my favor, right? The serial numbers will not match, Horne will come back with my money, I'll sign off on the receipt, and he'll apologize for having taken so much of my time.

I hope, he thought.

At five minutes to six that Thursday evening, Cass walked into Eyewear Fashions, Inc. on Stemmler Avenue and Twenty-second Street. The evening was clear and cold. Pinprick points of stars dotted a black sky, and the streets and sidewalks glistened with fresh snow, but Cass did not have a white Christmas on her mind. All she wanted to do was find the man who'd taken her money and her mink stole and her long sable coat, which should have been keeping her toasty warm on this frighteningly cold day. She'd been a cold puppy all her life, and the first thing she'd purchased from the money she'd earned on the Mexico job was the sable. Hell with people who went around in the nude protesting the wearing of furs. Anyone ever tried to spray paint on her furs was somebody who'd better already own a funeral plot.

Instead of the stolen sable, she was wearing the short red fox jacket over blue jeans and a green turtleneck sweater, freezing her ass off nonetheless. One of the reasons she'd left Fall River, Massachusetts, was that it had been so damn cold up there. That and her father shouting hell and damnation at her day and night. Her mother was a mathematics teacher. Cass guessed she thought it made sense to marry a Presbyterian minister and then present him with two daughters, one of whom grew up to be a holy person like Papa. The second and youngest, Cassandra Jean Ridley herself, fed up to here, ran away from home instead. Went to live on a commune in New Hampshire, which was even colder than it was here on this street corner in Isola. Left there when the group's youth advisor came into her room naked one midnight clear, determined to read to her out loud a short story from *Hustler* magazine. Cass clobbered him with a frying pan.

"Hi," she said to the man behind the counter, "my name is Harriet Daniels," which was the name of the woman who'd run the rooming house she'd lived in down in Eagle Branch, Texas. "I found an eyeglass case with your store name on it, and I was wondering if you could help me locate the owner of the glasses."

"Well, gee, I don't know," the man said.

"You are?" she asked.

"Wesley Hand," he said.

He was perhaps twenty-eight or twenty-nine, a round little man with moist blue eyes and a pleasant looking face except for the complexion. He looked sincerely concerned about the eyeglass case she now put on the counter top. He also looked bewildered. She guessed that was his natural expression.

"Is there some way you could do that for me?" she asked. "Help me locate the owner?"

"That might be difficult," he said. "Except for some very special prescriptions, most eyeglasses . . ."

"Isn't there some machine or something you can put them on?" she asked. "To see what the prescription is?"

"Well, sure, but . . ."

"Because maybe it's one of the *special* ones, you see."

"Well . . ."

"I would appreciate it," she said, and flashed what she hoped was a warm and convincing smile.

"I close at six," he said, and glanced up at the clock.

"Well, how long would it take . . . ?"

"And I have to be someplace."

"The thing is, I found them earlier today," she said. "So chances are he'll be missing them by now."

"Uh-huh."

"So could you put these on your machine and see if . . . ?"

"Not now," he said. He was already moving around the counter toward a small closet on the side of the shop. "Call me tomorrow morning," he said.

"Thank you," she said. He was putting on his coat. "I appreciate it," she said, and smiled sweetly.

You prick, she thought.

• • •

Horne came back to see Will at ten-thirty that night. He came unannounced, and when he pressed the buzzer downstairs to say he was there, Will was enormously surprised. He'd never expected to see those hundred-dollar bills again. Tonight, Horne was wearing a blue car coat with a faux fur collar, wide wale, dark brown corduroy trousers, and a brown fedora. By comparison to this afternoon, he looked positively dapper.

"Will, I must apologize," he said.

"Why's that?" Will asked.

"These are *not* the ransom bills."

"I didn't think they were," Will said, but he was tremendously relieved nonetheless.

"We checked the serial numbers, and except for that one bill they simply didn't match. So . . . I'm sorry for whatever inconvenience the Department may have caused you . . ."

"What department is that, by the way?"

"Why, the Treasury Department," Horne said, looking surprised. "The U.S. Secret Service is part of the Treasury Department."

"I didn't know that," Will said.

"Not many people do," Horne said. "So if you'll just let me have that receipt I gave you earlier today . . ."

"Okay," Will said, and fished in his wallet for it.

Horne carried the receipt to the kitchen table, sat,

removed from his briefcase a sheaf of hundred-dollar bills, and handed them to Will.

"If you'll just count these," he said.

"I'm sure I can trust the Treasury Department," Will said.

"Even so," Horne said, "I'd feel safer if you counted them."

Will sat across from him at the kitchen table, and began counting the bills. Horne took out his pen and drew a straight line under the list of serial numbers on the receipt. Just below the line, he wrote the words *Receipt of $8,000 acknowledged in full.* It took maybe a minute and a half for Will to count all eighty bills. They were all there.

"If you'll just sign this," Horne said, and handed him the pen, and passed the receipt across the table to him. Will signed his name to it. Horne folded the receipt and put it into his briefcase.

"Mr. Struthers," he said, and extended his hand. "Please keep your nose clean."

"You, too, David," Will said, and opened the door for him. Horne stepped out into the hallway. Will closed and locked the door behind him. He listened at the wood until he could no longer hear Horne's footfalls in the hallway or on the steps. Then he whirled away from the door, grinning, and slapped his hand on his thigh and shouted, "Will Struthers, you are one lucky son of a bitch!"

· · ·

Cass's phone rang at precisely two minutes past ten on Friday morning. Today was the first full day of Hanukkah, the twenty-second of December, three days before Christmas. The man calling was Wesley Hand.

"The optician?" he said.

"Yes, Mr. Hand?"

"I checked the glasses . . ."

"And?" she said at once.

"As I told you, most prescriptions fall into routine categories," he said, "what we call plus-one biopters, absolutely commonplace. That was the case here. But I remembered the frames. He insisted on the mocha brown frames, even though I said they wouldn't go well with his coloring."

"What *was* his coloring?" Cass asked.

"Dirty blond hair, blue eyes, the mocha brown frames were all wrong. He'd have done much better with the midnight blue."

"But he insisted on the brown."

"Yes."

"Which is how you remembered him."

"Yes."

"What was his name?" she asked at once.

"I have it right here," he said. "It's Wilbur Struthers."

"Do you have an address for him?"

"I do," Wesley said. "Are you sure it's okay for me to give this to you?"

"Oh, yes, I'm positive. May I have it, please?"

"Well . . ."

"Please?" she said.

"Well," he said again, and read off the address like a prisoner of war revealing under torture the location of an infantry division.

"I can't thank you enough," Cass said.

"Yes?" a man's voice said.

"Delivery," she said.

"What kind of delivery?"

"Pair of eyeglasses," she said.

"What?"

"I'm from Eyewear Fashions. Somebody found your glasses, brought them in this morning. Did you want me to bring them up?"

"Thank you, yes, come on up. Hey, terrific. It's 2C, on the second floor."

The buzzer sounded. Cass opened the entry door at once and felt in her tote bag for the reassuring grip of the Browning automatic. No elevator, of course. She climbed the steps to the second floor and yanked the gun out of the bag as she came down the corridor. She used the muzzle to tap gently on the door to 2C.

When Will opened the door, he saw the red-headed woman whose apartment he'd ripped off. Moreover, she was holding in her fist what appeared to be a .45 automatic. He tried to slam the door shut on her, but she hit it with her shoulder at once, shoving it in against him, almost knocking him off his feet, he hadn't realized she was that strong. She was

in the apartment in a wink, slamming the door behind her, and whirling on him with the automatic
pointed at his head.

"Where's my money?" she asked.

"Don't get excited," he said.

"My money," she said. "My furs," she said.
"You're a thief," she said. She kept using the gun for
punctuation, which made Will believe she was
somewhat unstable and therefore capable of hyster-
ically pulling the trigger.

"Don't get excited," he said again. "Everything's
here, all of it's here, no need to go waving the gun
around like that."

She was maybe five-eight, five-nine, taller than
she'd looked from the rooftop across the way, a tall
good-looking redhead wearing a red fox jacket
open over blue jeans and a bulky green turtleneck
sweater that made her look like Christmas although
it was still three days away.

"Get it," she said.

"Would you mind putting up the gun?" he said.
"Makes me nervous, you standing there with a gun
in your hand."

"Get my stuff," she said.

"Right away," he said.

"You fucking *crook,*" she said.

He wanted to tell her that a Khmer Rouge soldier
had once pistol-whipped him with a weapon just
like the one in her hand, but instead he went to the
closet and took from it the long sable coat and the
mink stole, and carried them to where she was

standing alongside the sofa, the gun still in her hand, and dumped them onto the cushions, and then went back to the closet to take down from the shelf the shoe box containing what he'd last counted out for Horne as $8,000 dollars in hundred-dollar bills. He was hoping she knew how to handle that big gun in her fist because he sure didn't want to get hurt here.

"Take off the lid," she said, and waved the gun again.

"It's all here, I just counted it last night."

"That what you do in your spare time, you crook? Count other people's money?"

"I'll be happy to count it for you now," he said, taking the rubber-banded white envelope from the box. "Or you might want to put down the gun and do it yourself."

"You count it," she said.

He removed the rubber band, took the bills from the envelope, began counting the money for the second time in as many days, a hundred, two hundred, five hundred, six hundred, seven hundred, eight hundred, nine hundred, a thous . . .

"Stop!" she said.

"What?" he said.

"Hold it right there!"

"Why? What . . . ?"

"That isn't my money," she said.

"What do you . . . ?"

"That is *not* my money! What are you trying to pull here?"

"Ma'am, I can assure you . . ."

"That is *not* my money! My money had funny marks on it. And it smelled sweet."

"Lady, *all* money smells sweet."

"Where are the marks?"

"What marks?"

"The writing, the funny writing!" She picked up a handful of bills, spread them open like a fan. "Do you see any writing on these bills? These bills are clean! Smell them! Do you smell anything sweet?"

"No, ma'am, but . . ."

"What did you do with my money?"

"This *is* your money."

"It is *not* my money! What'd you do with my money?"

"Lady, I'm telling you for the last time, this *is* your money. In *your* envelope. They even gave me a receipt with the serial numbers on it. I had to sign it to . . ."

"What do you mean? Who?"

"To get the money back. I had to sign the receipt."

"Get it *back?* Where *was* it?"

"At the Department."

"What department? What are you *talking* about?"

"The Treasury Department. A Secret Service agent took the money to check the serial numbers."

Oh Jesus, she thought. Those Mexicans tipped me with hot money. Slowly, trying not to lose control, reminding herself that she had been in worse situations than this—she had once flown a Chinook helicopter over a desert blooming with black shrapnel, she had flown through horrific firestorms from below and had not lost it, she was not going to lose it now—slowly, carefully, she asked, "Why did they want to check the serial numbers?"

"Don't worry, they didn't match," he said.

"But why did they want to check them?"

"They thought they were ransom bills."

Calm, she thought. Stay calm. Just hear him out. Just try to get to the bottom of this.

"What ransom?" she asked calmly.

"There was a kidnapping," he said. "The ransom was paid in hundred-dollar bills. They thought these might be the bills."

"What made them think that?" she asked evenly, calmly.

"Because the serial numbers on a bill I cashed . . ."

"You cashed *my* money?"

"Just that one bill. I didn't spend any more than that. And the serial numbers on it *did* match."

Don't shoot him, she thought. Just remain extremely calm.

"Did match *what?*" she asked.

"Did match the numbers on one of the ransom bills."

"A bill the Secret Service was looking for."

"Yes."

"Why the Secret Service?"

"I don't know."

"And you say they took the *rest* of the money . . ."

"Yes. To check the serial numbers. Which did *not* match. So they brought all of it back."

"Brought back *this* money here on the table."

"Yes. Your money. In your very envelope. Right there on the table."

She stood there nodding, looking down at the money, trying to make some sense of everything he'd told her. Then she said, "This is not my money."

Will wished she would stop repeating the same words over and over again when her goddamn money was sitting right there on the kitchen table, in plain view for the entire world to see. Why wouldn't she just let him *count* it, for Christ's sake, and then get out of here with her goddamn furs and her gun?

"Ma'am," he said, "I am telling you for the last time that this is your money that the Treasury Department returned to me. I gave them a signed receipt with all the serial numbers on it, stating that the money was all here because I counted it last night and there was indeed eight thousand dollars here. Now if you'll let me count it for you now, ma'am, I'm sure it will come to eight thousand dollars all over again because nobody has touched a cent of it since Mr. David A. Horne, with an 'e,' left here."

"I'll let you count it for me," she said. "But it isn't my money."

Goddamn broken record, he thought, and began counting all over again. She kept watching the bills as he passed them from one hand to the other, counting, "twenty-one, twenty-two, twenty-three . . . ," shaking her head as if trying to dope out the great mystery of what had happened here, when it was all so simple a caterpillar could grasp it, "thirty-four, thirty-five" and on and on, money, money, money, "fifty-seven, fifty-eight, fifty-nine, sixty," if he had to count these damn bills one more time, "seventy-one, seventy-two . . ." and at last he counted the eightieth and last bill, and looked up at her and said, "Satisfied?"

She did not answer him. She rubber-banded the bills again, and dropped the wad into her tote, leaving the white envelope on the table. Then she took off the red fox, put on the sable, draped the fox and the mink over her arm . . .

"Would you like something to carry those in?" he asked.

She looked at him.

"Little bulky that way," he said. "Let me see if I've got anything."

Not trusting him for a minute, she followed him into a bedroom with an unmade bed and what looked like a week's laundry strewn all over the floor. He opened a closet door, rummaged around inside there, and came up with a duffel that looked like the one she'd carried in the Army, except her name and rank weren't stenciled in black on the side.

"Thanks," she said, and folded her furs into the

bag, first the fox jacket and then the mink stole. Pulling the drawstrings tight through the grommets, she wondered if she should offer to pay for the duffel, and then asked herself if she was losing her mind, the man here was a thief who'd caused her a great deal of unnecessary trouble. She slung the duffel over her shoulder, backed toward the front door with the gun still in her hand, and without saying another word, walked out.

Will still considered himself lucky.

She'd forgotten to ask for the four hundred dollars and change he still had left over from the five he'd borrowed yesterday.

She stopped at a bank ostensibly to change three of the hundreds into twenties, tens, and fives, but actually to test the bills. She was still wondering why a Secret Service agent had exchanged her own world-weary hundreds for these obviously used but relatively fresh ones, and she was relieved when the teller held them up to the light to check the security strip, and then changed them without raising either an eyebrow or a fuss. It was close to three when she came out of the bank but yesterday had been the shortest day of the year, and with the heavy clouds overhead, the afternoon seemed already succumbing to dusk. The day was still piercingly cold. She was grateful for the sable, luxuriating in its long silken swirl, feeling like a Russian empress all at once, $8,000 in cash in her handbag, the city all aglitter for Christmas, what more could a person wish for?

How about caviar and champagne? she thought.

The two men were sitting in their overcoats, one on either side of the Christmas tree in her living room. They popped out of the dusky gloom the moment she turned on the lights. The larger of the two men had a gun in his hand and it was pointing up at Cass's head.

"Buenas noches," he said and smiled. "We are here for dee money."

She thought at once that it was really shitty of Wilbur Struthers to recruit two Latino goons to reclaim the money he'd stolen from her in the first place, the son of a bitch. But here they were, both of them smiling now, somewhat apologetically it seemed to her, but perhaps she was mistaken. She put down the brown paper bag with the caviar she'd bought at Hildy's Market and the Dom Perignon she'd bought in the liquor store on Twenty-sixth Street.

"What money?" she said.

"One million seven hun'red t'ousan dollars," the one on the other side of the tree said.

"I think you're in the wrong apartment," she said.

"I don't theenk so," the first one said.

Very heavy Spanish accents on both of them, something suddenly clicked. The men on the narrow dirt strip in Guenerando, Mexico, except that earlier this month they'd been wearing baggy white cotton pants and wrinkled shirts.

"I don't know what money you're talking about," she said.

"Dee money we paid you for a hun'red kilos of pure cocaine," the one with the gun said.

"I don't want to know anything about that cargo," she said.

"You delivered the money, we gave you dee fockin cocaine . . ."

"I didn't know what the cargo was. I don't know anything about the money, either. All I did was hand it over."

"We know that."

"We know you were only dee messenger."

"We want to know who *gave* you dee money."

"I don't know his name. Look, if the money was short, I'm sorry. You should have counted it more carefully. Anyway . . ."

"We did coun' it carefully."

"It took us a fockin *hour* to coun' it."

"We counted it *very* carefully."

"Dee money *wassen* short," the one with the gun said. "Who gave it to you?"

"I told you, I don't . . ."

"His name, *por favor.*"

The gun was in her face now.

"He called himself Frank. But I'm sure that wasn't his real name."

"Frank what?"

"All he gave me was Frank."

"Where wass this?"

"I was living in Eagle Branch at the time. He was introduced to me by someone I know."

"And *his* name? The one who introduce you?"

"I don't want to get anyone in trouble. If the money was short . . ."

"Dee money *wassen* short."

The gun in her face again.

"Then why . . . ?"

"We delivered quality cocaine. We expected . . ."

"I don't want to know about it."

"Where *wass* this in Eagle Branch?"

"A bar."

"Tell us his name. The one who introduce you."

She suddenly wondered how much Randy Biggs had got for introducing her to the man who'd paid her $200,000 for making four trips to Mexico, to transport—at least on the last trip, anyway—what now turned out to be cocaine.

"Wha' wass his name?" the one with the gun said again.

"I told you . . ."

"We don' want to kill you," the other one said.

"Then tell him to put the gun away."

"*Su nombre,*" the one with the gun said.

She knew with absolute certainty that he would kill her in the next instant if she did not give up Randolph Biggs. She wondered what she owed Randy, wondered what she owed the one who'd called himself Frank and who seemed to have offended these men in some unspeakable way. She decided this was not the Persian Gulf. She was not sworn to tell them only her name, rank, and serial number.

"His name was Randolph Biggs," she said.

2.

Detective Steve Carella wished that one of the lions hadn't dragged the victim's left leg into the 88th Precinct. That was what brought Fat Ollie Weeks into the case. As it was, most of the vic's body was being consumed by three lionesses, a young lion, and a big thickly maned patriarch, apparent leader of the pride, none of whom seemed at all disturbed by a fascinated audience of detectives, zoo personnel, and television reporters gathered outside the Lion Habitat at the Grover Park Zoo.

Half of the zoo was in the 87th Precinct.

The other half was in the 88th.

By Carella's rough estimate, four-fifths of the vic's body was in the Eight-Seven. The remaining fifth, the vic's leg, was over there in the Eight-Eight, where Fat Ollie—watching a young lion claw and gnaw at the leg—was beginning to get hungry himself.

This was Saturday morning, the twenty-third day of December, the true start of the big Christmas weekend that only yesterday had included the first

full day of Hanukkah, now history. Carella and
Meyer had caught the squeal some twenty minutes
ago, at a quarter past seven, when the man in charge
of the zoo's Animal Commissary called the police
to report that a woman had wandered into the habitat and was at that very moment being attacked by a
pride of lions who hadn't yet been fed this morning.

At seven-thirty-seven A.M., there was a heavy
layer of snow on the paths that wound past the
barred fence, and the moat beyond that, and then
the island habitat where the lions and lionesses
feasted. The television reporters were having a field
day. Never before had a photo op like this one presented itself, a pride of lions tearing apart a woman
wearing nothing at all on one of the coldest days of
the year, the animals greedily feasting on the
woman's flesh and bones. Some fifty feet away, in
the 88th Precinct, a solitary lion contentedly
gnawed on the victim's leg.

Detective Oliver Wendell Weeks had caught the
squeal some ten minutes after Carella and Meyer
had, which was when the young lion had dragged
the leg over into the Eight-Eight. None of the detectives were particularly happy to have caught a case
like this one—or *any* case for that matter—a half-
hour or so before their shifts ended, especially on a
holiday weekend, when they had shopping to do and
trees to put up and gifts to wrap.

On a morning when the temperature hovered at
just above freezing, Ollie was wearing only a sports
jacket over dark slacks, a white shirt, a food-stained

tie, white socks, black shoes, and a red woolen
watch cap. He had eaten breakfast an hour ago, but
all the activity out there on the island was making
him wonder if the zoo's coffee shop was open yet.
By contrast, Carella and Meyer were both wearing
heavy overcoats, gloves, and mufflers. They were
each and separately wishing Fat Ollie hadn't been
dragged into the case by the victim's leg. They were
each and separately wondering how they were
going to get the victim off the island before there
was nothing left of her but chewed-over bones.

The Emergency Services truck had arrived not
five minutes ago, and the captain in charge of the ES
Squad was talking to the zoo's Assistant Director, a
man named William Boyd, who had been notified at
home by the Commissary Superintendent who'd
told him that one of their people had just finished
feeding the great apes and was approaching the Lion
Habitat to deliver two hundred pounds of horse meat
enriched with vitamins and minerals when he spotted a woman being attacked on the island there.
Boyd was now advising the ES Captain that he
should take his truck and his team and go home.

"Our own personnel are quite capable of getting
onto the island and recovering whatever's left of the
dead woman," he said.

The ES Captain told him it might be very risky
for a "civilian" to go over there to retrieve the body
while the lions were in a "feeding frenzy," as he put
it, though in all truth the animals seemed to be taking their morning meal in a leisurely manner. The

ES Captain's team tended to agree with him. The team had rescued people trapped in elevators, had scissored open automobiles with people squashed inside them, had plucked charred bodies from sizzling electrical cables, had even picked the locks on cell doors when hookers plugged them with bubble gum to avoid court appearances. This, however, was the first time they'd ever seen a woman being chewed to ribbons by half a dozen lions. Which did not stop them from becoming instant experts.

One of the guys on the team suggested that maybe they should go for the leg first, as a sort of training exercise. Throw the young lion over there in the Eight-Eight something *else* to eat, lure him away from the leg, lay a ladder across the moat, snatch the leg away from him while he was thus distracted. The ES Captain was of the opinion that human flesh was something of a treat for these animals and it might not be easy to tempt them away from it with ordinary fare. Ollie was getting hungrier and hungrier. Carella and Meyer were watching the pride at work. Over on the island, the ground around the kill was disturbed, the snow trampled and spattered with blood.

Ollie wandered over to where the ES Captain and his team were discussing their next move. The Captain's name was Ernie Levine. This being the Hanukkah weekend and all, Ollie figured it wouldn't hurt to remind Levine that he was a Jew.

"Hey, Ernie," he said, "what're you doing on the job, your holiday and all?"

Levine knew Ollie from previous jobs. He greeted him with something less than enthusiasm.

"Hello, Ollie," he said briefly.

"You put up your Hanukkah bush yet?" Ollie asked.

"We don't have anything like that in our house," Levine said.

"You light all ten of your candles?"

"Nine," Levine corrected.

"You think that lady out there is kosher?" Ollie asked. "Cause I hear lions don't eat pork."

"Eat *this* a while," Levine said, and briefly grasped his crotch, and then walked over to where the zoo's General Director had just arrived in a dither. The director's name was Alfred Hardy. He was in his late thirties, Carella guessed, a tall slender man you'd figure for a lawyer or an accountant rather than somebody running a small city. Which was what the Grover Park Zoo was, in effect: a small city within a much larger city. Hardy took one look at the situation and told Levine he wanted everyone out of here while his people performed what to him was a simple rescue operation. Levine explained that there was nobody to rescue anymore. The victim was already dead and in fact being consumed at this very moment. Hardy said there were five healthy *lions* to rescue. Levine said he would have to clear that with his Deputy-Inspector.

"Fine," Hardy said heatedly, "you go do that. Meanwhile, I'll be getting my lions off that island." He turned to Boyd. "Make sure nobody tries to go out there. I'll be in the holding area," he said, and marched off in a huff. Carella figured that anyone who arrived in a dither and went off in a huff couldn't be all bad. Levine went back to the truck to call his superior. Ollie shrugged and turned to where Carella and Meyer were still watching the lions. A pretty blonde from Channel Four News sidled up to Carella and said, "Fascinating, isn't it?"

"Thrilling," Ollie said.

The blonde turned to him as if surprised to learn that a hippopotamus could speak.

"Want to go for some breakfast?" Ollie asked.

"Thanks, I've already eaten," she said.

"I didn't mean you, Miss," he said, and grinned. "I was talking to my colleagues here. These superior sleuths from the Eighty-seventh Precinct."

"Better wait till the ME gets here, don't you think?" Carella said.

"But now that you mention it, I'm Detective/First Grade Oliver Wendell Weeks," Ollie said, turning back to the blonde. "Want to interview me?"

"What for?"

"The leg over there is in my jurisdiction."

"Then why don't you go take it away from that lion?"

"I might in a little while."

"Good. You go get the leg, and then I'll interview you."

"I also play piano," he said.

"A shame we don't have a piano here in the park,"

the blonde said, and turned back to Carella. "How do you suppose the woman got out there?" she asked.

"I've been taking lessons for almost two weeks now," Ollie said. "Right now, I'm working on 'Night and Day.' "

Boyd had been told to make sure no one went out onto the island. But he had just heard the blonde's question and he wanted to get a little closer to someone who looked so leggy and all in a short skirt and high-heeled boots and a brown leather jacket. So he came over to explain that the way personnel got onto the island was through a tunnel under the moat . . .

"The lions are brought inside every night," he explained. "To cages in the holding area."

"That's very interesting," the blonde said.

"I'm gonna learn five songs," Ollie said.

"That's very interesting, too," the blonde said, and turned back to where Carella and Meyer were still watching the lions. It was a frighteningly cold morning, but neither of the men was wearing a hat. Carella's hair was brown, dancing on his head now in a brisk wind. Meyer was totally bald; his barren pate made him look colder than he actually was. The two detectives stood like bookends flanking Fat Ollie, whose little red watch cap was tilted at a rakish angle. Actually, Ollie thought he cut a fine figure of sartorial elegance.

"My name is Honey Blair," the blonde told Carella, "I rove for the Five o'Clock News."

"Hello, Honey," Ollie said. "I rove for the Eighty-eighth Squad."

Honey was thinking the two big detectives made a nice picture standing there watching the voracious lions. They were both tall and wide-shouldered, the bald guy looking solid and serious, the other one looking sexy as hell in a way she couldn't quite understand, he wasn't that good-looking. Something about the way his eyes slanted downward maybe, giving him a sort of Chinese appearance, though he certainly wasn't Oriental. Something about the *look* in the eyes, maybe. Dark and brooding. As if it pained him to see the woman out there being torn to shreds.

"You new in the job?" she asked him.

"New? Me?" he said, and smiled, and shook his head.

The smile got to her, too.

"Want me to take your picture?" she asked.

"Sure," Ollie said.

"You and your partner," Honey said. "Looking over at the lions."

"I don't think so, thanks," Carella said.

"Why not?"

"Wouldn't be professional," he said.

"Make a nice shot, though," Honey said, and beamed a dazzling smile at him.

Meyer raised his eyebrows.

"Thanks, no," Carella said again.

"Think it over," she said, and turned away and

walked back toward her camera crew, flirty little skirt fluttering about her elegant long legs. Ollie watched her go. So did Meyer. Carella walked over to where Levine was still on the phone with the DI.

"We're going to have to get on that island soon," Levine was saying. "Before the Five o'Clock News tells everybody we let wild animals eat 'em for Christmas." He listened, and then said, "You think so?" He listened again. "I'm not sure the CEO here is gonna buy that." He listened, nodded, said, "Okay, Boss, whatever you say," and put the phone back on its bracket in the truck's cab. He turned to Carella and said, "Quote: 'If a dangerous animal is threatening human life, destroy it.' Period. Unquote."

"So what does he want?"

"A team of sharpshooters."

"Mr. Hardy won't like that."

"Just what I told the DI."

"Let me go talk to him. You call SWAT, tell them we need enough sharpshooters to take care of five healthy lions."

Meyer walked over to the truck.

"What are we doing?" he asked.

"Shooting the lions," Carella said.

"I'll have them off that island before your sharpshooters get here," Hardy said. "What's the sense in killing them? The woman is already dead. Besides, it isn't as if they escaped confinement and went looking for prey. The woman found her own way onto the island somehow. These are wild animals. Carnivores. It was in their nature to attack her and devour her."

"Sir, I'm merely telling you what we plan to do," Carella said. He looked at his watch. "A SWAT team should be here in ten, twelve minutes. They'll dispose of the animals at that time."

"Meanwhile, I'll have them off the island. You have your plan, I have mine."

"What's *your* plan, Mr. Hardy?"

"I'll have my vets anesthetize the animals and carry them back here to the holding cages."

"Back here" was a bunker-like building connected to the island by a ramp and a tunnel that ran under the moat. By now, a considerable number of zoo people had gathered here in the holding area. In addition to zookeepers of various grade levels, there were people from the Curation Department, and two animal behaviorists, and the three veterinarians who would be handling the anesthetizing of the animals out there.

The way Hardy explained it to Carella and Meyer—and to Ollie, who had now joined them— the forthcoming operation was really a simple one. The vets would use either dart guns or blowpipes to administer the anesthetic. The holding cages inside the bunker were flanked by keeper walkways. Guillotine doors opened from squeeze cages on the walkways into the larger holding cages. A five foot high concrete wall formed the back of each cage. The front of each cage was constructed of steel wire mesh. The keeper work area ran down the center of the building. There were access doors to the cages on either side of the work area. The anesthetized animals would be carried from the island to the ramp to the walkways and into the holding cages.

Considering that Carella had told Hardy the shooters would be here in ten to twelve minutes, he took his time debating with his staff the procedures they would use in safely anesthetizing and transporting the lions from the island to the holding area. Should they use an explosive projectile dart or a blowdart? Should they use a dissociative anesthetic, a tranquilizer, a non-narcotic sedative, or a narcotic drug?

"Even smaller cats than the ones out there are dangerous to handle without anesthesia," Hardy explained. "The young lion who carried off that woman's leg must weigh at least four hundred pounds. I'd say he measures ten feet long including his tail and stands at least three feet at the shoulders. You try to put a net on a wild animal that size, you're asking for trouble."

The drug they debated using was ketamine hydrochloride, a dissociative anesthetic most commonly delivered intramuscularly in doses of 100 to 200 mg/ml. For a dose sufficient enough to provide a rapid effect, a larger dart and more powerful delivery force was required. One of the keepers argued that this heightened the possibility of injury to the animal. Another argued that ketamine HCl was a painful injection. One of the vets argued that the drug induced a tendency for the animal to convulse. With three minutes to spare, they agreed to use the drug, after all, and decided that instead of using a blowdart, which had a higher probability of successful injection, they would use an explosive projectile dart, which had a traumatic impact but which was necessary because the drug was ketamine HCl.

At seven minutes to nine, just as Carella thought he heard the approaching siren of the van bearing the SWAT team, Hardy's own team went through the steel guillotine doors, out onto the run, down the ramp, and into the tunnel that led to a second pair of guillotine doors that opened discreetly onto the jungle-like environment where the young lion was gnawing on the woman's severed leg. If the lion heard the guillotine doors opening, he gave no sign of it. He was still busy with the bone—which was what the woman's leg had now become—when the first of the darts hit him in the forehead. The vets were going for the frontal or dissociative cortex of the brain. But as often happened with explosive projectile darts, the impact was insufficient to detonate the charge. Freddie, which was the lion's name, lifted his head from the bone, spotted the three vets crouched behind one of the habitat bushes—

"Easy now, Freddie," one of vets whispered.

—crouched for just an instant, and then charged them.

They ran for the guillotine doors, the lion behind them, ran into the tunnel under the moat, and up the ramp, into the run behind the holding cages, startling Hardy, who realized too late that a lion was loose. He stabbed at the button that began closing the guillotine doors behind the three vets—but the lion was inside as well. The doors clanged shut. Everyone was suddenly in a long narrow holding cage with a lion who'd just had his first taste of human flesh.

The access door to the work area was at the far end of the cage. Between that door and the lion were four zookeepers, three veterinarians, two animal behaviorists, two curators, an assistant director, a director, three detectives, and a partridge in a pear tree.

One of the detectives was Steve Carella.

The lion went directly for him.

Maybe it was his smile.

But Carella wasn't smiling. In fact, he was terrified, his eyes bulging, his mouth falling wide open as the lion leaped into the air at him. He brought his hands up defensively. Four hundred and some odd pounds of animal force knocked him flat on his back to the concrete floor of the cage. Pinned by enormous paws, Carella looked up at a head the size of a beach ball, all tawny fur and yellow eyes and open jaws and teeth. The lion's roar resounded through every nerve in Carella's body. He twisted his head away just as the animal lunged for his face.

A shot rang out.

It took the lion clean between the eyes.

He collapsed onto Carella like a huge smelly rug in somebody's den.

Fat Ollie Weeks waddled over, grinning, a nine-millimeter Glock in his hand.

He flipped back his jacket, holstered the gun, and said, "You owe me one, Steve-a-rino."

Over Alfred Hardy's violent objections, the SWAT team disposed of the remaining four lions in short order. Honey Blair got some nice shots of the sharp-shooters doing their job, aiming down their rifle barrels and all, the lions happily munching away on the lady out there, whoever she was, unaware that in minutes they would be merely trophies. Hardy re-fused to let Honey take any pictures of the carcasses on the island, animal or human, and ordered her off the premises. She went over to where a pair of para-medics were searching Carella for any cuts or bruises caused by what they insisted was a "maul-ing."

"I was *not* mauled," Carella told them over and over again. "I was almost *eaten,* but I was not mauled."

"Sounds like a good idea either way," Honey said, and smiled. "Here's my card. You ever feel like discussing police work or television reportage, give me a ring. Or even just a cappuccino, mm?" she said, and smiled again. *"Ciao, bambino."*

Carella watched her walking off.

He looked at the card.

And tossed it into the trash bin near the railing where he sat.

The paramedics thought the lion mauling him had damaged his brain.

The thing that bothered Carella most about the dead woman—or what was left of her, which wasn't very much—was that she was naked.

"Woman wandering around the zoo without any clothes on, dead of winter," Carella said.

"Which does seem peculiar," Meyer agreed.

"Almost makes it seem as if she didn't *want* to be identified."

He was thinking that this was the worst time of the year for suicides. Girl loses her man, her job, her mind, her gold watch—she wasn't wearing a watch, he noticed, unless one of the lions ate it— she decides to end it all. Ashamed of the act she's about to commit, she strips herself naked, goes for a bare-assed walk in the zoo, straight into the lion's den.

Another thing that bothered him was the fact that Ollie Weeks had saved his life. Once upon a time, Bert Kling had saved a Puerto Rican courier from a near-fatal baseball-bat beating. The man's name was José Herrera, and he had informed Kling that in certain cultures—Asian or North American Indian, he wasn't sure which—if you saved a person's life, you were responsible for that person's life forever. The one thing Carella did not want was Fat Ollie Weeks being responsible for his life forever.

"You think somebody *threw* her to those lions?" he asked Meyer.

"Be a new one, all right," Meyer answered.

Carl Blaney hated examining bodies that were in parts. If he'd wanted to become a butcher, he would not have gone to medical school. This one was particularly disgusting. All chewed over and everything. Your cases involving severed parts were usually your blunt force injuries, where a person got run over by a truck or a subway train. The other times you got a bundle of disconnected arms and legs was when somebody was trying to dispose of a murder victim, and sawed the body up into pieces and packed them in a trunk. This particular corpse, he'd been told, had been attacked by lions, of all things, you'd think this city was the African veldt.

There was not much more than the bare bones remaining of the victim's left leg. All the tissue and muscle had been torn away, leaving the exposed femur, patella, tibia, and fibula, portions of which had been gnawed through as well. The right leg was in a similar state of obliteration, the bones cracked open, the marrow sucked out. The woman's right breast was completely gone, her left breast consumed to almost where it joined the chest. Her right arm was still connected to the body, but the hand had been consumed, bones and all, and from the wrist up to the elbow, the tissue and muscle were gone, exposing the ulna and radius.

The heart, the liver, the pancreas, the stomach—all the tasty parts—were gone. He was examining the woman's head and face, which had been partially consumed, the nose and ears gone, the lips gone, the eyes gone, when he noticed—

But how could that be?

He was looking at a tiny circular perforation in the skull, just above what was left of the woman's hairline.

To the naked eye, it looked a great deal like a small-caliber pistol wound.

It was two-thirty that Saturday afternoon when the phone on Carella's desk rang. He picked up the receiver.

"Carella," he said.

"Blaney here."

"Hey, Carl."

"On this dead girl who got eaten by lions?" Blaney said, as if he still couldn't quite believe it. "I've lifted a good thumbprint and two fingerprints. I don't imagine you know much about her . . ."

"Not a thing so far."

"Reason I'm asking . . . I've come up with something interesting."

"What's that, Carl?"

"I found a tiny perforation in the left temporal region of the skull. At first, it looked like a bullet wound, but upon further . . ."

"Looked like a *what?* " Carella said.

"But it wasn't."

"What was it?"

"An ice-pick wound. Somebody stabbed her with an ice pick."

He waited while Carella absorbed this.

"The tract passed into the brain as deep as the left cerebral peduncle," he said. "Now, the reason this is interesting, such a wound will rarely cause instant death. Absent concussion of the brain, we've had victims surviving for as long as five days after an assault."

"I'm not sure I understand what you're saying, Carl."

"I'm saying there are cases on record of victims walking long distances from the scene of the trauma. Eventually, there'll be either subcortical or subdural hemorrhaging from the wound, with subsequent compression of the brain and resultant death. But *before* then . . ."

"Before then, she could've walked to the park, is that it?"

"Yes. Or someone could have transferred her there from wherever the trauma occurred. In either case, I'm merely stating as a positive fact that she was stabbed first. With an ice pick."

"When will I have those prints?" Carella asked.

"They're on the way now," Blaney said.

• • •

The prints reached Carella by messenger at three-seventeen that afternoon. A half-hour later, AFIS—the automated fingerprint identification system—got back to him with a hit on a United States Army lieutenant named Cassandra Jean Ridley.

3.

The telephone directory gave them a listing for a C J Ridley on South Ealey Street in Silvermine. Carella and Ollie went there at once. They had phoned ahead and a pair of technicians from the Mobile Crime Unit were waiting for them downstairs. The building was a twelve-story red brick a block away from the oval. They introduced themselves to the doorman, and asked to speak to the superintendent, a man named Peter Dooley, who immediately took them up to apartment 9C and unlocked the door for them.

Carella and Ollie stayed out in the hall with Dooley while the techs got to work. The super was a tall, wide-shouldered man with a shock of black hair and piercing blue eyes. He was wearing wide-wale blue corduroy trousers and a navy blue sweater vest over a red plaid shirt. He told them the woman lived here alone, took the apartment in November, was gone for a little while, came back again early in December. He figured she was worth a little something, the fur coats and all, don't y'know.

"When's the last time you saw her?" Carella asked.

"She was in and out a lot the past few days," Dooley said. "Doing her Christmas shopping, I guess. This the same case as the other one?"

Carella and Ollie looked at each other, puzzled.

"Had some detectives from the Eight-Seven here the other day," Dooley said.

"Oh? When was that?" Ollie asked.

"The other day. Thursday."

"What do you mean by the other case?" Carella asked.

"The break-in. We had a patrol car come by and then two detectives."

"No, this has nothing to do with that."

"I thought . . . well . . . Miss Ridley and all."

"What do you mean?"

"It was her apartment got broken into. She had me change the lock on the door the very next day."

"Let me get this straight," Carella said.

"There was a burglary here?" Ollie said.

"On Thursday, yes, sir. I changed the lock on this door only yesterday."

"Because the apartment was broken into?" Ollie said.

"Yep. I was outside with the doorman when your two detectives come by to investigate," Dooley said. "One of them a redhead, the other one this short little fellow with curly black hair. Doorman called upstairs, Miss Ridley told him to send them right up."

"Who were they, do you know?"

"Thought you might."

Carella was already on the cell phone.

"Anybody else here for the lady in recent days?" Ollie asked.

"Not that I noticed. I'm busy in the office most of the time."

"Bert?" Carella said. "This is Steve. Can you check with the Loot, see if Willis and Hawes responded to a burglary here on South Ealey this past Thursday?" He listened. "321," he said. "Apartment 9C. Sure." He turned to Ollie. "Kling. He's checking."

"Did you see anyone coming out of the building with Miss Ridley late last night, early this morning?" Ollie asked the super.

"I go home at six," Dooley said. "You're lucky you caught me."

"Which doorman was on last night, would you know?"

"Same one as now."

"Can you send him up, please?"

"Sure," Dooley said, and walked off toward the elevator.

"Yeah," Carella said into the phone. "Just what I thought. Are either of them there now? Put him on, willya?" He turned to Ollie. "Willis and Hawes were here around four Thursday," he said. "He's getting Willis now."

They waited.

The apartment seemed suddenly very still.

"Hal, hi, it's Steve," he said. "Bert tells me you

investigated a burg here at 321 South Ealey this past Thursday. Can you tell me a little about it?" He listened. "No, this is a homicide. Right. The lady got stabbed with an ice pick and thrown into the lion exhibit at the zoo. No, I'm dead serious. Can you give me the back story?" He listened. "A sable worth forty-five grand, right. And a mink stole worth six. Initials in both of them, CJR. Is that it? Okay, good, thanks a lot." He hit the END button, flipped the lid shut, turned to Ollie. "You heard?" he said.

"I heard."

Dooley was back with a man wearing a blue uniform with gold trim, blue hat with a shiny black peak. He looked Hispanic to Ollie, but Dooley introduced him as Muhammad Hassid, which meant he had just arrived from the Sahara and was plotting to blow up the nearest municipal building. Ollie asked him if he'd seen Miss Ridley leaving the building with anyone anytime last night.

"No, sir, I have seen no one," Hassid said.

"What time did you leave here?" Ollie asked.

"I was relieved at eleven-forty-five," Hassid said.

"Who came on after you?"

"Manuel Escovar."

"We'll want his address and phone number," Carella told Dooley.

"I have them in the office," Dooley said. "Will you be needin either of us any further?"

"Not right now," Ollie said. "We'll stop by on our way out."

"Good luck to you, lads," Dooley said.

"Thank you, sirs," Hassid said.

It took a good hour and a half for the techs to vac-uum the place for fibers and hair and to dust for fin-gerprints. The lights were on when Carella and Ollie finally went in to join them.

"Got some nice latents," one of the techs said. "How urgent is this?"

"It's a fuckin homicide," Ollie said. "What do you mean, how urgent is it?"

"Cause what I can do . . ."

"The fuckin lady got chewed to bits by lions!" Ollie said.

"I can run the prints for you, was what I was gonna suggest, save a little time," the tech said, un-ruffled. "Call you if I get a make."

"That'd be a help," Carella said.

"My name's Murphy, here's my card," he said. "Probably be late tonight, early tomorrow morn-ing."

"Gee, that's a *big* fuckin help," Ollie said.

Murphy looked at him.

"Talk to you later," he said to Carella and walked out shaking his head.

The apartment was a one-bedroom with a good-sized living room and a utility kitchen. They started in the bedroom, which was where they hoped to learn the most about the woman.

Three furs were hanging in the closet there: an ankle-length sable, a mink stole, and a red fox jacket. The initials in each of the furs were CJR.

Ollie turned to Carella.

"Didn't you say . . . ?"

"That's what Willis told me."

"So what are they doing here?"

"Maybe she had two of each."

"Maybe my aunt has balls," Ollie said.

There were also two woolen cloth coats in the closet, and a fleece-lined brown-leather flight jacket. The jacket had a silver bar on each shoulder and a diamond-shaped leather name patch over the left breast: Lt. C. J. Ridley. Hanging lengthwise on trouser hangers were two pairs of blue jeans and three pairs of tailored slacks. Hanging in the rest of the closet were dresses, skirts, and several bulky sweaters.

The clothes in her dresser drawer were laid out like soldiers lined up for inspection, rolled nylons and pantyhose in one drawer, tank tops and cotton panties in another, T-shirts and sweaters in the bottom drawer, all precisely stored away.

In the top drawer of the night table on the left hand side of the bed, they found a candy tin with a floral design on its lid. They opened the tin. Inside the box was a stack of photographs, several airmail letters, and a small black ring box that contained a slender gold wedding band. The letters were from a Captain Mark William Ridley—the return address indicated he was stationed with the U.S. Air Force in Germany—to a woman named Cassandra Jean Ridley in Eagle Branch, Texas.

"Probably her husband," Ollie said. "Got killed over there in Germany for some reason or other, and the letter's from a chaplain or somebody, telling her he was dead and returning the wedding band."

"Very romantic," Carella said.

"Let's read 'em."

"Also there's no war going on in Germany right this minute."

"Be the only place there isn't," Ollie said.

They opened one of the letters.

It was dated November 13 of this year, and it was from the dead woman's brother. He was telling her he'd just received a Dear John letter from his wife back in Montana, and he was sending their wedding band to Cassandra Jean to dispose of because he couldn't bear doing that himself, nor could he bear even looking at it ever again.

"That's romantic, too," Ollie said.

The letter went on to say that the job his sister had lined up for the early part of December sounded good to him, "so long as you won't be flying anything that might get you in trouble."

"Might've got her in a whole *lot* of trouble," Carella said.

"Let's take these, read 'em all later."

Sitting on the living room desk was an appointment calendar for the current year. They immediately flipped to the week of December 3.

Someone—presumably Cassandra Jean Ridley—
had scrawled the word *Mexico* into the box for
Sunday the third. An inked arrow ran over the boxes
for the next four days, its point leading to the box
for December 7, Pearl Harbor Day, where the words
End Mexico were written in the same hand. The
single word *East* was written in the box for December 8.

In the top drawer on the right hand side of the
kneehole, they found a checkbook from Chase, another for Midlands, and a savings account passbook
from a bank called First Peoples. For yet another
bank called Banque Française, they found a safe deposit box key in a little red packet with a snap catch.

A pile of rubber-banded hundred-dollar bills was
resting on edge, at the right hand side of the drawer.

There were eighty of them.

$8,000 in cash.

They wished they could take a peek at her
Banque Française safe deposit box, but this was the
Saturday before Christmas Day, and the bank had
closed at noon. Even a court order would not get it
to open again before Tuesday morning, the twenty-
sixth.

They went to see Manuel Escovar instead.

The streets of Little Santo Domingo were ablaze
with light when they got there at eight that night.
Stringed white lights hung from sidewalk to sidewalk, and dancing red and green lights flashed in

every window overlooking the street. Spotlighted
banners wished *Feliz Navidad* to the world. All up
and down the street, pushcarts lighted with flash-
lights displayed last-minute gifts ranging from Louis
Vuitton handbags to Hermès scarves and Rolex
watches. Christmastime was the biggest thriller of
the year, and the countdown had begun in earnest.

"All of this shit fell off the back of a truck," Ollie
commented.

They found Escovar in a little bar off Swift
Street, where he was enjoying a few beers with his
cronies before heading off to work at eleven. Ner-
vously, he told them his shift began at midnight and
ended at eight in the morning. Anything more than
two beers would be dangerous, he told them, but he
assured them he was all right with just two. Ollie
suspected Mr. Escovar here did not have a green
card. He suspected the man did not wish the slightest bit of trouble with the law. Which was why his
hands were trembling as he smilingly explained that
he was just a mellow little man with a sporty little
mustache enjoying a few peaceful brews with his
pals. My ass, Ollie thought. Instinctively, he knew
Escovar had something to hide if only because he
was a spic.

"There's a woman who lives at 321 South Ealey,"
Ollie said. "Her name's Cassandra Jean Ridley.
Does that name mean anything to you?"

"Miss Ridley, yes," Escovar said, nodding at
once. "Appar'menn nine C."

"That's the one," Ollie said. "Did you see her

leaving the building at anytime late last night, early this morning?"

Escovar thought this one over. Because he's getting ready to lie, Ollie thought. He had never met anyone of Spanish descent who gave you a straight answer. Then again, he had never met any Jew, Chinaman, Polack, Irishman, or Wop, for that matter—present company excluded—who could look you in the eye and give you an unequivocal yes or no. Ollie was a consummate bigot. He knew that virtually everyone he met in this business was inferior to Detective/First Grade Oliver Wendell Weeks. That was simply the way it was, kiddies, take it or leave it. Otherwise, a fart on thee.

Escovar's drinking buddies had moved from the bar to one of the booths, but they were watching the action here with intense interest now. Ollie glanced in their direction, and they all turned their heads away. He figured *they* didn't have green cards, either. Escovar was still thinking.

"Take all the time you need, ah yes," Ollie said, doing his world-famous W. C. Fields imitation.

Escovar took the suggestion to heart, the dumb little spic. The detectives waited.

"This might have been very early in the morning," Carella suggested. "Four, five o'clock, around then."

"I'm trine to remember," Escovar said.

Try speaking a little English, Ollie thought.

"She might have seemed disoriented," Carella said.

She might have had an ice pick in her forehead, Ollie thought.

"I thought she wass drunk," Escovar said.

The way he finally tells it, Miss Ridley got out of the elevator at about four-thirty this morning, accompanied by two girls—he called them "gorls"—one on each side of her, each holding one of her arms to support her, it looked like to him.

"Can you describe these girls?" Carella asked.

"They wass big gorls. Very tall."

"White? Black? Hispanic?"

"White," Escovar said.

"What color hair? Black? Blond? Red?"

"It wass two blondies," Escovar said.

Blondies, Ollie thought. Jesus.

"Skinny? Fat?" he asked.

"They wass wearin overcoats."

Ollie wondered what the fuck that had to do with the question.

"You can still tell if a person's skinny or fat," he said. "Look at me. Am I skinny or fat?"

Escovar hesitated.

"Go ahead, you won't hurt my feelings, I know I'm fat."

"If you say so," Escovar said shrewdly.

"In fact, I like being fat. It means I eat good."

"Okay," Escovar said.

"So were these two broads skinny or fat?"

"They wass healthy," Escovar said.

"What does that mean, healthy? Big tits? Did they have *tetas grandes, amigo?*"

Escovar grinned.

"Big *tetas,* huh?" Ollie said, grinning with him.

"Bigger than they gorlfrenn, anyhow," Escovar said, still grinning.

"How do you know she was their girlfriend?" Ollie asked. He was no longer grinning.

Neither was Escovar.

"How do you know Miss Ridley was their girlfriend?" Ollie asked.

Escovar looked at him blankly.

"Answer the question, Pancho."

"My name iss Manuel," Escovar said.

"Answer the fuckin question!"

"Slow down, Ollie," Carella warned.

"Never mind that man behind the curtain," Ollie said, jerking his thumb at Carella. "He's just being Good Cop. I'm the *Bad* Cop, Pancho, you dig? And in a minute I'm gonna ask you for your green card."

"I hass a green card."

"Oh, I'm sure you do."

"I hass it home."

"I'm sure that's just where you have it. How'd you know they were Miss Ridley's girlfriends?"

"They tole me they wass."

"Oh? When was this? When they carried her out of the fuckin elevator? They stopped and told you they were all good girlfriends here, is that it?"

"*Sí,* that wass when."

"You're lying, Pancho."

"That wass when."

"You sure it wasn't when they came *in?*"

Escovar looked at Carella again.

"Don't look at him, he ain't gonna help you. What'd they do, slip you a few bills to let them upstairs without buzzing the apartment?"

Escovar went pale.

"That's it, ain't it, Pancho?"

"They had a bahl of champagne," Escovar said. "They tole me it wass her burr'day. They said they wass good frenns, they wann to sorprise her."

"How much did they give you?"

"Ten dollars."

"To let them in, huh?"

"They said they wass frenns."

"Some friends, they stuck a fuckin ice pick in her head. What was she wearing, Pancho?"

"I tole you. Overcoats."

"Miss *Ridley.* What was *she* wearing when they carried her out of there? She wasn't naked, was she?"

"Naked? No. A gray suit. Jacket, skirt, a suit."

"Was she wearing shoes?" Carella asked.

"Shoes?" Escovar said, looking offended. "Of course, shoes, *señor.* The two gorlfrenns walk her by where I am holdin dee door open for them, out in the street. I thought she wass drunk," he said. "I thought it wass dee champagne. I wash them . . ."

He watched them as they walked up the street to a black Lincoln Town Car parked just outside the Korean nails place. Both of the girls got in the back seat with Miss Ridley. The car drove off around five, five-fifteen.

"Chauffeur driving the car?"

"I theenk so, yes."

"You didn't happen to notice the license plate number, did you?" Carella asked.

"I'm sorry, *señor,*" Escovar said. "I did not."

It was too early for Christmas presents.

Or maybe not.

At nine that night, when Carella went back to the squadroom to check on any phone calls and to sign out, there was a message that a detective named John Murphy had called to say he'd run the prints he'd lifted from the vic's apartment and had got hits on an Army lieutenant named Cassandra Jean Ridley and a guy named Wilbur Colley Struthers who'd taken a burglary fall in this city seven years ago. Struthers had dropped the better part of a five-and-dime at Castleview before getting released on parole two years ago. His last known address was 1117 South Twelfth . . .

"Right up there in the Eight-Seven," Murphy said. "Now ain't *that* a stroke of luck?"

Carella figured maybe it was.

He went there with three other detectives as backup; the man was a convicted felon whose fingerprints had been found all over the vic's apartment. The building on South Twelfth was a brick walkup, no doorman. The name under the doorbell was W. Struthers. Carella rang every other doorbell in the row. To the first voice that erupted on the speaker, he said, "Police, want to buzz me in, please?"

"What?" the voice said.

"Detective Carella, Eighty-seventh Squad," he said. "Please buzz me in, sir."

"What is it?"

"We need access to the roof. Buzz us in, sir."

"But what is it?"

"An air vent," Carella said.

Hawes shook his head, suppressed a smile. The buzz sounded a moment later.

"Thank you, sir," Carella said to the speaker, and the four detectives entered the building. Hawes was still shaking his head and smiling. Outside the door to 2C, Carella put his ear to the wood. Meyer was behind him, on his right. Brown was standing to the left of the door. This was ten o'clock on the Saturday night before Christmas, the building was alive with sound. Radios and television sets going, toilets flushing, people talking behind closed doors, there was a city in miniature inside the walls of this building. They had no warrant, hadn't even bothered to approach a judge for one because they'd felt certain Struthers' fingerprints alone would not constitute probable cause for arrest. They had to hope that the man inside there did not bolt for a window the minute they knocked on the door and announced themselves as policemen. Like most cops, they considered burglars—even convicted burglars—people who were not particularly dangerous. The "Burglars-Are-Gents" myth persisted, even though a surprised burglar could turn as violent as any other thief in the world.

There was music behind the closed door, coming from either a radio, an audio system, or a TV set, Carella couldn't tell which. Christmas music. He kept listening. He heard nothing but the music.

He turned to the others, shrugged.

Nobody said anything.

They all stood there with drawn weapons pointing up at the ceiling. Meyer Meyer, bald and blue-eyed and burly, looking patient and attentive and somewhat bored, to tell the truth; Cotton Hawes standing tall and square and redheaded, a white streak in the temple over his left ear, memento of an assailant whose name he'd long since forgotten, still looking amused by Carella's doorbell bullshit; Arthur Brown resembling nothing so much as a dark, scowling Sherman tank. Stalwarts of the law. Waiting for a signal either to come down the chimney or go home.

Carella shrugged again, knocked on the door.

There was silence except for the music, and then, "Yes?"

A man's voice.

"Police," Carella said, what the hell.

"Shit, what is it *this* time?" the man said.

They heard footsteps approaching the door. Heard a lock turning, tumblers falling, a chain coming off. The door opened wide. The man inside backed away the instant he saw four guys standing outside there with guns in their hands. He was about six feet tall in his bare feet, Carella guessed, wearing blue jeans and a brown woolen sweater with the sleeves shoved up to his elbows. His hair was a muddy blond color and his eyes were blue, opened wide now in either fear or surprise or both. A Christmas special was on the television set behind him.

"For Christ's sake, don't shoot," he said, and threw his hands up alongside his head. The cops in the hallway suddenly felt like horses' asses.

"Okay to come in?" Carella asked, and showed the tin.

"Yes, fine, come in," the man said, his hands still up. "Just watch how you handle them pieces, okay?"

"Your name Struthers?" Brown asked.

"Yes, sir, that's my name," Struthers said.

"Wilbur Struthers?"

"But you can call me Will, sir. Is this the kidnapping again?"

"What kidnapping?" Carella asked at once.

The detectives were maneuvering so that he was the center of a loose circle, their guns still drawn, nobody even dreaming of holstering them now that they'd heard the word "kidnapping," which was a federal offense that carried with it the death penalty.

"Is it the President's been kidnapped?" Struthers asked, and Carella thought, Oh dear, we've got ourselves a nutcase here, but he still didn't put up the gun.

"Know anybody named Cassandra Jean Ridley?" he asked.

Recognition flashed in Struthers' eyes.

"Do you know her?" Carella asked.

"I have met her, yes. But I do not *know* her, sirs. I would not say I truly *know* her. Excuse me, Officers, but it's been my experience that when there are firearms on the scene, one of them is bound to go off, either because of undue excitement or some other impulse of the moment. So, if it's all right with you, I'd appreciate it . . ."

"How'd your fingerprints get in her apartment?" Carella asked.

"Her goods and her money have already been returned," Struthers said.

The detectives looked at each other.

"What goods? What money?" Carella asked.

"I gave it all back to her yesterday," Struthers said.

"What are you saying?"

"He's saying he burglarized the joint," Brown said.

"Is that it?"

"No, no. There was a misunderstanding, that's all," Struthers said.

"What kind of misunderstanding?"

"Two of her furs came into my possession, was all. And a little cash, too. But everything was returned to her yesterday. Officers, if you think I'm armed and dangerous, why not simply frisk me, so I can put my hands down?"

Hawes frisked him. He was still smiling. He was
finding all of this somehow very comical. He nodded okay to the other detectives. They all holstered
their guns except Brown, who had grown up in a
neighborhood where people sometimes hid weapons up their asses. Struthers lowered his hands. He
looked relieved.

"When yesterday?" Carella asked.

Struthers blinked at him, puzzled.

"Did you return her stuff?" Carella explained.

"Oh. She came here around ten-thirty in the
morning."

"How'd she know where to find you?"

"I think through my eyeglasses," Struthers said.

Carella was still thinking the man was a bit off
his rocker. Hawes was still smiling. Brown still had
his gun in his hand. Meyer was wondering what the
man had meant about a kidnapping.

"What kidnapping?" he asked.

"What do you mean, through your eyeglasses?"
Carella asked.

"I think she may have found my eyeglasses. She
said she was delivering my eyeglasses."

"Found them where?" Carella asked.

"I don't know."

"What kidnapping?" Meyer asked again.

"The man from the Secret Service said there'd
been a kidnapping."

Next comes the CIA giving him instructions,
Carella thought. Through his radio or his television
set.

"Said the President had been kidnapped?" he asked.

"No, that was *my* notion."

"You thought the President had been kidnapped."

"Well, why else the Secret Service?"

Why else indeed? Carella thought.

Hawes was still smiling. Nodding his head and smiling. This was turning out to be a very amusing evening after all. Meyer was thinking if the Secret Service had really been here, then maybe someone in the White House had really been kidnapped. Brown was beginning to think along the same lines as Carella: the man was a loonie. He kept his gun in his hand, just in case.

"When was the Secret Service here?" Meyer asked.

"Day before yesterday," Struthers said, "around four in the afternoon. And he came back again that night, around ten, ten-thirty."

"Who was this? Did he give you a name?"

"Yes, sir, he did. Special Agent David A. Horne. With an 'e.' "

"Show you any ID?"

"Showed me his badge, yes, sir."

"What'd it look like?"

"You know that gold star the Texas Rangers carry? It looked a lot like that."

"And he told you he was with the Secret Service, is that right?"

"Yes, sir. The U.S. Treasury Department."

"What'd he want here?"

"He said a hundred-dollar bill I'd spent earlier in the day had serial numbers that matched the ones paid as ransom in a kidnapping. Which is why I thought it might be the President, the Secret Service and all."

"Naturally," Carella said.

"He took the rest of the money with him," Struthers said.

"The rest of *what* money?" Hawes asked.

"The money that was part of the misunderstanding between me and the Ridley woman."

"The money you *burglarized,"* Brown said, and waved the nine for emphasis.

Struthers looked at the gun.

"I'm not admitting to any burglary here," he said. "Or anything else."

"Like what?" Carella asked.

"Like anything at all," Struthers said.

"Maybe you'd like to tell us how your prints got in her apartment," Brown said.

"I took down her drapes," Struthers said.

Carella tried to remember if there'd been any drapes in the dead woman's apartment.

"Because I was going to paint the place for her," Struthers said. "Which is why I thought she wanted the furs moved. So they wouldn't get any paint on them." He nodded to the detectives, seeking approval and encouragement. "That was the misunderstanding," he said. *"I* thought she wanted the furs moved, whereas *she* didn't want them moved."

"How about the money?" Brown asked.

"That, too," Struthers said.

"You didn't want to get paint all over the money, is that it?"

"Exactly. There was just a misunderstanding, is all. She didn't know I was planning to move it, you see."

"Maybe she thought you'd be painting the place green."

"Huh?" Struthers said.

"The color of money."

"No, no . . ."

"In which case it wouldn't've mattered if you got paint all over it."

"No, it was beige."

"Which made a difference, of course."

"Yes."

"So you moved the furs and the cash before you took down the drapes and got your fingerprints all over everything."

"Well . . . yes."

"Man, you are so full of shit," Brown said.

"It wouldn't have been eight thousand in cash, would it?" Carella asked.

"The money was returned to her," Struthers said. "And I didn't kill her."

Whoa now, Carella thought.

"Who said anything about her being *dead?*" he asked.

"Television," Struthers said.

They all looked at him.

"I saw you and some fat cop on television early

this morning. At the zoo? Where some lady got tossed to the lions? That was her, wasn't it? That's what this is all about, ain't it?"

The man they knew only as Frank Holt was waiting in the other room while they tasted and tested the cocaine. What he was selling them here was a hundred kilos divided into ten-kilo packets. He was getting a million-nine for the lot, so they wanted to make sure it was good stuff. If it was anything but what he'd advertised it to be, they would kill him. He knew that, he was no fool.

The apartment they were in was a second-floor walkup on Decatur and Eighth. Tigo and Wiggy the Lid were in the second bedroom, such as it was. The man who called himself Frank was waiting outside, in what passed for a living room, chatting with a third man whose name was Thomas, and who was carrying a nine-millimeter Uzi. A radio playing rap music was on in the living room. Frank was the only white man in the apartment. He and Thomas were talking about recent movies they had seen. Thomas was saying he didn't believe none of the gunplay shit in any of the so-called action-adventure movies because all that ricochet stuff and sparks flying and sound effects like zing zang zing was all full of shit. Most gun fights didn't last an hour and a half, anyway. You shot somebody, he was either dead or gonna shoot you so *you* were dead. Frank tended to agree, though he himself had never been in a gun fight. He admitted this to Thomas now.

"You never shot nobody?" Thomas said.

"Never," Frank said.

"Shit, man," Thomas said unbelievingly, and began chuckling. "Where you from, man, the planet Mars?"

"I've just never found the opportunity."

"How long you been doing this?" Thomas asked.

"Almost eight years now."

"And you never found no opportunity to shoot nobody?"

"Most people I deal with aren't interested in ripping anyone off. We're traders, pure and simple."

"I got to tell you bout Wiggy," Thomas said. "He ain't such a pure and simple trader, man."

"He seems like your average businessman."

"He ain't so average, neither. You know how many people *he* has found the opportunity to kill?"

"I'd rather not know," Frank said.

"He got the name Wiggy not ony cause his lass name's Wiggins. It's also cause he wigs *out* whenever things don't go his way. Blows his *lid,* that's the second part of the handle, he Wiggy the *Lid,* man. Reason he so tempermennul, is he doped up day and night. This is one man involved in dealing shit who don't believe shit is *shit,* you take my meanin? He believes shit is *good* for a person. I don't know how much you sellin him in there . . ."

"A hundred keys."

"Wiggy goan snort half that fore the week is out."

"I know you're exaggerating."

"I am. But the man *do* like his cocaine. And when he's stoned, why, man, that's when he wigs out, that's when he blows his lid, that is when you has to shoot him first or he goan shoot you dead, man. He shot and killed . . ."

"I don't want to know. Really."

". . . twelve niggers ony last year," Thomas said, and shrugged. "It was Nigger of the Month Club roun here."

Frank never felt safe when black men—especially black men named Thomas—began calling themselves niggers in his presence because he never knew when the inside familiarity would suddenly turn against him. And whereas he'd never shot a man, he did not particularly encourage situations where gunplay might be called for. He himself carried a P-38 Walther. It made him feel like a Nazi in a war movie. They had not relieved him of the gun when he'd come up here. Perhaps because they knew he'd be crazy to attempt a shootout. Anyway, he'd have handed it over in a minute because there was no need to worry about his cocaine failing any test put to it.

The stuff Frank was selling had been grown in Bolivia and processed in Colombia for about $4,000 a kilo. That came to a growing-and-manufacturing cost of $400,000. The Mexicans he'd purchased it from in Guenerando had probably paid $800,000 for it, and had sold it to him for

$1,700,000. He was now about to turn it over for $19,000 a key—$1,900,000. That's the way it worked. A pyramid with everyone making a profit from top to bottom. Eight hundred large in Colombia, a million-seven in Guenerando, and now a million-nine in New York.

But Frank served a much higher cause than any of these assholes knew about.

Besides, he had a decided edge.

Wiggy had tasted the coke, and so had Tigo, but tasting it meant nothing because you could get bad stuff'd fool the keenest taste buds. Ony way to make sure was the trio of tests Wiggy called the TNT, for "Tried 'N' True."

First test you got straight from the water tap.

Opened the faucet, filled the glass with a few ounces of plain water, then scooped a spoonful of shit out of the plastic bag and dropped it in. If it dissolved directly, it was pure cocaine hydrochloride. If any of it stayed solid, the dope had been cut with sugar.

Second of the TNT was Clorox.

Put a little in a glass jar, drop a spoonful of the powder in it, and watch the movie. If you got a white halo trailing the powder, it was cocaine, my dear. If you got red following the powder as it fell, the stuff was cut with some kind of synthetic, and somebody was going to get killed.

Last of the three was the best of them all, cobalt

thiocyanate. What you did with the chemical was you dropped it onto the cocaine, also known as the White Leash, or the White Lady, or Lady, or sometimes just plain Girl, or any one of a thousand other cute little names to lure the kiddies in. If the powder turns blue, you've got cocaine. The brighter the blue, the better the Girl. Is what they say, man. The brighter the blue.

Frank's stuff lit up the sky like neon.

Wiggy had been taught to distrust every white man in the universe. He turned to Tigo and said in something like astonishment, "Why, the honkie's honest!"

But Wiggy also served a much higher cause.

Himself.

And he, too, had a decided edge.

4.

Ollie Weeks had called his sister to tell her he might not be able to make it there on Christmas Day cause he'd caught a leg being chewed on by a lion, and she'd said, "You ought to find yourself another job." Typical Isabelle Weeks remark, the jackass.

Now, to make matters worse, here was a dead guy stuffed in a garbage can, with a bullet hole at the back of his head. Your classic Mafia-style murder, except that the gangs up here in the Eight-Eight were all either black or Hispanic. Ollie could remember a time when the Mob ruled this part of the city, and all the Negroes and spics were running around doing the legwork for them while the Wops pulled in all the hard cash. Now it was different. The Wops should have learned to speak Spanish or so-called black English, which meant saying, "I done gone sell some dope to school chillun."

Ollie loved using the word "Negro" because he knew it pissed off "people of color," as they sometimes chose to be called. "Blacks" was another favorite, they should make up their fuckin minds.

Same thing with the spics up here, which word he
didn't dare use to their faces or they would cut him
up and serve him from a *cuchifrito* stand. They
didn't know whether to call themselves "Hispanics," which sounded too much like "spics," or "Latinos," which sounded like a team of tango dancers.
Ollie thought maybe they should concentrate instead on calling themselves "American," huh? and
not flying Puerto Rican or Dominican Republic
flags from their car antennas. Or marching in
Columbus Day parades, the Wops. Or St. Patrick's
Day parades, the Irish micks, getting drunk and
puking all over the city streets, while cops got paid
time and a half for overtime. Ollie hated all this
high-profile nationalism for countries that weren't
the U.S. of A. If they liked Santo Domingo or
San Juan or Islamabad or Jerusalem or Dublin
or Calcutta so fuckin much, they should go back
home instead of leaving dead bodies in garbage
cans. Ollie hated everyone and everything except
food.

They had stuffed the corpse in the garbage can
feet first, knees up, which was considerate of them.
It meant that you could look the dead man right in
the eyes. Looked like some kind of sculpture you
could find in one of the elite, highbrow, so-called art
museums downtown. Ollie could remember a time
when a person could stroll along the avenue and
buy an artistic landscape in real oil paints for
twenty-five bucks. Nowadays, you got a dead man
in a garbage can who looked like he was alive and

posing for some *artiste* except that he had a bullet hole at the base of his skull.

The medical examiner had come and gone, offering his learned opinion that the guy in the garbage can was indeed dead and that the possible cause of death . . .

"Possible," he'd actually said.

. . . was a bullet wound in the head.

With the help of the Mobile Unit techs—who had arrived some ten minutes ago and were dusting the alleyway as if it would reveal anything surprising about the corpse in the garbage can—Ollie lifted him out, and spread him on the alley floor. He was aware of the fact that in about ten minutes, an ambulance would arrive to pick up the body and carry it to the morgue, where they would cut it open to make sure the guy hadn't been poisoned *before* he got shot, a distinct possibility in police work, where nothing was as it appeared to be, ah yes, m'dear. Sometimes, Ollie even *thought* like W. C. Fields.

The dead man was carrying a wallet with a lot of identification in it. There was a driver's license that gave his name as Jerome L. Hoskins (no relation to the disease, Ollie hoped) and his address as 327 Front Street in Calm's Point—shit, he'd have to make a trip all the way to a section of the city for which he had no particular fondness. There was an American Express credit card made out to Jerome L. Hoskins, and MasterCard and Visa cards made out to the same name. There was a MetTrans card for the subway and bus lines in this considerate city,

and also a health plan card from an outfit called
MediPlan, whose main offices were in Omaha, Ne-
braska, wherever that was. There was seven hundred dollars in hundred-dollar bills in the wallet,
plus three twenties, a ten, and eight singles. A little
card said that the person to notify in case of an
emergency was Clara Hoskins at the same address
in Calm's Point, who could be reached at 722-1314.
Great. He just *loved* breaking the news to somebody's wife, mother, or sister.

A handful of change was in the right hand pocket
of the stiff's trousers, along with what appeared to
be a house key, a mailbox key, and a car key with a
big gold L for Lexus in a circle on its black plastic
head. The luxury car maybe spelled dope, though
the vehicle of choice these days was a Range Rover,
there being not much difference between big-city
dope dealers and Hollywood producers, ah, yes.
Strengthening the possibility of the stiff being
drug-connected (as who wasn't up here these
days?) was a carry pistol-permit tucked into one of
the wallet flaps.

The carry was for a P-38 Walther, however, a
somewhat ancient weapon for anyone in the drug
trade, but perhaps the man was merely a diamond
merchant who'd wandered uptown in search of
black pussy and flirted by mistake with the girlfriend of a Negro warlord named High Five or some
such. The gun itself was in a shoulder holster under
the man's hand-tailored suit jacket. He was wearing
no overcoat; when you're about to shoot a man at

the back of his head, you don't dress him for the cold weather outdoors.

Well, Ollie guessed he had to talk to this Clara Hoskins, whoever she might turn out to be, find out if she was home, and then go all the way out to Calm's Point to give her the sad tidings, ah yes. He gave one of the techs his card, and asked him to call if he came up with any valuable fingerprints, Fat Chance Department. He also advised them to keep an eye out for a meat wagon from St. Mary Boniface, which should be along any minute now. He could tell the techs didn't like fat people. Hell with them. *He* didn't like nerds who tip-toed around alleyways treating garbage as if it was some priceless piece of evidence instead of the messy shit it actually was.

"Have a merry Christmas," he told them.

"You, too," one of the techs said cheerlessly.

A fart on thee, Ollie thought, and smiled in farewell.

This was now twenty-seven minutes past ten on Sunday morning, the twenty-fourth day of December—Christmas Eve, by Ollie's own reckoning, ah yes.

His jackass sister was probably in church.

Carella's phone directory for law enforcement agencies gave him a number for the U.S. Treasury Department at 427 High Street, all the way downtown, close to where the old police headquarters building used to be located. A recorded message told him the offices were closed for the holiday and would not reopen until Tuesday morning, December 26.

On the off chance that Special Agent David A. Horne might be listed in one of the city's five telephone directories, Carella tried the Isola book first and came up with dozens of listings for the surname Horne, but none for a David A. Horne. He began dialing, anyway. On his twelfth try, he hit paydirt.

"David Horne, please," he said.

"Who's this?"

"Detective Steve Carella, Eighty-seventh Squad."

"This is David Horne."

"Mr. Horne, we're investigating a homicide here, woman named Cassandra Jean Ridley . . ."

"Yes?"

". . . whom we've linked to a man named Wilbur Struthers . . ."

"Yes?"

"Did three and a third at Castleview on a burglary fall . . ."

"Yes, I know the man. I questioned him about some suspect hundred-dollar bills."

"Related to a kidnapping," Carella said, nodding.

There was a silence on the line.

"Can you tell me which kidnapping that was?" Carella asked.

"No, I'm afraid that's classified information," Horne said.

"Even to a fellow law enforcement officer?"

"I'm afraid so."

"This is a homicide, you know."

"So you told me."

"Well, can you at least tell me how it worked out?"

"How what worked out?"

"The questioning."

"I confiscated eight thousand dollars in hundred-dollar bills, checked the serial numbers against our list, and came up negative. I returned the bills to Mr. Struthers that very same day. End of story."

"Which list would that be? That you checked the bills against?"

"I'm afraid that's classified, too."

"Who was kidnapped, Mr. Horne? Can you tell me that?"

"Classified."

"If I showed you the bills we recovered in the victim's apartment, could you tell me if they're the same ones you checked against this mysterious list of yours?"

"Do I detect a note of sarcasm in your voice, Detective Coppola?"

"It's Carella."

"Oh, forgive me. But this is Christmas Eve, you know . . ."

"Yes, I know that."

"And I'm home here with my family. If you can . . ."

"Gee, *I'm* still here at the office," Carella said.

"That's admirable, I'm sure. Call me on Tuesday, okay? Perhaps we can talk then."

"Mr. Horne, the victim won't *ever* be talking again."

"That's unfortunate. But I'm certain our separate cases aren't at all linked."

"Then why were the serial numbers on her money being checked against bills paid in ransom, isn't that what you said?"

"I said nothing of the sort."

"Then it's what Struthers told me."

"A man with a criminal record."

Carella could almost hear the dismissive shrug.

"He seemed to be telling the truth," Carella said.

"Be that as it may."

"Mr. Horne, I'm trying to find out who . . ."

"It's Special Agent Horne, by the way."

"Oh, forgive me. But somebody tossed a woman to the lions the other day . . ."

"Is that a metaphor, Detective?"

"I wish. We're trying to find out who. Any help you can give us . . ."

"I have no help to offer. Our case is, as I said, classified. Besides, the bills we checked have nothing to do with that woman's death."

"How do you know that?"

"I feel certain they're unrelated."

"Then why were you checking them?"

"Detective . . ."

"Please don't sound so annoyed," Carella said.

He wanted to say, Don't sound so fucking annoyed, okay, Mr. Special Agent Horne?

"I can subpoena those serial numbers," he said.

"You'd never get a court order."

"Why not?"

"Detective," Horne said, and paused. "Let it go, okay? Leave it alone."

"Sure," Carella said, and hung up.

He had no intention of leaving it alone.

Clara Hoskins, as it turned out, was Jerome Hoskins' wife. On the phone, Ollie told her he was investigating something or other . . .

Actually, he mumbled the words "identification process" so that they were unintelligible, a bullshit ploy that did nothing to quell Mrs. Hoskins' curiosity.

"You're investigating *what?*" she asked.

"Routine matter," he said. "Better to discuss it in person. Okay to come out there, Mrs. Hoskins?"

"Well, all right, I guess," she said. "But you'd better have identification."

The drive to Calm's Point took him half an hour from the North Side of the city to the bridge and over it into a community only recently reclaimed from urban decay. Hillside Commons consisted of low-rise tenements which had been inhabited by runaway hippies during the Sixties and Seventies, immigrant Hispanics in the early Eighties, Koreans in the Nineties, and now—here in the bright new

millennium—upwardly mobile Yuppies yearning
for a glimpse of the distant towers across the River
Dix. The way Ollie looked at it, all those former immigrant residents could move right next door to
Hillside Heights, where there were still street gangs
and dope pushers and prostitutes and all the other
amenities they were used to. Not that he liked the
fuckin preppie Yuppies, either, but if an individual
couldn't speak the fucking language, he had no
right living in a nice neighborhood.

Clara Hoskins spoke the language just fine.

She would not open the door until Ollie had
flashed both his ID card and his gold detective's
shield, and then she unlocked two locks and took off
a security chain before letting him in. She was a
blonde in her early forties, Ollie guessed, dressed in
tailored gray slacks and a tight red sweater with a
little Santa Claus pin over the left breast. Five-
seven, five-eight, he supposed, good-looking
woman except for the suspicious blue eyes and the
frown. She led him into the living room, where a
Christmas tree was ablaze with light in one corner
of the room. There was the scent of greenery all
over the apartment, in fact. All the place needed was
a log burning on the hearth, but this was the city,
and only cannel coal was allowed, and not even that
was in evidence.

"Mrs. Hoskins," he said, figuring he'd get straight
to the point, "I'm afraid I have bad news for you."

"Oh Jesus," she said.

"Your husband is dead, ma'am, I'm sorry to have to tell you this way."

"Oh Jesus," she said again.

They all reacted in different ways. Some of them burst into tears, some of them staggered around the room like drunks, some of them looked as if they'd been hit by a locomotive, some of them couldn't speak for ten, fifteen minutes, some of them denied it, told you you'd made a mistake, or this was all a horrible joke, anything to get away from the fact that the Grim Reaper had come to the door and knocked on it and found somebody home. Clara Hoskins just stood there staring at him.

"Tell me what happened," she said.

"He was murdered," Ollie said.

"Are you a homicide detective?" she asked.

"No, ma'am, that's not the way we work it here. The precinct detective who catches the squeal . . ."

He caught himself.

"The responding detective follows the case through to its conclusion, ma'am, is the way we work it here in this city."

"Where was this?" she asked.

"In a section of the city called Diamondback, ma'am."

"That's black, isn't it?" she said.

"Largely, ma'am. And Hispanic."

"What was Jerry doing up there?"

"I thought maybe you could help me with that."

"Diamondback," she said, and shook her head.

"Do I smell something baking, ma'am?" Ollie asked.

"Oh my God," she said, "thank you," and turned away from him and rushed into the kitchen. He watched as she yanked open the oven door and took from it a steaming cake. "Caught it just in time," she said, and put it down on the counter top. "I bake one every Christmas," she said.

"What is it, ma'am?"

"An apple upside down cake."

"I'll bet it's delicious," Ollie said.

But she didn't offer him any.

Instead, she suddenly burst into tears. Sometimes apple upside down cakes did that to people. Or maybe she had just realized her husband was dead. Either way, if she wasn't going to offer him any-thing to eat, he had no sympathy at all for the woman.

"Ma'am," he said, "weren't you concerned when your husband didn't come home last night?"

"He's often gone a lot," Clara said.

"Were you expecting him home?"

"Not necessarily."

"Well, did he call to say he *wouldn't* be home?"

"No, he didn't. But that's usual. I don't worry about him. He comes and goes."

"What does he do for a living, ma'am?"

"He sells books."

"He works in a bookstore?"

"No, he's a book *salesman*. For Wadsworth and

Dodds. The publishing house. His territory is the entire northeast corridor. He goes all the way up to Maine and down to Washington, D.C. He's gone a lot."

Ollie tried to think if there were any bookstores in Diamondback. He couldn't recall a single one.

"Does he make stops in Diamondback?" he asked.

"I don't know where he makes stops," Clara said, and yanked a Kleenex from a box on the counter. "Can't you see I'm crying here?" she said. "Don't you have any sensitivity at all?"

"I'm sorry, ma'am, but I'm trying to learn who might have killed him. Your husband wasn't doing drugs, was he?"

"What!"

"I said . . ."

"I heard what you said. How *dare* you?"

"Mrs. Hoskins, I was simply asking a question. Your husband was found in a garbage can in Diamon . . ."

"A garbage can!"

"Yes, ma'am, with a bullet hole in the back of . . ."

"A bullet hole!"

"Yes, ma'am, which all sounds very strange for a man who sells books for a living, wouldn't you say? Did you know that he carried a gun?"

"A gun!"

"Yes, ma'am, a P-38 Walther was the make. In a

holster on his right side. Was he left-handed, ma'am?"

"Yes. I have to tell you, Detective Weeks, I find all of this extremely upsetting." She pulled another tissue from the box, and blew her nose. Ollie hoped she wouldn't get snot all over the cake. She still hadn't offered him a piece. "I can't imagine *what* my husband was doing up there in Diamondback, or why he was carrying a gun, or why anyone would want to kill him. This is all simply beyond belief," she said, and blew her nose again.

"Yes, well, I'm terribly sorry it happened, too, ma'am, or even that I had to report it to you."

He was thinking he would like a piece of her apple upside down cake.

He was also thinking he would like to grab her ass.

"Your husband had a permit for the gun," he said.

"A permit!"

She had a very bad habit of repeating the key words in everything he said and shouting them back at him, very loudly, as if he were deaf. Each time she did that, he winced. The kitchen was redolent with baking smells. He felt like grabbing that cake in both his hands and gobbling it down.

"You sure he wasn't doing drugs?" he asked.

"No, I'm *not* sure, how would I *know* if he was doing drugs or not? He was on the road two, three weeks at a time, for all I know he was robbing banks with his goddamn P-36 . . ."

"Eight, ma'am."

"Whatever, and shooting heroin in his veins, how the hell would *I* know what he was doing when he wasn't here? He ends up in a garbage can, how the hell do *I* know what he was or even *who* he was?"

"That's just my point, ma'am."

"I fail to see your point."

"Just that it seems so strange."

"It does," she agreed, and burst into tears again.

He wanted to take her in his arms and comfort her. He wanted to reach up under that tight red sweater.

"I wish I could play piano for you sometime," he said.

She looked at him.

She had very blue sad wet eyes.

"To ease your pain," he said.

"Thank you," she said, "that's very kind of you."

"I play piano," he said.

"I wouldn't have suspected it," she said.

"I'm sorry for your trouble," he said. "Here's my card. Call me if you think of anything."

"What would I think of?" she asked.

"Anything that might help us find your husband's murderer."

She burst into tears again.

"Where do I go to . . . to claim . . . to . . . to . . . where is he now? His body?"

"At the St. Mary Boniface morgue," Ollie said. "You can identify the remains . . ."

"Remains!" she said.

"Yes, ma'am, his body, ma'am. You don't think he had a black girlfriend up there, do you?"

"A what!"

"I guess not," he said. "Call me, okay? I know 'Night and Day,' if you happen to like that song."

She was sitting by the Christmas tree in the living room, weeping, when he left the apartment. He could smell the goddamn apple upside down cake all the way down to the street.

The halls of justice were somewhat less than thronged with judges eager to hand down rulings at three o'clock on this Christmas Eve, which also happened to be a Sunday. Most pickpockets, shop-lifters, and daytime burglars had called it a day yes-terday, packing it in at six o'clock, when all the stores closed. Most of the judges had done the two-step at around the same time, the Christian judges eager to get back to their homes and hearths so they could start the Yuletide festivities, the judges of other faiths heading to vacation spots where they could escape a holiday that excluded them so completely. Only skeleton crews manned the courtrooms. The entire Criminal Courts build-ing resembled nothing so much as a marble mau-soleum.

Abe Feinstein was the judge who read Carella's petition for a search warrant. He was sixty-three years old, and he'd been a criminal court judge for twenty-three years now, having been appointed at the age of forty, which was relatively young for such a judgeship. He read the signed affidavit and then peered over the rims of his eyeglasses and the top of his bench, and said in a rather astonished voice, "You want a warrant to search the offices of the U.S. *Treasury* Department?"

"Yes, Your Honor."

"Because—if I'm reading this correctly—you wish to examine a list of *serial* numbers . . ."

"Yes, sir."

". . . for hundred-dollar bills that you believe may have been used as *ransom* money in a kidnapping?"

He still sounded astonished.

"Yes, Your Honor," Carella said.

"Which kidnapping would that have been, Detective?"

"I don't know, sir. That's what I'm trying to find out."

"I must be missing something," Feinstein said, and shook his head.

"Your Honor, a special agent named David A. Horne confiscated eight thousand dollars in hundred-dollar . . ."

"Hold it, hold it, where's that on the affidavit?"

"Paragraph number three, Your Honor."

" 'Upon personal knowledge and belief,' " Feinstein quoted, " 'and facts supplied to me by . . .' "

"Yes, Your Honor, by an ex-con named Wilbur Struthers, who burglarized the suspect money from the apartment of a woman now deceased, the victim of a homicide. That's all in paragraph three, Your Honor."

"Eaten by *lions,* does this say?"

"Yes, sir. At the Grover Park Zoo yesterday. But that wasn't the cause of death. The woman was first stabbed with an ice pick."

"I see that, yes."

"In the head, Your Honor."

"Yes. And you think her murder may be related to this kidnapping you mention?"

"Yes, Your Honor, I do."

"But you don't know anything about this kidnapping?"

"Only what Struthers reported to me."

"Does he seem reliable?"

"As reliable as any thief can be, Your Honor."

"Have you contacted the Secret Service?"

"I spoke personally to Special Agent Horne, yes, Your Honor."

"And what did he have to say?"

"He advised me to leave it alone."

"Any idea why he would have made such a suggestion?"

"He told me the case was classified, sir."

"I see. And you're asking for a search warrant that would invade this confidentiality, is that it?"

"A woman was murdered, Your Honor. An ice pick . . ."

"I have no idea what this kidnapping case is about—and neither do you, I might add. Which means you don't have probable cause, Detective. If the Secret Service has deemed its case classified, I'm not going to allow you to poke around confidential documents. Take Horne's advice, Detective. Leave it alone. Petition denied."

"Thank you, Your Honor," Carella said.

"Merry Christmas," Feinstein said.

Ollie Weeks called the offices of Wadsworth and Dodds at four that afternoon. He got a message telling him the firm was closed for the holidays and would not reopen until Tuesday morning, December 26.

He figured he was the only person working in this fucking city, so he went home.

5.

So this is what the family has turned out to be, Carella thought.

This is what this family has become on this Christmas Day in the new millennium.

There's still me and Teddy, thank God, and the twins, thank God again, although he didn't appreciate the fact that they were slowly inching their way toward puberty. Before he knew it, Mark would be reading *Penthouse* and April would be dating seniors, and he and Teddy would be in wheelchairs in a nursing home. Forty years old, he thought. Jesus. Where did it all go so soon?

There was his sister Angela, too, of course, with her own twins—they ran in the family—and their older sister. Tess was eight, the twins four, all three far distant from puberty. Angela had named the twins Cynthia and Melinda, and then had begun calling them Cindy and Mindy, as if they were a tap-dancing team in Vegas, shame on you, Sis, even though their father had insisted they be called Cynthia and Melinda as originally planned, a noble thought.

Tommy wasn't here this Christmas, the little girls' father was God-knew-where on this bright cold afternoon as everyone was called to dinner, or lunch, or whatever it was at two in the afternoon. Tommy Giordano wasn't here today because he and Angela were divorced now—but not because he'd insisted on calling his daughters by their true and proper names. Tommy Giordano had been caught having a love affair, was still having a love affair, but the lady in question wasn't a lady at all, although she was often called that. Tommy Giordano was having a love affair with cocaine. He had tried psychiatric help, had tried rehabilitation, had tried every damn thing he and the family could think of, but he was hooked through the bag and back again, and nothing had worked. The marriage had fallen apart when Angela just couldn't take it any longer. Tommy was still snorting the Devil's Dandruff, *wherever* he was—the last time they'd heard it was Santa Fe, New Mexico.

In Tommy's place today was an assistant district attorney named Henry Lowell, who had received his undergraduate degree from Duke, his law degree from Harvard, and a smattering of lesser education from Oxford University, or so the precinct locker-room jive maintained. Lowell had been with the D.A.'s Office for almost five years now. In that time, he had racked up thirty-eight convictions, an impressive record, four of them on murder cases.

The only murder case he'd ever lost, in fact, was the one he'd prosecuted against the man who'd killed Carella's father.

Maybe this was why Carella didn't like him too much.

Gee.

What Carella couldn't understand was why his *sister* was sleeping with the son of a bitch, and bringing him around to his mother's house on every goddamn holiday that came along. That was what Carella couldn't understand, but maybe he was just old-fashioned. Maybe he thought real life here in the big bad city wasn't the same thing as Greek tragedy where you slept with your father's murderer or ate your own children. Given that the murderer had finally been gunned down by Carella himself or maybe Brown, who'd been standing by his side and firing at the same time . . .

Or maybe both of them . . .

Given that bygones should be bygones . . .

Justice had been served . . .

An eye for an eye and all that . . .

Given all that . . .

Should Angela *really* be considering marriage to the man?

But even worse than *her* defection . . .

How could his *mother* have forgotten so soon?

The second interloper at the table today was a man named Luigi Fontero from Milan, Italy. Henry

Lowell was sitting on Angela's right, and Luigi Fontero was sitting on Louise Carella's right— Carella's mother's right, right! Nor was this the "Luigi" of ancient television fame, a fruit peddler or whatever the hell he'd been, a man who spoke broken English the way the immigrants at the turn of the century had, although the show took place in the Fifties, Carella guessed, he'd only seen a single rerun on the Nick at Nite channel or one of the other hundred and ninety-nine channels proliferating like fleas on a dog.

This Luigi was a furniture manufacturer. *This* Luigi made furniture fashioned by some of Europe's most important designers. *This* Luigi spoke fluent English with merely the faintest trace of an accent. *This* Luigi wore suits hand-tailored in Rome, and shoes hand-cobbled in Florence. *This* Luigi was holding his mother's hand. If this were Greek tragedy, Carella would have cut off *this* Luigi's hand at the wrist.

"How was the weather when you left Milan?" Lowell asked pleasantly.

"Milan is always the same this time of year," Fontero replied pleasantly. "Drizzly and cold. Very much like Paris."

Two old buddies chatting about the weather.

Carella wanted to kill them both.

"Could *we* go to Paris sometime?" April asked her mother, simultaneously signing.

Teddy signed back, *Yes, next weekend, darling.*

"Really?" April said, her eyes opening wide.

Image of her mother, black hair and brown eyes. Talked up a storm, a constant chatterer—well, exactly like her mother in that respect as well, except that Teddy could only talk with her hands and her eyes. Born deaf, she had never heard a human voice, never heard any sound at all. Almost everyone at this table knew how to sign, some perfectly, some to a lesser degree. Except the interlopers, of course. They looked at Teddy's hands as if she were scribbling Sanskrit on the air.

April was wearing lipstick. Not yet thirteen, and wearing lipstick. Teddy assured Carella it was all right. Carella didn't want to think his daughter was growing up. He didn't want to think his sister would be marrying the man who'd let their father's killer go free. He didn't want to think his mother was starting up with some Italian gigolo so soon after his father's death. On Christmas Day a year ago, she'd burst into tears whenever his father's name was mentioned. Now she was openly holding hands with a man who looked too fucking much like a young Marcello Mastroianni.

Maybe I've had too much wine, Carella thought.

"I love Italian furniture," Angela said.

Right, Sis, Carella thought. Aiding and abetting.

"Yes, it is quite beautiful," Fontero said.

In all modesty, Carella thought.

"Lamps, too," Angela said.

Compounding the felony, Carella thought.

"What's the name of your company?" Lowell asked.

"Mobili Fontero."

"Could I have more lasagna, please?" Mark asked.

The conversation ebbed and flowed, washing the table in familiar sound, except for the voices of the inept district attorney and the sartorially resplendent furniture man from Milan. Carella's mother had been on a diet for the past two months. Now he knew why. She was styling her hair differently. Now he knew why. He wondered how long they'd known each other. Wondered how they'd met. Wondered . . .

"How'd you two guys meet, anyway?" Lowell asked.

You two guys. As if they were teenagers. His mother was sixty-three years old. Fontero was sixty-seven if he was a day. You two guys.

"You tell him, Luigi," his mother said, and patted his hand.

Looking like a schoolgirl. The funeral meats not yet cold upon the table. He suddenly remembered his brief stay in college, remembered playing a bearded Claudius to Sarah Gelb's Gertrude, a girl he'd later taken to bed—if you could call it that—in the back seat of his father's car.

He missed his father so very much.

Luigi was telling them about Louise's best friend—

That was Carella's mother he was talking about. Louise. Louise Carella. Luigi and Louise. And, of course, Luigi was Louis in Italian, Carella's middle name, Louis and Louise, oh how *cute!*

—Louise's best friend Kate, who lived next door, and who was related somehow to Luigi's brother in Florence (Firenze, Luigi said) who had suggested that Luigi stop by to say hello while he was on his business trip to America, which he had done, taking a taxi the first time . . .

"That was a mistake," Louise Carella said, his mother said, rolling her eyes. "Luigi didn't know how much it would cost, all the way up here to Riverhead."

"You should have asked for a flat rate," Angela suggested.

"Well, at home they warn us all the time about the taxi drivers in this city, but I must tell you I have never once been cheated on any of my visits here."

"How often do you come here?" Lowell asked.

"Three, four times a year. To sell my line to American dealers. But also because I love this city." He smiled. Beautiful white teeth. Marcello Mastroianni teeth. "Now I have reason to come more often," he said, and squeezed Louise's hand, squeezed Carella's mother's hand.

"To make a long story short," his mother said, Louise said, "I was there having coffee with Katie when this taxi pulled up and Luigi stepped out . . ."

"This was in October," Luigi said.

"He was wearing a gray coat with a black fur collar . . ."

Like a Russian diplomat, Carella thought.

"No hat," Louise said.

Carella noticed that he had thick black hair, Luigi
did.

"He came up the walk, and rang the doorbell,"
Louise said. "Katie was expecting him, of course,
but not until much later. He introduced himself . . ."

"I soon forgot I was there to say hello to my
brother's friend," Luigi said, and squeezed her hand
again, Carella's mother's hand, Louise's.

"We went out to dinner, the three of us," Louise
said.

"I asked Katie to join us for the sake of courtesy,"
Luigi said.

A beard, Carella thought.

"And that's how we met," Louise said.

"I came back the very next month."

"Before Thanksgiving."

"We talk every day on the phone."

"We've known each other since October fif-
teenth," Louise said.

Birthdate of great men, Carella thought, but did
not say.

"Seventy-one days today," Luigi said.

But who's counting? Carella thought.

His sister's eyes met his.

There was something like a warning in them.

Et tu, brute? he thought.

He'd played Caesar, too. And had gone to bed
with Portia after the opening-night party. A year
and seven months in college, and he'd been able to
score with only two girls, big Lothario. How did he

suddenly get to be forty? It occurred to him that he had never been to bed with another woman since the day he met Teddy. Nor did he ever plan to. Nor had he ever felt the slightest desire for any other woman. He wondered how many women *Signore* Marcello over there had been to bed with, *Signore* Casanova, wondered if he'd already been to bed with Carella's mother, Louise, with her stylish new clothes and her svelte new figure and her elegant new coiffure, wondered if his mother had already forgotten that once upon a time there'd been a gentle, loving man named Anthony Carella who'd been shot to death during a holdup in his bakery shop, wondered if sooner or later everyone who dies is forgotten, and thought, curiously, Shakespeare isn't forgotten, I was Claudius, I was Caesar.

He poured himself another glass of wine.

This time, it was his wife's eyes that shot a warning across the table.

He smiled at her and raised his glass in a silent toast.

She sighed and turned away.

She did not say anything to him until she was certain the children were asleep. Carella was already in bed when she came to him. She sat on the edge of the bed, and in the light of the lamp burning on the night table, her fingers and her eyes told him what was on her mind.

You're drinking too much, she said.

"Come on," he said, "a few glasses of wine, what's wrong with you?"

It started in November, when Danny Gimp got killed . . .

"Danny was a stool pigeon," he said.

He was your friend.

"I never considered him a friend."

He came to the hospital.

"That was a long time ago."

He came when you were hurt. And now he's dead. And you never cried for him.

"He meant nothing to me," Carella said.

Did your father mean something to you?

Carella looked at her.

You didn't cry for him, either.

"I cried," Carella said.

No! her hands shouted. Her eyes were flashing. He realized all at once that she was containing enormous anger.

"I cried inside," he said.

Why are you still so angry with Henry?

"Oh for Christ's sake, is he *Henry* already?" Carella said.

Your sister's going to marry *him!* Teddy said. *You have no right to make her feel guilty about it! She* loves *him!*

"Love!" Carella said.

Is that all at once a dirty word?

"He lost the case!"

Do you think he wanted to?

"He let the man who killed my father . . ."

Steve, she said, and put her hand on his arm. *Sonny Cole is dead. You killed him, Steve. He's dead. Let it go, honey. Leave it alone.*

"Seems everyone's asking me to do that these days," he said, and shook his head.

What does that mean?

"Nothing," he said. "Forget it."

You never used to say Nothing, forget it.

Her hands stopped, the room went suddenly still. She looked at him for what seemed a very long time.

Steve? she said at last. *Do you still love me?*

"I adore you," he said.

Then what is it? Is it the job?

He shook his head.

Is it?

"No. No, I love the job."

She took a deep breath.

And in the stillness of the night, she asked him why he'd drunk so much at his mother's house today, and at first he told her he hadn't drunk that much at all, a glass or two of wine, and then he admitted he'd had at least a full bottle, but this was Christmas Day, so what the hell, she didn't have to start talking to him as if he was some kind of *drunkard,* this wasn't Tommy Giordano here sniffing his life up his nose in Santa Fe or wherever. Then he admitted that he was annoyed that his sister would even *consider* marriage to the man who'd let Sonny Cole walk out of that courtroom . . .

"Never mind that it ended with me shooting him, do you think that's something I *enjoy* doing?" he asked. "Gunning down a man? Do you think I became a cop so I could shoot people dead in the street, twenty yards from the house where my wife and my children are sleeping, do you think I *enjoy* doing that?"

I think the job is getting to you, she said, and he told her Don't be ridiculous, and she said I think the job is beginning to get to you, honey, you're not the same since your father got killed, you just aren't the same man I married, and she began sobbing into his shoulder. He told her Come on, nothing's changed, I *love* the job. And I *did* cry for my father, you don't know how much I cried. I cried for Danny, too, he *was* a friend, I know he was, he practically died in my arms! Jesus, Teddy, don't you think I *care* for people, don't you think I have any feelings?

And suddenly he was crying again—or perhaps for the first time.

She moved out of his arms.

She sat up.

Listen to me, she said.

He nodded. His nose was running. Tears were rolling down his cheeks.

If it's the job, she said, *I want you to leave it.*

He shook his head. No. Kept shaking it. No.

I don't want to lose my husband to the job.

Tears kept streaming from his eyes.

I don't want you eating your gun one day.

He kept sobbing.

At last, she turned out the light and went to bed with him cradled in her arms.

He fell asleep thinking that only two days ago, he'd seen a woman chewed to pieces like raw meat.

Visions of sugar plum fairies danced in Ollie's head, even though Christmas Day had come and almost gone. Visions of roast beef slices, too. And candied yams. And buttered beans. And thick apple pie with vanilla ice cream sitting on its flaky crust. And Red Delicious apples, and Bartlett pears, and Baci chocolates with a sort of fortune-cookie message that read A woman's soul is like an angel's kiss. Lying alone in bed, he thought of all the delicious things his sister had served for Christmas dinner today, and he forgot all about the two separate—or so he thought—cases he was currently investigating. Suddenly famished, he got out of bed and went to the refrigerator.

He fixed himself a thick Genoa salami sandwich on rye bread smothered with butter and mustard, and poured himself a glass of whole milk, and carried these to the upright piano he'd rented.

It was almost midnight.

He sat down and started playing "Night and Day."

Somebody in the building yelled, "Shaddup, you jackass!"

A fart on thee, Ollie thought, and continued playing.

He had to admit he wasn't yet a jazz giant, but tomorrow was another day.

Walter Wiggins, better known as Wiggy the Lid, liked to frequent a bar on St. Sebastian's and Boyle because there were very often white hookers in here. Wiggy was in the mood for a white hooker tonight. Not any of your Puerto Rican hookers who looked white because they were of Spanish and not African descent. What he wanted was a genuine white hooker.

As a black kid growing up in America, Wiggy had played basketball in the schoolyard, had joined a street gang when he was thirteen, had convinced a twelve-year-old deb member of the gang that slobbering the Johnson wasn't the same thing as having sex, had killed two other black kids from opposing gangs when he was sixteen, had decided when he was eighteen that gang-busting was for the fools of this world, had become fond of cocaine while serving as a mule for a Colombian dope dealer whose business he'd later acquired after he'd shot the man with a Desert Eagle semi-automatic he purchased from a black gun dealer.

As a grown man living in America—Wiggy had just turned twenty-three—he earned more each year than the head of General Motors did, but he still lived in Diamondback, the almost exclusively black section of the city, and he still dated black women, and went to a black barber who knew how to cut his hair, and wore expensive clothes he bought from a shop on Concord Av because the black owner knew what looked best on a black man. He liked eating steak and potatoes, but he also liked collard greens, and fried chicken, and grits. He enjoyed television shows and movies with all-black casts. He didn't read much, but when he did it was mostly novels about crime—none of them by white writers, who he felt didn't know shit about black thieves, and shouldn't even try. In fact, Wiggy distrusted *all* white people because the men believed he was a criminal—which he happened to be, by the way—and the women believed he was a rapist, which he *didn't* happen to be, and had *never* been, by the way. He especially distrusted cops because he'd suffered too many beatings from them when he was coming along, and he was now paying off too many of them to look the other way when it came to this small matter of dealing controlled substances. Having a few dozen cops in your pocket did not engender faith in the criminal justice system.

Wiggy generally steered away from white neighborhoods altogether because he felt reviled there, observed, suspected, never treated with the respect he earned on his home turf. As a result, his universe was largely defined by the *absence* of white people in it. This was why he liked to go to bed with white hookers. Same way lots of white dudes came uptown looking for black hookers, because these girls were something outside of they purlieu, so to speak. The Starlight Bar often had white hookers in it, which is why he was not surprised when along around twelve-fifteen or so on Christmas night, this leggy blonde walked in all alone and took the stool to his right at the bar, and crossed her legs to show enough gartered stocking to qualify her for porn stardom. This little girl seemed most definitely for sale. If she was Puerto Rican, however, he didn't want her. Because to his mind, that meant she wasn't white, she was just a spic.

America was a peculiar place.

"Merry Christmas," he said.

"Merry Christmas," she said and turned to him, and smiled.

"Merry Christmas, Miss," the black bartender said. "Something to drink?"

"I'll have a Tanqueray martini," she said. "On the rocks. A twist."

"Another scotch, Mr. Wiggins?" the bartender asked.

"No, John, I think I'll try what the lady's drinking," Wiggy said, and swung his stool around to face her. "What'd you just order there, Miss?"

"A Tanqueray martini."

"Sounds good to me," Wiggy said.

"It is," she said, and smiled.

He had never drunk a martini in his life. He did not know what Tanqueray was, either. He had, however, seen a lot of James Bond movies.

"Stirred or shaken?" he asked.

He did not like Bond making it with black girls. The girl here looked very white indeed. But if so, what was she doing in a black bar at midnight on Christmas Day?

"Shaken is better," she said, and smiled.

"Shakin it, huh?" he said. "Is better, you think?"

"Oh yes," she said. "Much."

"Then, John," he said, "you best shake it for me, too."

"Two martinis comin right up, Mr. Wiggins," the bartender said.

"So," Wiggy said to the blonde, "how was your Christmas?"

"Very nice, thank you," she said. "And yours?"

"Spent it with my mama," he said, which was the truth. His mama didn't know he was dealing drugs. She thought he got lucky as a day trader. Only person in his family knew he was thus involved was his cousin Ashley, who was one of his runners. Kid made more money than Wiggy's father did, who was a mailman. "How about you?"

"Uh-huh," she said, but he noticed she hadn't mentioned who with, or exactly how she'd spent the day.

"Santa treat you nice?" he asked.

"Oh yes," she said.

"Two martinis on the rocks, a twist," John said.

"Thank you, m'man," Wiggy said, and raised his glass to the blonde. "Cheers," he said, "Merry Christmas."

"Merry Christmas," she said again, and clinked her glass against his.

Wiggy tasted the drink.

"Mm," he said. "Good."

"Told you, didn't I?"

"So you did."

Not a trace of Spanish accent, but lots of these third-generation spics spoke English good as he did. Last thing he needed was a roll with a girl had six diseases she'd picked up in San Juan.

"Walter Wiggins," he said, and put his glass down, and extended his right hand. She took it in her own hand; it was cold from holding the drink.

"I'm Sheryl," she said.

"Nice to meet you, Sheryl."

Didn't sound like any Spanish name he knew, maybe she was white, after all. Or Jewish maybe, which was even better. You got some of these Jew-girls in bed, they screamed down the whole fuckin hood.

"You live up here in Diamondback?" he asked.

Smattering of spics lived up here, maybe she was one of them, after all. He was tempted to take John aside, ask him who the blonde with the long legs and the big tits was. A Spanish working girl or an import?

"No, I spent the day here with a girlfriend," she said.

"She live up here?"

"Her mother does."

"She a black girl?"

"No."

"Spanish?"

He looked her dead in the eye.

"White," she said. "Same as me."

"Where do *you* live?" he asked.

"Same place my girlfriend does. We're room-mates."

"And where's that?"

"Downtown. Hastings and Palm. Near the Triangle."

"Nice neighborhood," he said. "So what are you doing up here?"

"I told you. My girlfriend's mother invited us for Christmas."

"White woman living up here?" he asked.

"On the *park,*" she said. "What is it with you?"

"I thought you might be Puerto Rican."

"I'm not. But what difference would it make?"

"None at all."

"So what's the bullshit?" she asked. "I mean, what is it, are *you* so fucking white?"

All at once, he liked her.

"Have another drink," he said.

"Oh, am I suddenly white enough for you?"

"You're white enough, honey," he said, and put his hand on her thigh. She looked into his eyes.

"Another Tanqueray," she told the bartender.

"How about you, Mr. Wiggins?"

"I'll join the lady, sure," Wiggy said, and squeezed her thigh. She kept looking into his eyes.

She was jiggling her foot now. She had terrific tits in a very low-cut black dress.

"So what are you doing here at the Starlight?" he asked.

"What are *you* doing here at the Starlight?"

"Hoping to meet a gorgeous blonde from downtown on Hastings and Palm," he said. "Near the Triangle."

"So you met her," Sheryl said, and covered his hand on her thigh with her own. Her hand was no longer cold.

"Seems I have," Wiggy said.

Sheryl looked at her watch. "My girlfriend's picking me up in five minutes," she said. "We've got a car and a driver. You want to come downtown with us, honey?"

"Let's have our drinks first," Wiggy said.

The limo was a black Lincoln Town Car driven by a black chauffeur. There was another blonde on the back seat, wearing a black dress like Sheryl's, high-heeled black shoes like her, a black cloth coat identical to hers, little black fur collar at the neck. The car felt warm and smelled of expensive perfume. "Hi," the other blonde said, extending her hand. "I'm Toni." Wiggy slid onto the seat beside her, took her hand. "Hi, honey," she said, and leaned across him to kiss Sheryl on the cheek. He felt her breasts against his arm. Her dress was high on her thighs. The door on Sheryl's side slammed shut. She moved closer to him. The brother came into the car, made himself comfortable behind the wheel.

"We're going home," Toni told him, and the tinted glass separating front from back slid up at once.

"Excuse me, ladies," Wiggy said, "but how much is this going to cost me?"

"One million, nine hundred thousand dollars," Toni said.

He turned to look at her.

She was holding an AK-47 in her lap.

6.

The offices of Wadsworth and Dodds were in a side street off Headley Square, close to the Municipal Theater and the Briley School of Art. As Ollie crossed the small park outside the school, and then the square itself, a fierce wind almost blew his hat from his head. He clutched at it with both hands, cursed at the wind, and at God—who was also on his list of people, places, things, and supernatural beings he hated—and then proceeded across the square to the building in which the publishing firm was housed. The wind moaned beneath the eaves of the old landmark building as he mounted the low flat entrance steps and walked into the lobby, stomping slush from his shoes. He checked the lobby directory—Wadsworth and Dodds was on the fourth floor of the six-story building—and walked toward the waiting elevator, its fancy grillwork door looking like it had come out of a spy movie set in Vienna.

"Whoosh!" he said to the elevator operator, and took off his hat when he noticed there was a lady in the car. The gesture did not go unnoticed. The woman, a good-looking broad in her late fifties, Ollie guessed, with still splendid legs and *poitrine,* ah yes, smiled almost imperceptibly. He figured she worked out a lot. One of these days, he'd have to go to a gym, lose a few pounds, though not anytime soon. Maybe after he learned his five songs. His next lesson was tomorrow night, he could hardly wait.

Wadsworth and Dodds occupied the entire fourth floor of the building. Ollie took one look at the receptionist behind the desk and figured she could have profited from the same aerobics classes the broad in the elevator most likely attended. Ollie hated fat people. He considered them unsightly and weak-willed whereas he thought of his own girth as perfectly suited to his height and his large bone structure. When Fat Ollie Weeks looked into a mirror he saw an impressive figure of a man, whose very presence struck fear into the hearts of underworld types.

"May I help you, sir?" the fat lady behind the desk asked.

Ollie flashed the tin.

"Detective Weeks," he said, cutting to the chase. "I'd like to talk to whoever runs the place here."

"You'd want Mr. Halloway, our publisher."

"Okay," Ollie said, and snapped the leather case shut. "Could you let him know I'm here, please?"

The fat lady picked up her phone, pressed a button on her desk panel, listened, said, "A Detective

Weeks to see you, sir," listened again, said, "Yes, sir," looked up at Ollie, and asked, "May I ask what this is in reference to, sir?"

"No," Ollie said.

The fat lady looked startled. "Uh," she said into the phone, "he won't tell me. Yes, sir," she said. "Yes, sir." She hung up, smiled at Ollie, and said, "He'll be with you in a moment, sir. Won't you please have a seat?"

"Thanks," Ollie said, and began roaming the waiting room.

Framed posters of Wadsworth and Dodds books lined the walls. The firm's logo was a distinctive open hand with a silver globe sitting on the palm and radiating rays of light, the fingers tentatively closed around it. Ollie didn't recognize any of the titles.

Behind him, he heard a buzz from the phone on the fat lady's desk.

"Mr. Weeks?" she said. "He'll see you now. It's the end of the corridor, the door on the right."

Ollie nodded.

The corridor leading to Halloway's office was similarly lined with framed posters of books Ollie never heard of. The closed walnut door on the right, at the end of corridor, had no markings on it. He knocked, heard a man's voice call, "Come in, please," twisted the brass doorknob, and entered. He was in a corner office with floor-to-ceiling bookcases on two walls. The other two walls were windowed, enclosing a walnut desk that matched the entrance door. A white-haired man in his early fifties, Ollie guessed, sat behind the desk. He rose the moment Ollie entered the room. Extending his hand, he said, "Richard Halloway, how do you do?"

Ollie took the hand.

"Detective Oliver Weeks," he said, "Eighty-eighth Squad."

"Sit down," Halloway said. "Please," and gestured to a brown leather wingback chair studded with brass buttons. Ollie sank into the chair.

"How can I help you?" Halloway asked.

"One of your salesmen was murdered on Christmas Eve," Ollie said. "His name . . ."

"What?" Halloway said.

"Yes, sir. His name's Jerome Hoskins. From what his wife . . ."

"Oh my God!" Halloway said.

"From what his wife tells me, he sold books in your northeast corridor."

"Yes. Yes, he did. Forgive me, I'm . . . forgive me."

He was shaking his head now, demonstrating how overwhelmed he was. Little white-haired guy in a gray flannel suit and a bow tie with red polka dots on a black field, shaking his head and looking appalled and overcome with sudden grief, all of which seemed somewhat phony to Ollie. Then again, he'd never met a book publisher before.

"Did his territory include Diamondback?" he asked.

"Yes, it did."

"Lots of bookstores up there, I guess."

"Not many. But enough. We're a small firm, last of the family publishing houses in this city, in fact. We're constantly trying to expand our market."

"You sell your books for cash, Mr. Halloway?"

"I'm sorry, I don't understand the question."

"Hoskins had seven hundred dollars and change in his wallet. Seemed like a lot of cash to be carrying around."

"I have no idea why he would have . . ."

"Any idea why he might have been carrying a gun?"

"Diamondback is a dangerous section of the . . ."

"Tell me about it."

"Perhaps he felt he needed protection."

"Do all of your salesmen carry guns?"

"Not to my knowledge. In fact, I didn't know *Jerry* carried one until this very moment."

"How many salesmen are there?"

"Including Jerry, only five. As I told you, we're a small firm."

"Is Mr. Wadsworth still alive? Or Mr. Dodds?"

"Both dead. Christine Dodds is the sole stockholder now. Henry Dodds's granddaughter."

"How about you? Are you a member of the family?"

"Me? No. No, what gave you that idea?"

"Well, you being the *publisher* and all . . ."

"Oh, that's just a title," Halloway said airily. "Like President or Vice President or Senior Editor."

"Pretty important title, though, huh?"

"Well . . . yes."

"Who are these other four salesmen? I'll need to talk to them."

"Jerry was the only one based here, you know. In this city."

"Where are the other ones?"

"Illinois, Minnesota, Texas, and California."

"Can you give me a list of names and phone numbers?"

"Yes, of course."

"And the names, addresses, and phone numbers of the bookstores Mr. Hoskins visited in Diamondback."

"I'll ask Charmaine to get those ready for you," he said.

Charmaine, Ollie thought. A slender wraith who weighs a ton and a half bone dry. He watched as Halloway picked up the receiver, pressed a button, and told his receptionist what he needed. There was something crisp and efficient about his motions and the way he rapped out instructions. When at last he replaced the receiver on the cradle, he seemed to suddenly realize that Ollie had been observing his every move. He smiled pleasantly. "She'll have those for you when you leave," he said.

"Thanks," Ollie said. "Tell me what you know about Jerry Hoskins, okay?"

"Tell me what you're looking for."

"Well," Ollie said, "I guess I want to know what a

book salesman was doing with types who'll shoot a man at the back of his head and drop him in a garbage can."

"Good Lord!" Halloway said.

Ollie didn't know there was anyone still left on the planet who said, "Good Lord!" He had the feeling all over again that Richard Halloway was faking surprise and sorrow.

"Most of the gangs in Diamondback are dealing drugs," he said, and watched Halloway's eyes. Nothing flickered there. "Hoskins wasn't doing dope, was he?"

"Not to my knowledge."

"Who *would* know?" Ollie asked.

"Pardon?"

"If he was doing drugs. Or dealing drugs. Or involved in any way with controlled substances."

"I can't possibly imagine Jerry . . ."

"Who *could* possibly imagine it, Mr. Halloway?"

"I suppose our sales manager would have known him better than anyone else in the firm."

"What's his name?"

"She's a woman."

"Okay," Ollie said.

"I'll ask her to come in."

Carella and Meyer went to the Banque Française at ten that morning of the twenty-sixth with a court order to open Cassandra Jean Ridley's safe deposit box. The manager of the bank was a Frenchman from Lyon. His name was Pascal Prouteau. In a charming accent, he said he had read about Mademoiselle "Reed-ley's" death in the newspapers and was very sorry. "She was a lovely person," he said. "It is a shame what 'appen."

"When did she first open the box, can you tell us?" Meyer asked.

"Oui, messieurs, I 'ave her records here," Prouteau said. "It was on the sixteenth of November."

"How many times has she been in that box since?"

Prouteau consulted the signature card.

"She was 'ere a great deal," he said, looking surprised, and handed the card to Carella. He and Meyer looked at it together. "We'll need a copy of this, please," Meyer said.

"Mais, oui, certainement," Prouteau said.

"Let's take a look in the box," Carella said.

What they found in the box was $96,000 in hundred-dollar bills.

There was also a sheet of paper with a lot of figures on it.

They asked Prouteau for a copy of that as well.

They knew the lady had been smurfing even before they checked the figures against her two checkbooks and her passbook.

The handwritten notes in her safe deposit box looked like this:

Deposit: November 16	*$50,000*
Current Balance:	*$50,000*
Withdrawals:	
November 20:	*$6,500*
November 21:	*$9,000*
November 22:	*$7,000*
November 24:	*$5,430*

"Missed a day," Meyer said.
"Thanksgiving," Carella said.

November 25:	*$6,070*
November 27:	*$8,000*
November 28:	*$4,000*
Current Balance:	*$4,000*

The next deposit was made almost two weeks later.

"According to her calendar, she came East on the eighth of December," Carella said.

Deposit: December 11	*$150,000*
Current Balance:	*$154,000*
Withdrawals:	
December 12:	*$4,000*
December 13:	*$9,000*
December 14:	*$7,500*
December 15:	*$7,500*
December 18:	*$8,300*

December 19:	$9,400
December 20:	$8,600
December 21:	$3,700
Current Balance:	$96,000

On the identical dates she had listed for withdrawals from the safe deposit box, there were corresponding deposits in either of her two checking accounts or her savings account. Each deposit was for a sum of money less than $10,000, the maximum cash deposit allowed under a federal law that had gone into effect almost three decades ago. Anything more than that sum had to be reported to the Internal Revenue Service on a so-called CTR, the acronym for Currency Transaction Report. Cassandra Jean Ridley, it would appear, had been engaged in money laundering, albeit on a relatively minor scale. Smurfing, as it was called in the trade.

In order to be charged with laundering, a person had to disguise the origin or ownership of illegally gained funds to make them appear legitimate. Hiding legitimately acquired money to avoid taxation also qualified as money laundering. The U.S. Treasury Department cautiously accepted a State Department Fact Sheet estimating that as much as four hundred billion dollars was laundered worldwide annually. Of this, fifty to a hundred billion was said to have come from drug profits in the United States alone.

If Cassandra Jean Ridley's transfers of cash were

indeed necessitated because the money came from drugs, she was small potatoes indeed. According to the evidence they now possessed, she had introduced a mere $200,000 into the banking system, and had then separated it from its possible criminal origins by passing it through several financial transactions. In police jargon, this was called "placement" and "layering." But street sales of drugs were usually transacted in five- or ten-dollar bills, and the $96,000 they found in her safe deposit box was in hundreds. It seemed certain she hadn't been running around the street selling dime bags of coke to teenagers.

Her checkbooks showed somewhat substantial amounts written to department stores all over the city in the weeks before her murder. The lady had been moving money around and spending it profligately. The only sum they could not account for was the $8,000 in $100 bills they'd found nestling in the top right hand drawer of her desk—presumably currency suspected in a kidnapping that had drawn the attention of the Secret Service.

They knew several other things about Cassandra Jean Ridley.

She had been a pilot in the U.S. Army.

She had lived in Eagle Branch, Texas.

This last bit of information might not later have proved significant if Ollie Weeks wasn't at that very moment speaking to Jerome Hoskins' sales manager in the publishing offices of Wadsworth and Dodds.

Karen Andersen was a tall brunette wearing a char-
coal black business suit with wide lapels and white
pin stripes. Her handshake was firm and her smile
was welcoming. Ollie wondered at once if she was
wearing black thong panties and a garter belt under
the tailored slacks. Halloway filled her in on the reason for Ollie's visit—

She seemed equally appalled by the news of
Hoskins' murder.

—and then left them alone in his office while he
attended a meeting in the firm's conference room.
Karen asked Ollie if he'd care for a cup of coffee. It
was close to twelve noon; he was beginning to get
hungry. He wondered if the offer included a crois-
sant, a donut, or at least a slice of toast. He accepted
it nonetheless, watching Karen's ass as she walked
to a folding door that opened to reveal a small
kitchen unit. A coffee maker was already prepared
for brewing. She hit a button. A red light went on.
Karen walked to a chair facing him. She crossed her
long legs. He wished she was wearing a skirt. She
tented her hands. Long narrow fingers, the nails
painted a red to match her lipstick. The savory
aroma of perking coffee set Ollie's salivary glands
flowing.

"So," she said, "what is it you want to know?"

"What was he doing in Diamondback?" Ollie
asked.

"Selling books, I'd expect."

"At one A.M. on Christmas Eve?"

Karen looked at him.

"That's the ME's estimated postmortem interval. The time of his death. The time someone fired a nine-millimeter pistol into the base of his neck."

"I can't even *imagine* what he was doing up there at that hour."

"How many bookstores was he selling to?" Ollie asked. "In Diamondback?"

"Four. We're trying to expand our market there."

"What sort of books do you sell?"

"Mostly non-fiction. We have a small fiction list, but nothing significant."

"Books that would appeal to a Negro audience?"

"To a what?"

"A Negro audience."

"You said Negro."

"Yes."

"Some of them."

"Like what?"

"Oh, any number of our titles."

"Was Hoskins having any kind of trouble with his accounts?"

"Trouble?"

"Deadbeats. Slow payers. Whatever. Personality differences?"

"No problems that I know of. We're an easy firm to deal with. As I said, we're trying to expand our markets. Not only in Diamondback, but all over the United States. Coffee's ready," she said, and un-crossed her legs. She rose, walked to the kitchenette, poured coffee for both of them. "Sugar?" she asked. "Cream?"

"Both," he said.

He was hoping she'd offer him something to eat. His eyes whipped the counter top, saw nothing but an open box of granulated sugar. She knelt to open a mini-fridge under the counter, took from it a container of skim milk. She spooned sugar into his cup . . .

"Two, please," he said.

. . . added milk, carried it to where he sat. She smelled of expensive perfume. He wondered what the hell she was doing selling books for a rinky-dink firm like Wadsworth and Dodds.

"Five salesmen," Ollie said. "Was what Mr. Halloway told me. Charmaine's supposed to be getting me their names and phone numbers."

"Why?" Karen said.

"I want to talk to them. See what they can tell me about him."

"I doubt if any of them knew him that well. Aside from sales conferences, their paths wouldn't have crossed all that often."

"Worth a few phone calls," Ollie said, and shrugged.

"I'll see how she's doing," Karen said.

She lifted the phone on Halloway's desk, stabbed at a button on the face of the cradle. "Hi," she said, "it's Karen. Have you got that information for Detective Weeks?" She listened, hung up, nodded, said, "She's bringing it in," and then folded her arms across her chest, and looked across the room at Ollie.

"Would you guys be interested in a book by a bona fide police officer?" he asked.

Karen looked surprised.

"Would you?" he asked.

"What kind of a book?"

"You know, make-believe."

"Fiction?"

"Sure, fiction. But by somebody who really *knows* police work, never mind these faggots who make it all up."

"Who'd you have in mind?" Karen asked.

"Me," Ollie said.

"I didn't know you were a writer."

"You probably didn't know I play piano, either."

"I confess I didn't."

"Do you like 'Night and Day'? I can play that for you sometime."

"It was never one of my favorites."

"I can even play it with a Latin beat, if you like."

"I don't think so, thanks. Why? Do I look Latin?"

"Well, the dark hair and eyes."

"Actually, my parents were Swedish."

"So would you be interested?"

"In what?"

"A fictious book about police work? I've had lots of experience."

"Would it have a Latin beat?" Karen asked, and smiled.

"I had more of an American cop in mind."

"We sell lots of books in the Southwest."

"What's that got to do with the price of fish?"

"Large Latino audience," Karen said, and shrugged.

"I could throw in a few wetbacks, I suppose," Ollie said dubiously. "But it might ruin the subtle mix."

"Oh, you already have a mix in mind, is that it?"

"No, but I thought if I could talk to somebody up here, one of your editors . . ."

"I see."

". . . he could maybe fill me in on your needs, and I could prepare an outline or something. I have to explain something to you, Miss Andersen . . ."

"Yes, what's that?"

"If a person is creative in one way, he's usually creative in another. That's been my experience, anyway. Take Picasso, you ever heard of Pancho Picasso?"

"Does he write police novels?"

"Come on, he was a famous painter, you heard of him. The point is, he also made pots."

"I see."

"What I'm saying is, if you're creative in one way, you're creative in another. My piano teacher says there's no limits to where I can go."

"Maybe you'll even play at Clarendon Hall one day."

"Who knows? So have you got an editor up here I can talk to? Give your company an exclusive look at the book?"

"I'm not sure any of our editors are free just now," Karen said. "But we may have something you can look at."

"What do you mean *look* at?"

"Something one of our editors may have prepared. Defining our needs. As I said, we don't publish much fiction . . ."

"Always room for a bestseller, though, am I right?"

"Always room."

"You had more bestsellers, maybe your salesmen wouldn't end up in garbage cans with bullet holes in their heads."

"Maybe not."

"Was he doing drugs?" Ollie asked.

"Not to my knowledge."

"Did he have a black girlfriend up there?"

"He was married."

"Did he have a black girlfriend up there?" Ollie asked again.

"He was *happily* married."

Dainty Charmaine came in with the names and addresses of Hoskins' customers in Diamondback, and the names and addresses of his fellow sales reps in the United States.

One of them lived in Eagle Branch, Texas.

Walter Wiggins had grown up to believe that beating the system was the only way to cope with the system. The way he looked at it, the system was stacked against the black man, and any man of color would be foolish to try living within the rules white men had established to control and punish the black man.

Wiggy committed his first theft—a two-dollar water pistol from a variety store on Hayley Avenue, the wide thoroughfare that skewered Diamondback north to south—when he was six years old. His mother forced him to take the toy pistol back to the owner, which Wiggy did after much wailing and protesting. Two days later, he went back to the store again—without his mother this time—and stole the water pistol all over again.

The owner of the store was white, but Wiggy didn't feel he was striking a blow for black power— which words were all the rage then—or anything else. He merely felt he was getting a water pistol for free, fuck his mother. He kept committing petty thefts until the time he was thirteen and joined a street gang named Orion, after which his life became a merry round of rumbling, doing drugs, dealing drugs, and eventually masterminding (he thought of it as such) the ring (he called it a posse, in the Colombian style) that now supported him in the life style to which he had become accustomed. It would never have occurred to Wiggy that living within the system was a possible alternative to the life he'd chosen. Wiggy the Lid was a big man in this part of the city. He even fancied himself to be famous outside of the six square blocks he controlled in Diamondback.

It annoyed him enormously that he'd had to pay for cocaine being peddled by a man he thought of as an amateur. It annoyed him even further that he'd had to hand over the money to a pair of white chicks holding guns bigger than they were. This guy Frank Holt—if that was his name, which Wiggy doubted—had come recommended by a cousin of Wiggy's in Mobile, Alabama, who said he'd met him with a man named Randolph Biggs in Dallas, Texas, when the three of them were setting up a run from Mexico, this was four years ago. Apparently this Frank Holt person—who'd later found himself stuffed feet first in a garbage can with a bullet hole at the back of his head, courtesy of Wiggy the Lid himself—had recently purchased some very good shit in Guenerando, Mexico, and through various levels of subterfuge had smuggled it into the metropolitan area where he was peddling a hundred keys for a million-nine. One look at the guy, you knew he was new at the trade, however long ago Wiggy's cousin had worked with him. Patted him down, found him carrying an ancient piece out of *Casablanca,* trusted Tigo and him alone to test the shit while he sat outside with a brother named Thomas who could've broke him in half with his bare hands. Beating the system was what this was all about. Why pay a white man a mill-nine when you could shoot him in the head and take the booty home free? Like the water pistol.

Not that there wasn't profit enough in the trade even if Wiggy had played it by the book. Pay Frank

Holt—or whatever his name was—the money he wanted for his hundred keys of truly very good shit, and then take it from there. In the long run, because Wiggy'd been careless or stupid or both, he'd had to fork over $19,000 a key to the two blondes in the Lincoln Town Car, who'd driven him back to his so-called office on Decatur and watched while he'd opened the safe, the one named Toni—which he was sure wasn't *her* goddamn name, either—sitting there with the AK-47 leveled at his head while he twirled the combination dial, a smile on her face, her splendid white-cunt legs crossed.

Wiggy had failed to beat the system.

Oh yes, he knew he'd be selling off his newly ac-quired ten-key lots for twenty-three grand a key, a twenty-one percent profit on each key, for a virtual overnight gain of $400,000 on his $1,900,000 in-vestment. Yes, he knew that, and that wasn't bad for a kid who'd stolen his first water pistol at the age of six. He knew, too, that there'd be profits for every-one down the line, but he didn't give a shit about anyone but himself. His one-kilo buyers would step on the drug by a third, diluting it to produce 1,333 grams or some 47 ounces of cocaine. This would be sold for about $800 an ounce, the profit margin ris-ing the closer the drug came to the street. What had started in Mexico for $1,700,000 would end up on the streets of Diamondback at a retail price of close to $9,000,000. From door to door, all anybody made was money, money, money, but Wiggy was in this for Numero Uno alone. It did not disturb him to know that some of the kids buying highly diluted shit from sad-assed street dealers were scarcely older than he himself had been when he swiped that water gun.

What bothered him was that he'd allowed two titty blondes to cold-cock him and deprive him of an even greater profit. He would have to get that money back somehow.

What he didn't know was that his $1,900,000 had already been wire-transferred to Iran—where it would buy even more money at a huge discount.

The redheaded pilot had told them the man's name was Randolph Biggs and had said he lived in Eagle Branch, Texas. She'd given them a fairly good description, too: a tall, broad-shouldered man with thick black hair and a black mustache. She had told them he was a Texas Ranger, but they couldn't go ask about that, eh, amigo? And besides they felt she was either lying or had been lied to. How could a Texas Ranger be involved in a scheme flying dope out of Guenerando, Mexico?

Eagle Branch was just across the Rio Grande from Piedras Rosas, Mexico—where, legend held, a former U.S. Marine had broken an American drug-prisoner out of jail there, oh, twenty, thirty years ago. Legends die hard. The people in Eagle Branch still talked about the daring escape. To them, it had become almost mythic. They insisted that the escaped prisoner's girlfriend had lived and taught school right there in Eagle Branch. Who knew? It could be true. The people in Piedras Rosas were indifferent to the story. They wouldn't have cared if a whole Marine *battalion* had freed the entire prison population. They were of a mind to believe that the corrupt guards at the local jail, if paid enough *mordida,* would let everybody go free, anyway. Most of the people in Piedras Rosas were more intent on crossing the river and making their way north, where Wiggy the Lid was selling cocaine to dealers lower down the chain of command who would eventually step on the drug and sell it to Mexican immigrants without green cards living in shitty neighborhoods where they pined for the good old days in Piedras Rosas.

Both Francisco Octavio Ortiz and Cesar Villada possessed green cards and were therefore free to come and go as they pleased, taking trips hither and yon in pursuit of their chosen occupation, which was earning—if that was the word—millions of dollars smuggling drugs up from Colombia and selling them to assorted gringos from across the border. On the seventh day of December this year, they had turned over to a pretty redheaded pilot one hundred keys of very high quality cocaine they'd purchased from the Cali cartel, a notorious association of traffickers operating out of Colombia's third-largest city. She had given them in return $1,700,000 in hundred-dollar bills, which they'd counted to ascertain the proper value and then—

generously, they felt—had skimmed ten thousand dollars off the top, to give to her as a gratuity.

They had smiled all around.

Gracias, gracias, muchas gracias.

Now, in this little border town of what they estimated to be fifteen, twenty thousand people, they were looking for a man named Randolph Biggs, who had given the lady the money she'd subsequently passed on to them.

They didn't mind losing the ten thousand, which, after all, had been offered of their own free will, in gratitude, as an act of South of the Border generosity.

What annoyed them was that *all* the money was counterfeit.

7.

The restaurant specialized in Middle Eastern and Mediterranean cuisine. Here, in the virtual shadow of the mosque near the ramp approach to the River Dix Drive, one could feast upon delicious dishes from Turkey, Israel, Lebanon, Morocco, Tunisia, Syria, Iran, Iraq, the United Arab Republic. The restaurant was smoke-filled even at lunch time, when it was packed with men and women—but mostly men—on breaks and longing for the taste and the aroma of the food and drink they had enjoyed in Damascus or Baghdad, Beirut or Teheran. The entertainment, even during the lunch hour, helped to remind them of their homelands, but it was the fare that drew them here, exquisite to the taste and to memories too long submerged in an accursed foreign land.

Mahmoud Gharib looked the most benign of the three men sitting at the little round table near the small stage where a Raqs Sharqui belly dancer gyrated to a recorded mix of electronic instruments and violins. Resembling a chubby cheerful standup

comic from the good old days before comedians
turned lean, mean, and obscene, he sported a tiny
mustache somewhat uptilted at the tips, giving him
the appearance of a man who was perpetually smiling. His complexion was the color of bread lightly
toasted, his eyes the color of the very dark brown
Turkish coffee they brewed here. His comrades
knew him as Mahmoud. The dispatcher at the cab
company for which he worked called him Moe,
which Mahmoud knew was a Jewish name, and
therefore a hundredfold more offensive. He looked
plump and jolly and content. He was the most dangerous of the three men.

The men were talking about the proper way to
prepare a fish dish that was enormously popular
throughout the Middle East. Jassim, the smallest of
the men, was saying that the secret was in refriger-
ating the fish for an hour before it was cooked.
Akbar, who worked for a sporting goods store on
the South Side, told him that refrigeration had nothing to do with it, he had eaten the fish in poor little
villages where no one had even *heard* of ice. Jassim
insisted it was the refrigeration. You had to keep the
fish on ice for an hour before placing it in the skillet,
skin side down, and cooking it. It was the refrigeration, he said, that caused the skin to crisp so swiftly
and effectively. Mahmoud said that was nonsense.

"The fish is inconsequential to the dish," he said,
waving his hand in a manner that defined leadership
and dismissed argumentation. The gesture seemed
exceptionally grandiose in light of the comic little

mustache under his nose. "You can use any kind of white-fleshed fish," he said. "So long as you wash it clean and season it with salt, pepper, and lemon juice, you can let it stand outside while you make the sauce. I'm not saying forever. It is dangerous to let any fish stand forever. But it's the sauce and the nuts that give the dish its succulent flavor."

"The onions," Akbar agreed.

"The caramelized onions, yes," Jassim said, nodding.

"But especially the pine nuts," Mahmoud said, again superseding all discussion. "Swiftly fried in oil, browned to a pale golden perfection, and then *showered* on the fish."

"On a bed of rice," Akbar said.

"On a bed of rice," Mahmoud said, and kissed his fingertips.

It was odd that the men were discussing fish because at the moment they were eating pancakes stuffed with cheese. In Morocco, where they were cooked on one side only and served with only a warm honey-butter sauce, these little semolina-yeast crepes were traditionally served on the feast of *aid el seghir,* toward the end of the Islamic month of fasting called Ramadan. Here in this restaurant, the pancakes were prepared in the Lebanese manner, stuffed with ricotta and shreds of mozzarella, broiled on both sides to a succulent crispness, and then drizzled with a syrup made of sugar, lemon juice, orange blossom honey, and orange flower water. The men ate ravenously. Jassim licked his

lips. Mahmoud found this disgusting, but he made
no comment.

A dark-eyed, dark-haired waitress brought them
thick black coffee. The belly dancer was wearing a
beaded bra and matching belt, a sequined skirt over
a body stocking. Her veil work was hardly Egyptian. To Mahmoud, it looked more like the modified
strip tease one would find in the so-called American
Nightclub style. The girl was wearing finger cymbals, although they had for the most part gone out of
style in Egypt. She was more adept at twirling her
veil and snapping her hips than she was at playing
the cymbals.

"When does the Big Jew arrive?" Akbar asked.

Given the origins and political dispositions of the
trio, this could have been a derogatory remark, but
it was not meant to be. Svi Cohen was in fact an Israeli Jew, and he was in fact a very big man, standing some six feet, three inches tall and weighing
close to two hundred and forty pounds.

"Tomorrow," Mahmoud said.

"And his performance at Clarendon?" Jassim
asked. He was still licking traces of syrup from
his lips. His fingernails were grimy with traces
of his trade; he worked as an automobile mechanic
in a garage at the foot of the Calm's Point Bridge.
Mahmoud found the filthy fingernails disgusting, too.

"On the thirtieth," he said. "This Saturday night."

"So where's the money?" Akbar asked.

It was a good question.

• • •

The squadroom was relatively calm on that Wednesday morning two days after Christmas. Today was only the twenty-seventh and the week was lurching steadily forward into another big weekend that would culminate on Sunday with the tolling of the bells and the falling of the ball in the square. But the squadroom was enjoying a comparative period of calm, a respite from the usual hubbub and hullabaloo that accompanied its normal pace.

Carella and Meyer sat poring over the letters Mark Ridley had written to his sister in the months and weeks preceding her death. From references he made to her own letters, it became clear almost at once that she was terribly excited about a job she'd be flying early in December, which would change her circumstances considerably, enabling her to move East, where she'd always wanted to live, be there long before Christmas, in fact. In the letter they'd already read—the one dated November 13— her brother wrote to say that the job sounded good to him, "so long as you won't be flying anything that might get you in trouble."

The words still rang meaningfully in the stillness of the squadroom.

On November 16, Cassandra Jean Ridley opened a safe deposit box at Banque Française here in this city and placed in it $50,000 in cash. Apparently, her circumstances had in *fact* changed considerably by then. They were to change even more dramatically. Her calendar for December 7 was marked with the words "End Mexico." On December 8, she presumably flew East again. Three days later, she placed another $150,000 in the safe deposit box. Twelve days after that, she was dead.

Their computer told them there'd been seventy-four reported incidents of kidnapping in the United States during the first three weeks of December. Most of these were abductions of children from parents in divorced or separated circumstances. Some of these cases might have attracted the attention of the FBI, in that state lines had been crossed. None of them would have warranted the attention of the Secret Service.

Yet the Treasury Department had braced a small-time burglar named Wilbur Struthers, confiscating bills he'd stolen from Cassandra Jean Ridley's apartment, checking out the serial numbers against ransom notes used in an alleged kidnapping, and then—remarkably—giving him a clean bill of health and returning the bills to him that very same day.

Something stank in the state of Denmark.

They figured it was time they paid a personal visit to Special Agent David A. Horne.

A whole lot of hundred-dollar bills were fanned out on Horne's desk.

"A hundred and four thousand dollars," Carella said.

"Some of it recovered in the dead woman's apartment," Meyer said.

"The rest from her safe deposit box."

"All receipted and accounted for," Meyer said.

"So?" Horne said.

He looked like a used car salesman who'd eaten and drunk too much over the weekend, jowly though not paunchy in a dark blue suit, brown shoes, a white button-down shirt, and a blue tie. The circular seal of the Department of the Treasury hung on the wall behind his desk, its gold shield decorated with a pair of scales representing justice, a key symbolizing official authority, and a blue chevron with thirteen stars for the original thirteen states. A little black plastic placard, with Horne's name on it in white lettering, sat near his telephone.

"We think the eight thousand we found in her apartment is the money you appropriated from Wilbur Struthers," Carella said flat out.

"What makes you believe that?"

"Struthers does. Apparently, Miss Ridley located him and went to get her money back. At gun point, incidentally."

"I'm assuming Struthers told you this as well."

"Yes."

"A petty thief," Horne said, dismissing him.

"Big enough to have captured your attention, though," Meyer reminded him.

Horne looked at him. "I don't like unannounced visits," he said belatedly.

"We'd like to see that list of ransom-note serial numbers," Carella said.

"As I told you on the phone . . ."

"We'd like to know just which kidnapping you were investigating," Meyer said.

"I have no authority to release that information to you. And you have no authority to request it."

"We're investigating a murder," Carella said.

"Top of the food chain," Meyer reminded Horne.

"I'm sorry," Horne said, and shook his head.

"We won't go away, you know," Carella said.

"Detective," Horne said, and paused to give the word weight. "Go home, okay? Go arrest some pushers around the schoolyard. Keep your nose out of affairs that don't concern you."

"Gee," Carella said, "all at once I'm *really* interested."

"Me, too," Meyer said.

Horne looked at them both. He sighed heavily.

"I'm not free to discuss any case currently under investigation," he said. "I can, however, show you the list of suspect serial numbers for you to make a comparison check. You'll have to do it here in this office, under my supervision. If that's satisfactory to you . . ."

"It's a start," Carella said.

. . .

The serial numbers were a random lot.

There were numbers in the A series . . .

A63842516A, A5315898964A, A0615286 0A . . .

. . . and numbers in the B series . . .

B35817751D, B40565942E . . .

. . . and numbers in the C and F and H and G and E and L and K and D series . . .

But none of these numbers matched those on the separate caches of hundred-dollar bills they'd seized by court order from Cassandra Jean Ridley's desk and her safe deposit box.

They thanked Horne for his time and courtesy . . .

"Always a pleasure," he said.

. . . and went back to the squadroom.

It was not yet twelve noon.

David Horne was trying to convince his boss that the two Keystone Kops had no idea the bills had been switched.

"This is like the old shell game," he said. "You have to guess which shell the pea is under. But the pea is really in the palm of our hand."

"I'm not familiar with the shell game," Parsons said.

His full name was Winslow Parsons III, and he had been recruited into the Secret Service when he was twenty-two and a senior at Harvard. He'd been present in Dallas, walking alongside the presidential limo when Kennedy was assassinated, but he hadn't been the one to protect the President with his own body—well, no one had, for that matter. Similarly, when John Hinckley, Jr., shot Ronald Reagan in 1981, Parsons had missed his big chance at immortality by not hurling himself in the path of the bullet. At the age of sixty-four, he was still tall and lean and he had all his hair, albeit turning gray, and he thought he looked like Charlton Heston, whom he greatly admired, but he bore no resemblance to him at all. In any case, he didn't know what a shell game was. In Cambridge, they did not have such things as shell games.

"You palm the pea," Horne explained. Or tried to explain. "Same way we palmed the bills."

He was thinking this is four days before New Year's Eve, and we're having a big party, and I should be checking my booze, see how much I have to order. Setups, too.

"How did they come across the bills in the first place?" Parsons asked.

"A case they're investigating."

"What kind of case?"

"A woman was murdered."

Parsons looked at him.

"It gets complicated," Horne said.

"Life gets complicated," Parsons replied.

"Yes, sir, it does."

"Life *is* complicated."

"Yes, sir, it most certainly is."

"How'd *we* get involved in this, is what I'd like to know," Parsons said. "If you please."

"A flagged super showed up on our list, sir. Man who passed it had eight thousand total in similar bills. We yanked them out of circulation. Should have been the end of the story." Horne shrugged. "Instead, the woman got killed and suddenly it's Mickey Mouse time."

"What's the woman got to do with it?"

"He stole the bills from her."

"The eight thousand?"

"Yes, sir."

"He admitted that?"

"No, sir. He told me he won them in a crap game."

"Is that likely?"

"Hardly."

"And you say you recovered eight thousand supers?"

"Yes, sir, and replaced them with clears. The old shell game, sir," he said, and smiled.

Parsons did not smile back.

"Why the hell did you do that?" he asked.

"Do what, sir?"

"Give the man good money for bad?"

"In retrospect, I'm glad I did, sir. All this sudden police interest."

Parsons looked at him skeptically.

"Never mind in retrospect," he said. "Why did you do it in the *first* place?"

"I thought he might make a fuss, sir, if we simply grabbed eight thousand dollars of his."

"Has this man got a record?" Parsons asked.

"Yes, sir. Took a burglary fall seven years ago, did three and a third at Castleview."

"Ex-cons don't usually make fusses."

"But he might have, sir."

"Any chance we can pop him back in?"

"Not unless he commits a crime, sir."

"How'd this woman get the eight thousand?"

"I have no idea. But, sir . . ."

"Yes?"

"There's more."

"Let me hear it."

"The locals found close to a hundred thousand in her safe deposit box."

"Supers?"

"I didn't check them, sir."

"Why not?"

"Well, they had them in their possession, sir. They were here to look at the list of serial numbers used in a kidnapping . . ."

"What kidnapping?" Parsons asked at once. "Has there been a kidnapping?"

"No, sir, that was just confetti."

"But you say they were here with a hundred thousand dollars . . ."

"Ninety-six, actually, sir."

". . . that they found in her safe deposit box?"

"Yes, sir."

"And you didn't check the *bills?*"

His eyes were wide open now.

"I had no opportunity to do so, sir. Without arousing suspicion."

"Suspicion is *already* aroused," Parsons said. "Why the hell do you think they came here? They're *already* suspicious!"

"I don't think so, sir. They're a simple pair of flat-foots investigating a murder. Nothing more."

"Nothing more," Parsons said sourly. "Nothing more than a murder."

"That's all, sir."

"Ninety-six thousand dollars in cash and you don't think they're going to smell something fishy?"

"Sir, my job was to yank those supers out of circulation. That's what I did, sir."

"Splendid," Parsons said.

Horne never knew when he meant it.

"But how long do you think it'll be before these nitwits realize there are *more* phony hundreds out there?" Parsons asked. "How long will it be before they come back to us?"

The room went silent.

"Why was the woman killed, do you know?" Parsons asked.

"I would suspect to keep her quiet," Horne said.

"Do you think this may be Witches and Dragons again?"

"It could be, sir."

Parsons nodded.

"Find out," he said. "Give Mother a call."

• • •

The sign over the cash register read:

WE WILL NOT CASH BILLS
LARGER THAN $50. SORRY FOR
ANY INCONVENIENCE.
THANK YOU.

Wilbur Struthers took umbrage at this.

Perhaps this was because the only money he had in his wallet was a pair of singles and $400 in hundred-dollar bills. A glance at the cash register total informed him that he had spent $95.95 for two bottles of Simi Chardonnay, two bottles of Gordon's gin, and a bottle of Veuve Cliquot champagne.

"I'm afraid I only have hundred-dollar bills," he told the cashier.

"We accept American Express, MasterCard, and Visa," the cashier said.

"I only have cash."

"Take a personal check, too, if you have proper ID," the cashier said. "Driver's license, or even a MetTrans card with a photo on it."

"I only have cash."

"We can't accept a hundred-dollar bill, I'm sorry," the cashier said.

"Why's that?"

"Been burned too often. Lots of phonies in circulation."

"These aren't phonies," Struthers said.

"Hard to tell 'em apart nowadays," the cashier said.

So much easier to stick up the fuckin joint, Struthers was thinking.

"Tell you what I'm gonna do," he said. "I'm gonna lay a hundred-dollar bill right on the counter here and forget all about the four dollars and change I got coming. You can either pick up the bill and put it in your cash register and tell me 'Thanks for your business, sir,' or you can shove it up your ass. Either way, I'm walkin out of here with my purchases. Good day to you, sir."

The Eighty-seventh Precinct car patrolling Adam Sector picked him up before he'd walked three blocks from the store.

First thing Detective Andy Parker learned about the perp the blues brought in was that he'd walked out of a liquor store with purchases totaling close to a hundred bucks without paying for them—or at least paying for them with a bill the cashier had refused to accept because it might have been counterfeit. Nobody—least of all Parker—as yet knew whether the bill was queer or not. That wasn't the point. You could not simply walk out of a store without paying for your purchases even if you kept insisting afterward that you had paid for them—which Struthers was insisting now, over and over again, bending Parker's ear and breaking his balls.

This was not a court of law here. This was a police station. Parker was a detective and not a judge. He was not being paid to administer justice here, any more than cops in a park during a riot were expected to determine whether a crowd of unruly assholes were *actually* sticking their hands up under girls' skirts. Those cops were being paid to sit on park benches and watch the parade go by. Parker was being paid to sit here and write up a DD form that would follow this man through the criminal justice system—where, by the way, the dude had been before, Parker was just noticing on his computer. This did not bode too well for Mr. Wilbur Struthers here, who seemed to have taken a burglary fall not too long ago and done some fine time upstate. This was enough to put Mr. Struthers in serious trouble here, though certainly Parker did not wish to seem judgmental.

"What you did, it looks like," he said, "was walk out of a store with close to a hundred bucks in merchandise, without paying for it. Is what you seem to have done, Willie."

"I paid for the merchandise," Struthers said.

"Man said you placed a possibly phony . . ."

"Man had no reason to believe the bill was phony."

"Says you forced it on him even though he told you it was store policy not to accept . . ."

"No one forced anything on him. I merely placed the bill politely on the counter top . . ."

"And told him to shove it up his ass."

"He could've also just put it in the cash register and shut his fuckin mouth."

"Language, Willie, language."

"Well, he could've avoided a lot of unnecessary trouble here."

"Which he chose not to do because his boss has been stung with queer C-notes before."

"This one was not queer."

"How do you know?"

"The Secret Service told me," Struthers said.

This was not exactly true.

The Secret Service had told him that $8,000 of the $8,500 he'd stolen from Cassandra Jean Ridley's apartment was not part of a ransom paid in some mysterious goddamn White House kidnapping, but they had not said the bills weren't counterfeit. In any case, the lady had reclaimed the eight large and had been eaten by lions for her boldness. The $100 bill Struthers had subsequently passed across the counter of S&L Liquors on Stemmler Avenue was one of the bills first Special Agent David A. Horne and later the redheaded lady herself had overlooked in their zeal to make everything right again. Struthers had no idea whether it was phony or not.

Besides, intent was ninety percent of the law, a jailhouse attorney had once informed him, true or not. He'd had no intention of passing counterfeit money. His only intention was to stock up on alcoholic beverages for New Year's Eve, which he hoped to perhaps spend with that girl Jasmine he'd tried to introduce to good champagne, if ever he could find her again. He now had $300 left of the money he'd stolen from the Lion Lady, as he thought of her, and if Jasmine would accept that in trade, he would be willing to pay for a woman for the first time in his life. What the hell, a new year was coming. After which, he figured he might have to run out and do another little burglary, provided this asshole detective here in the rumpled suit and the razor cuts all over his face let him go. Struthers didn't see that anybody had a case here. He'd paid for the goddamn booze!

"Here's the way I look at it," Parker said. "If the bill you gave that guy was genuine, then you in fact paid for the merchandise, and we've got no beef. If, however, the bill is phony, then not only were you passing bad money, you were also committing Petit Larceny, a class-A misdemeanor as defined in Section 155.30 of the Penal Law, punishable by a term not to exceed a year in the slammer. I'm not paid to be judgmental," Parker said judgmentally, "but why waste the city's time and money if in fact the bill is genuine?"

Struthers held his breath.

"Let's take a walk over to the bank," Parker said.

"Let's," Struthers said confidently.

"Well, well, look who's here," Meyer called from the corridor. He swung open the gate in the slatted wooden railing, walked into the squadroom, tossed his hat at the hat rack, and missed. Kneeling to retrieve it, he asked, "What's it this time, Will?"

"Walkaway," Parker said.

"Oh dear," Meyer said.

"Hello, Will," Carella said, just behind him.

Struthers didn't like all this fucking cordiality. He wanted to go to the bank, show the bill to whoever understood counterfeits there, and get on with his preparations for New Year's Eve.

"Also he insisted on passing a C-note may be phony," Parker said.

"I was paying for my merchandise. Incidentally," he said, "there's no law against innocently passing a counterfeit bill if there is no intent to deceive."

The detectives looked at him.

Parker sighed.

"We were just on our way to the bank," he said.

"Where'd you get that bill?" Carella asked.

Struthers didn't answer.

"Will? Where'd you get that C-note?"

Still no answer.

"Was it part of the money you stole from Cass Ridley?"

Struthers didn't know what he might be getting into here. He figured maybe he just ought to keep still.

"Was it?"

No answer.

"Cause I'll tell you what," Carella said. "We've got a whole pile of *other* hundred-dollar bills here. Why don't we all walk over to the bank?"

It was ten minutes to three when Struthers and the detectives walked through the revolving doors of the First Federal Bank on Van Buren Circle. Not too long ago—well, perhaps longer ago than Carella chose to admit—a criminal alternately known to the squad as "Taubman" or "L. Sordo" or most commonly "The Deaf Man"—had tried to rob this bank, twice. Carella still felt a faint shiver of apprehension at the memory. They had not heard from The Deaf Man in a long, long time—well, perhaps not as long a time as Carella might have wished—and he had no desire to hear from him again anytime soon.

The manager back then had been named Somebody Alton, Carella no longer remembered the first name, if ever he'd known it. The new manager was a woman named Antonia Belandres, a stately plump brunette in her forties, wearing no makeup and a dark gray suit. She looked up at the clock the moment they approached her desk.

"Little late for business, gentlemen," she said.

Carella showed his shield.

"Detective Carella," he said. "Eighty-seventh Squad."

"This is the Eighty-*sixth* Precinct," she said.

Carella didn't know what that had to do with anything. The bank was on the Circle, directly across Tenth, the wide avenue that slivered the two precincts roughly in half, north to south. First Federal was most convenient to the station house, and besides it was a federal bank. If anybody should know anything about counterfeit money, it was the Feds.

"We're just across the avenue," Parker explained helpfully.

"We're investigating a homicide," Carella said.

She looked at the clock again.

"We need some suspect bills checked," Meyer said.

"We're kind of in a hurry here," Struthers added.

Antonia turned to look at him. Something flashed in her dark eyes. Perhaps she was wondering if he was in charge of this little band of Homicide detectives. He certainly looked intelligent enough. Perhaps she liked the long rugged cowboy look of him. Whatever it was, she addressed her next question to him. With a smile.

"May I see the bills, please?" she said.

They spread the bills on her desk.

$96,000 in hundreds from Cass Ridley's safe deposit box . . .

$8,000 in hundreds from the desk drawer in her apartment . . .

And next the solitary hundred-dollar bill Struthers had placed on the counter at S&L Liquors in payment for his various alcohol purchases.

"You have to understand," Antonia said, as she delicately leafed through the money, "that for every man, woman, and child in the United States, there are six or seven hundred-dollar bills in circulation. That means for every person in the work force, there are more than a *dozen* hundred-dollar bills out there. That comes to something like a billion and a half dollars."

It had begun snowing again. The snow was fierce. Tiny little needle-like crystals blown by a bitter wind. The snow and the wind lashed the long windows of the bank where they sat around Antonia's desk covered with hundred-dollar bills.

"Now who do you think is in possession of *most* of those bills?" she asked, and smiled at Struthers.

"Who?" he asked.

"Vicious criminals, drug dealers, and tax cheats," Antonia said.

"I'm not any one of those," Struthers explained to the detectives.

They did not appear impressed.

"The Secret Service gave me a clean bill of health," he explained to Antonia. She seemed more impressed than the detectives. She raised her eyebrows appreciatively, gave him an approving little nod.

"You may not know," she said, "that the United States Secret Service is part of the Treasury Department."

"Yes, I *did* know that, in fact," Struthers said. "It was explained to me."

"They don't merely protect the life of the President of the United States. Actually, the *major* part of their job is the detection and prevention of currency counterfeiting. Not many people know that," she said.

"*That* I didn't know till this very minute," Struthers said—kissing ass, Parker thought.

"I'm happy you came to me today," Antonia said.

"I've had occasion to work with the Secret Service before, you see, on cases regarding counterfeit United States currency." She was carefully turning over the stack of hundreds on her desk, bill by bill, checking for whatever. "Though at first glance, I must say these bills do not strike me as being super-bills. Or super-dollars, whichever terminology you gentlemen prefer. Or even super-notes. Which *do* you prefer, Lieutenant?"

Struthers realized she was addressing him.

"I never heard any of those terms in my life," he said.

"The Arabic writing on the face of some of these bills is suspect, of course," Antonia said, "but not all bills passing through the Middle East are fake. In fact, sixty percent of *all* United States currency is in circulation abroad. You probably didn't know that, either."

"I certainly didn't," Struthers said.

"In fact, the hundred-dollar bill is the most widely held paper currency in the world. Which is what makes it such an attractive target for counter-feiters," Antonia said. "What I'm trying to tell you, however, is that the signature of a money-changer—on this bill, for example, the handwriting means 'Son of Ahmad'—in itself does not indicate a fake bill. As a matter of pride, a money-changer will sign or put some other personal mark on a stack of bills. It's like an author signing his book at Barnes & Noble."

Struthers thought a money-changer was some guy who cashed checks on Lambert Av, up in Diamondback. And he didn't know any authors who signed books.

"In the Arab world," Antonia said, "money-changers are financial middlemen. They've been around since well before Jesus. You need to buy commodities in the West? Simple. You just take your cash to a second-story office in the old quarter of Damascus. The money-changer will arrange for the transfer. I've seen these money-changers' signatures many times before," she said, exhibiting another of the bills. "They don't necessarily indicate a bill is counterfeit. We see entire *families* of counterfeit bills . . ."

Families, Struthers thought.

". . . with the same serial numbers on them," Antonia said. "But none of this larger stack of bills belongs to any of those families."

"Then they're genuine," Carella said.

"They're not counterfeit, that's right," Antonia said, and shoved the stack of bills to one side of her desk, summarily dismissing $104,000 as beneath further scrutiny. "But let's look more closely at this lone hundred-dollar bill here," she said, and picked up the bill Struthers had used in the liquor store. "Henry Loo," she said, staring at the face of the bill.

The man on the bill looked like Benjamin Franklin to Struthers, but he didn't say anything.

"The manager of Ban Hin Lee," she said. "The

bank I worked for in Singapore, many years ago. On Robinson Road."

"I know Robinson Road," Struthers said.

"You do?"

"I was in Singapore many years ago, too," Struthers said.

"What's Henry Loo got to do with this bill?" Carella asked.

"He was the first person who showed me a super-bill," Antonia said. "Or a super-dollar, if you prefer. Or a super-note."

Struthers was trying to figure what the rap might be for passing a phony hundred-dollar bill he hadn't known was phony to begin with.

"I studied economics in Manila," she told Struthers, trying to impress him, Parker figured. "After graduation, I got a job at Ban Hin Lee . . ."

"I spent some time in Manila, too," Struthers told her—still kissing ass, Parker thought. "After I escaped from the Khmer Rouge. But that's another story," he said, and Antonia noticed for the first time the almost imperceptible tic and small white scar near the corner of his left eye.

"And later in Singapore," he said. "That's how I happen to know Robinson Road."

"It's a small world," Antonia said.

"I'm amazed we didn't meet there," he said. "In Singapore. We probably passed each other all the time on Robinson Road."

"Yes," she said. "We probably did."

Staring at each other across the desk where the genuine bills were stacked to one side, and Struthers' lone C-note was sitting in front of her.

"I started as a bank messenger," Antonia said. "Worked my way up to teller and then assistant manager, which was when Henry Loo showed me a hundred-dollar bill so *real*-looking I thought old Ben Franklin would any minute go fly a kite off it!"

Antonia laughed at her own witticism.

"But it was as queer as monkey soup," she said, on a comic roll. "A lot of these C-series hundreds were coming through at the time, all of them printed in Teheran on high-tech intaglio presses."

"*What* kind of presses?" Carella asked.

"Intaglio," she said.

"What's intaglio?" Meyer asked.

"An embossing technique that uses a very thick gummy ink."

"Is that what intaglio means?" Parker asked Carella. "Thick and gummy?"

"How should I know what intaglio means?" Carella said.

"Maybe it means embossing technique," Meyer suggested.

"I thought you were supposed to be Italian," Parker said, and shrugged.

"Intaglio produces a three-dimensional effect you can't get with any other printing technique," Antonia said. "Whatever the engraver designs, intaglio gives you *exactly*."

"And you say these presses exist in *Teheran?*" Parker asked. He was thinking *Teheran?* Where they wear baggy pants and turbans?

"Yes," Antonia said. "Identical to the ones used by the Bureau of Engraving and Printing."

"Bureau of Engraving presses in *Teheran?*" Meyer said. He was thinking *Teheran?* Where they shoot guns in the air and burn American flags?

"Oh yes," Antonia said.

"Let me get this straight," Carella said. "You're saying . . ."

"I'm saying that the late Shah of Iran bought two high-tech intaglio presses from the United States to print his own currency. When the mullahs took over, they put the presses to their own use."

"Printing counterfeit hundreds, you're saying," Parker said.

"Printing super-bills, yes. On plates and paper purchased from the East Germans, yes. Is what I'm saying."

"Printing high-quality . . ."

"Printing *super*-bills," Antonia repeated, stressing the word this time. "Notes so close to the original, they're virtually impossible to tell apart. In fact, I suspect *this* may be a super-bill," she said, and gingerly tapped Struthers' hundred-dollar note.

Uh-oh, he thought.

"How can you tell?" Carella asked.

"Experience," she said.

He looked at her.

"How?" he asked. "If they're so close to the original . . ."

"There are detection machines at the Federal Reserve," she said.

"Do you have one of those machines here?"

"No. I'm judging by eye."

"I thought you said it was virtually impossible . . ."

"Yes, well, I have a trained eye."

He looked at her again. It suddenly occurred to him that she didn't *know* for sure whether or not that hundred-dollar bill was a phony.

"But if it's so *easy*," he said.

"No one said it's easy."

"Well, you took one look at that bill . . ."

"I've been looking at it all along."

"Without a machine, without even a magnifying glass . . ."

"There are machines at the Federal Reserve. I told you . . ."

"But not here."

"That's right. We send any suspect bills to the Fed."

"How many suspect bills do you get on any given day?"

"We get them every now and then."

"How often?"

"Not very often. Now that the Big Bens are in circulation . . ."

"The what?"

"The new hundreds with the big picture of Franklin on them. Little by little, they're replacing all the old hundreds. That means all the super-bills will eventually be pulled out of circulation, too."

"When?"

"That's difficult to say. It might take years."

"How many years?"

"Five? Ten? Why are you being so hostile?" Antonia asked.

Struthers was wondering the same thing.

"Maybe because a woman was killed," Carella said. "And you're telling me a bill stolen from her apartment may be one of these *super*-bills that are so good nobody can tell them from the real thing."

"The Federal Reserve can detect them. They have machines."

"But how about mere mortals? Can *we* detect them?"

"I just told you this bill looks suspicious, didn't I?"

"Which means you'll be sending it to the Federal Reserve to check on one of its secret machines, right?"

"They're not *secret* machines. Everyone knows they exist."

"How many of these super-bills find their way to those machines?"

"I'm sorry?"

"How many of the bills end up in the Federal Reserve's vaults?"

"The Fed doesn't release those figures."

"Well, how many of them are still in *circulation?* I'm not talking about the ones you see here at your bank, I'm talking about . . ."

"I don't understand your question."

"I'm asking how *many* of these super-bills are still floating around out there."

"I've heard an estimate."

"And what's the estimate?"

"Twenty billion dollars," Antonia said.

8.

In this business, you do not expect fake money.

Fake names, yes, but not fake money.

Fake money can get you killed, whereas a fake name can save your life. Even the two Mexicans, whose real names *were* Francisco Octavio Ortiz and Cesar Villada, used fake names when they were doing business with types trading in controlled substances. No one buying or selling a hundred keys of dope gives you his real name, unless he is *loco*—which, by the way, was a distinct possibility with the people who'd paid a million-seven in fake hundreds to two dangerous *hombres* like themselves. They suspected that the man the redheaded pilot had fingered as Randolph Biggs wasn't a Randolph Biggs at all, nor was he even the Texas State Ranger he'd pretended to be. The problem was in finding him first in a good-sized town like Eagle Branch, and next in Piedras Rosas, the teeming border town just across the river.

If you are dealing in controlled substances, you do not buy radio commercials or newspaper ads announcing that you are in town looking for a man who paid you with bad money. You play it cool, which is difficult to do when you are eager to tie a man to a chair and pull out his fingernails. Villada and Ortiz merely kept flashing money everywhere they went. They were either rich tourists from Barcelona—in a shitty border town like Piedras Rosas?—or else they were looking to make a drug deal. There were drugs and drug dealers in Eagle Branch, and there were drugs and drug dealers in Piedras Rosas, too. You could not go anywhere in the world today and not find drugs or drug dealers, even in those nations where the penalty for possession was death. This was a very sad fact of life to Ortiz and Villada, but what could one do in a world obsessed with money?

The color of their money blinked like green neon. Money, money, money. The scent of human greed on their hundred-dollar bills floated on the hot Mexican air. Prostitutes blatantly tendered their sloppy favors. Men proffered high-stakes card games, cock fights, dog fights. Lower-level street pushers looking like *bandidos* out of old black-and-white movies offered rolled sticks of marijuana, dime bags of diluted cocaine. Urchins asked if the gentlemen would care to fuck their sisters. Ortiz and Villada were even afraid to drink the water.

Randolph Biggs—or someone who could have been Randolph Biggs—surfaced that afternoon.

• • •

They were sitting at a table in an outdoor bar, flashing the green as always, trolling. The white man who took a table adjacent to theirs was tall and broad-shouldered, with a broad neatly trimmed mustache under a nose that sniffed the air disdainfully as he sat and signaled to a harried waiter. He was wearing a neatly pressed tan tropical suit. White linen shirt open at the throat. Tan loafers. No socks. A huge man, the redhead had told them. Randolph Biggs?

Looking bored, he ordered tequila, lime, salt. His dark brown eyes grazed their table. He looked at his watch. Sniffed again, as if he'd just smelled an open toilet, which in all likelihood he had. Looked around as if expecting cockroaches or rats in a place like this, another likelihood. The waiter brought his drink and the props. He thanked him in fluent Spanish, told him to keep the tab running. Villada and Ortiz were impressed.

He squirted lime juice on the back of his hand, sprinkled salt onto it, licked at the solution, drank some tequila. They were further impressed. He signaled to a man selling cigarettes from a tray hanging around his neck. Loose or by the pack? the man asked in Spanish. He bought an unopened package of Marlboros, paid with Mexican *pesos* he peeled from a grubby roll of bills.

The three men, at separate adjacent tables, sat drinking in the gaudy heat of the Mexican afternoon. There were guitars somewhere. There was the liquid laughter of women from alleyways and upstairs rooms. Everything smelled sweaty and smoky. Buses rolled past. Taxicabs honked their horns. This was a busy bustling little city the size of some neighborhood ghettos in North America. Walk into any one of those ghettos, you'd see the same faces you saw here, you'd hear the same language. The man sitting here in his fancy tropical suit and his neatly groomed mustache looked as out of place as Meg Ryan might have.

"Perdoname," he said. *"¿Tiene usted un cerillo?"*

He was holding one of the Marlboros between the forefinger and middle fingers of his right hand, close to his lips, leaning over toward them now. Ortiz triggered a gold Cartier cigarette lighter into flame. The man inhaled, let out a cloud of smoke, grinned in satisfaction. In Spanish, he said, "I've been trying to quit."

"A bad habit," Ortiz agreed in Spanish, and snapped the lid of the lighter shut.

Randolph Biggs?

"What brings you to this lovely city?" the man asked, and raised his eyebrows to emphasize the sarcasm.

"Passing through," Villada said.

"On your way to?"

"Mexico City."

They were still speaking Spanish. His Spanish was very good.

"And you?" Ortiz asked.

"I live in Eagle Branch," the man said.

They waited for his name. Nothing came.

"Manuel Arrellano," Ortiz said, reaching his hand across the tables, giving the name he frequently used during drug transactions, though he did not yet know whether or not this man was at all involved in the trade. "My partner Luis Larios," he said, giving Villada's *nom de guerre*.

"Randolph Biggs," the man said.

Ortiz's eyes narrowed just the tiniest bit.

The men shook hands all around.

"What business are you in?" Biggs asked. "You said you were partners."

"We export pottery," Villada said in Spanish.

"And you?" Ortiz asked in English. Shift to the man's own tongue, make him feel a little more comfortable about asking if the gentlemen here were in reality selling high-octane shit and not some crockery worth a buck and a half.

"I'm a law enforcement officer," Biggs said. "Texas Rangers." He raised the flap of his jacket, reached into his side pocket, took out a thick leather billfold, opened it to show a gold star pinned to the flap. Ortiz and Villada were impressed all over again. But the redheaded pilot had told them all this. A Texas Ranger named Randolph Biggs was the man who'd introduced her to Frank Holt, another bullshit name, who'd arranged for her to fly to Guenerando to pick up the dope. And pay for it with focking fonny money.

"Do you know a woman named Cassandra Jean Ridley?" Villada asked in English.

Stick to English now, he was thinking.

Make this all perfectly clear to Mr. Randolph Biggs here.

The name registered.

Biggs looked across the table to where Ortiz was sitting with a pistol in his lap, pointing at his belly.

"We have a car," Villada said.

Ollie's piano teacher was a woman named Helen Hobson. She was in her late fifties somewhere, he guessed, he'd never asked, a rail of a woman who always wore a green cardigan sweater over a brown woolen skirt, he wondered if she had any other clothes in her closet. He thought it ironic, the way fate worked. In November, he'd caught a little dead colored girl in an apartment downstairs, turned out Helen had been the one who discovered the body. Now he was taking piano lessons from her and well on the way to becoming an accomplished musician. It was all so strange and wonderful.

It seemed odd to find a grand piano in what was basically a slum apartment, but Helen had crowded one into a corner of her small living room, and it was here that Ollie shared a piano bench with her while he pored over the sheet music for "Night and Day." Helen sat perched to his right on one scant corner of the bench, Ollie's wide buttocks overwhelming the remainder of it. He kept pecking away at the keys.

"I'm having trouble with the notes in the first few bars," he said.

He loved musical terms.

Until now, a bar was just a place where you went to have a beer.

Helen looked at him.

"The notes in the first few *bars?*" she asked.

"Yeah. They're giving me trouble," he said.

"There is only *one* note in the first few bars," she said. "It is the same note repeated three times. G. The note is G. Three times. Bom, bom, bom. Night. And. Day. That is the same note, Mr. Weeks. How can it be giving you trouble?"

"I don't know, it's just giving me trouble."

"Mr. Weeks, we've been working on the first six measures of this song for the past little while now . . ."

"Yeah, I know."

"Without, I must confess, noticeable progress. Are you *sure* you want to take piano lessons?"

"I am very sure. Yes, Miss Hobson. My ambition is to play five songs on the piano."

"Because . . . and this is a possibility you may wish to consider, Mr. Weeks . . . perhaps you have no talent."

"Oh, I have talent, all right."

"Perhaps not."

"I have talent to spare. I think I'm just in some kind of slump, is all. Not bein able to get past those first three notes."

"But those first three notes are one and the *same*

note! Bom, bom, bom," she said, demonstrating, striking the note three times in succession. "Night. And. *Day!*" she said, striking the same note again and again and again. "It is impossible for you to be having trouble with the identical note struck three times. It is physically impossible, Mr. Weeks. Bom, bom, bom," she said, hitting the note again. "It's so simple a *rodent* could tap it out with his nose."

"It isn't that I haven't been practicing," he said.

"Bom, bom, bom," she said.

"It's just I caught these two murder cases . . ."

"Please," she said, and lowered her eyes.

"I'm sorry, I know you don't like to hear about . . ."

"I truly don't."

"I'm just trying to explain I've been very busy. And also, I've begun writing a book."

Helen turned to look at him.

"Yeah," he said, and grinned. "A novel."

She kept staring at him.

"A novel," she said. "My."

"Yeah," he said. "I know."

He went on to explain that he'd been a cop for almost twenty years now, and a detective for fifteen of those years, so he knew a little bit more about police work than your average run-of-the-mill aspiring writer, didn't he?

"I'm sure you do," Helen said.

So he'd picked up what he guessed was some sort of form letter this editor at Wadsworth and Dodds . . .

"Which is where I'm investigating the second murder . . ."

. . . writes to people who make inquiries and it had really been very helpful, and had probably started him on yet another worthwhile career, though not one so satisfying as yet as playing the piano . . .

"If I can just get past those first three notes," he said.

"The *same* note, Mr. Weeks. It is the *identical* note. Bom, bom, *bom*," she said, pounding the G key.

"His name is Henry Daggert," Ollie said.

"Whose name?"

"This editor at Wadsworth and Dodds. He's a senior editor and vice president. I practically memorized everything he wrote."

"But you can't memorize the first note of this song," Helen said, tapping the sheet music. "Such a *simple* note, too. Just think of the three notes as the *same* note, can you do that? Place your index finger over the G key, and strike it once, bom. Let it resonate, and then strike it again, bom. Can you do that?"

"Oh sure," Ollie said.

Helen looked at the keyboard somewhat despairingly. "We have a few more minutes," she said. "Do you think we can try it one more time?"

At first, he insisted he knew no one named Cassandra Jean Ridley. Knew no one named Frank, either.

Of any last name whatever. No Franks at all in his busy life as a Texas Ranger.

But this was sunny Mexico.

So they used a cattle prod on his testicles.

He all at once remembered the good-looking redhead and this man named Frank Whoever, but all he'd done was introduce the pair, *"Verdad,"* he said in Spanish, he scarcely knew them at all, really. Cassie—the guys in the bar used to call her Cassie—was an attractive redhead, and Frank was just someone he'd seen around, nice-enough fellow, he thought they might hit it off together, didn't even know his last name, *verdad, amigos.*

"I'm a Texas Ranger," he told them. "What I do mostly is border patrol, trying to keep the wetbacks out, you know . . ."

He actually used the word "wetbacks" in the presence of two Mexicans who were holding a cattle prod an inch away from his quivering balls . . .

"No offense meant," he said immediately. "The point is . . ."

The point was he knew nothing about any money that was flown south of the border by Lieutenant Ridley or anyone else, knew nothing about any deals made between these two obviously fine gentlemen here and anyone in the entire universe, did not know anything about Frank Whatever-His-Last-Name-Was, whom he'd only met in a bar, did not know how much a key of cocaine was worth, did not even know what cocaine *was,* ask him any other question, he was very good at geography.

They gave him a longer jolt this time.

His balls shriveled right up into his throat.

Okay, he told them, the man's name is Frank Holt, I knew him only as an independent contractor who was normally very reliable. I had no idea what kind of deal was going down in Mexico, I merely put together a man and a pilot. The man needed a delivery and pickup, and the pilot had to be willing to take risks—which, by the way, Lieutenant Ridley had taken plenty of during the Gulf War, from what he'd heard about her. He believed she'd been decorated for valor, in fact. An honorable woman who'd served her nation well in times of dire stress, he felt sure she would not have had any part of a scheme designed to bilk anyone out of fair payment in exchange for his goods, whatever those goods might have been, though he'd had no idea the lady would be picking up cocaine across the border. He told them he'd certainly hadn't the faintest *notion* that counterfeit money was being flown to Mexico in exchange for what was undoubtedly very high-grade coke indeed, the two gentlemen here seeming trustworthy and entirely professional. In short, he'd been a mere instrument of convenience, an enabler, a facilitator, so to speak, an all-around nice guy who'd tried to be helpful, was all. If the gentlemen here had got stung, Randolph L. Biggs hadn't had anything to do with it. They would have to look elsewhere for satisfaction.

"So, gentlemen . . ."

Villada nodded to Ortiz.

Ten seconds later, Biggs was telling them that Frank Holt's real name was Jerome Hoskins and that he worked for a company called Wadsworth and Dodds, back East in the big bad city.

Carella finally reached Captain Mark William Ridley at a little past six that evening. He was cognizant of the fact that it was already midnight in Binsfeld, Germany, but when he'd tried earlier that day, he was informed that the captain had still not returned to base.

Now—at six-oh-six exactly on the face of the squadroom clock—Carella listened to the captain's voice coming over the line from somewhere outside Frankfurt, explaining at great length that Spangdahlem's commanding officer, the brigadier general in charge of the 52nd Fighter Wing, had decided to divide more or less evenly among the base's five thousand U.S. active-duty military members and their seven thousand dependents, the holiday season's twelve-day sequence that had begun on December 21, the start of Hanukkah, and would end on New Year's Day.

"That is because our wing mission is to be constantly ready at all times to promote stability and thwart naked aggression," he said.

"I see," Carella said.

"In order to achieve U.S. and NATO objectives," Ridley added, "yessir."

Carella wished the man didn't sound as if he'd been drinking.

"I drew December 21 to December 27," Ridley said. "I just got back from Italy fifteen minutes ago. Did I understand you to say you are a detective, sir?"

"Yes, I am," Carella said.

"Why are you calling me here in the Rhineland, may I ask, sir?"

Carella was calling to tell him his sister was dead.

He took a deep breath.

He guessed he'd performed this drill a hundred times before, perhaps a thousand times before, telling a wife or a mother or a father or a son or a brother or an aunt that someone near and dear was suddenly, inexplicably dead, and then listening to the silence or the tears or sometimes the hysterical laughter that greeted this unexpected, unwanted news from a total stranger, he guessed he had spoken these same damn more or less identical words a million times before it sometimes seemed.

Ridley was silent for several moments.

Then he said, "It comes in bunches, don't it, sir?" He sounded suddenly quite sober. "First my wife leaves me . . ."

He fell silent again.

Carella waited.

"I'm sorry," Ridley said.

Carella suspected he was crying, but he could hear no tears over the crackling line. He waited.

"Captain," he said at last, "I wonder if I could ask you some questions. I know this is a bad time . . ."

He let the sentence trail.

Ridley said nothing.

"Captain?" Carella said.

"Yes. Yes, sure," Ridley said. "Go ahead. Sure. I'm sorry. Go ahead."

"We read some letters you sent to your sister . . ."

"Yes, we corresponded a lot."

"In one of them, you made reference to one of *her* letters . . ."

"Yes."

". . . where she told you she'd be flying a job early in December . . ."

"Yes."

". . . which apparently she felt would change her circumstances considerably, was how she put it in the letter to you, which you were quoting."

"Yes."

"What was that job, Captain Ridley? Would you know?"

The captain was silent.

"Sir? Apparently she wrote to say she'd be moving East sometime after this job . . ."

"Yes."

". . . be there long before Christmas, in fact, was apparently what she wrote to you, if your letter was quoting her exactly. "

Again, the captain was silent.

"You see, sir, she was killed just before Christmas, and we were wondering if this job she flew had anything to do with her murder."

"How was she killed?" Ridley asked.

"Someone stuck an ice pick in her," Carella said. And waited.

"She was flying dope," Ridley said.

"To Mexico, is that right?"

"Yes. Four runs."

"On December seventh, she flew to Mexico for the last time, is that right?"

"Yes. How do you know that?"

"There was an entry in her calendar."

"She called me right afterward."

"Called you there in Germany?"

"Yes."

"To say what, Captain?"

"That she'd flown the four runs, and they turned out to be a piece of cake."

"How do you know they were drug runs?"

"She told me."

"On an open phone?"

"No, in one of her letters. After I warned her not to do anything that might get her in trouble. She assured me these would be short flights, simple pickups and deliveries. Just like chickens or sandals, she said. Just like that."

"Where was she flying? From where to where?"

"Texas to Mexico to Arizona."

"What kind of pickups and deliveries?"

"Money for drugs."

"How much money?"

"They didn't tell her. It was in locked suitcases."

"What drug? Heroin? Cocaine?"

"I don't know. I don't think she knew, either."

"Who was she working for?"

"A man named Frank Holt. He was the one who gave her the suitcases with the money in them. He was the one buying the stuff."

"Who is he, do you know?"

"Some guy she got introduced to in a bar in Eagle Branch. This is why I thought it all sounded so risky. I mean who the hell *were* these people? She said they were okay. Ordinary guys, she told me. Guys trying to make a buck. One of them was a Texas Ranger she'd dated once or twice. The guy who introduced her to Holt."

"What was *his* name? The Ranger?"

"Riggs? Briggs? Something like that."

"How much were they paying her?"

"A *lot* of money."

"How much?"

"Two hundred thousand dollars."

"That's a lot," Carella agreed. He was thinking they had to be big buys. You didn't pay fifty grand a pop for a two-bit pickup and delivery.

"How'd they pay her, did she say? Was it in hundred-dollar bills?"

"I don't know. She got fifty on a handshake, the rest after the last run." Ridley paused. "Plus what they tipped her."

"What do you mean? Tipped her?"

"Yeah, they tipped her."

"Who did?"

"The Mexicans in Guenerando. They gave her a ten-thousand-dollar tip. She told me she was going to buy a couple of fur coats."

The line went silent.

"Did she ever buy the coats?" Ridley asked. "Would you know?"

"She bought the coats," Carella said.

Fat Ollie Weeks stopped by after his piano lesson to see if anybody up the Eight-Seven wanted to go for pizza or anything. They went to a place on Culver and U. Ollie ordered a large pie for himself. Meyer and Carella shared a nine-incher. The men were off-duty, they ordered beers all around.

"You look tired," Ollie told Carella.

"Must be all this accounting work," Carella said.

Ollie bit into a wedge of pizza. Cheese and sauce spilled onto the lapel of his sports jacket. He dipped up a dollop of mozzarella with the tip of his forefinger, and daintily brought it to his mouth. Licking it off, he asked, "What accounting?"

"On the Ridley case."

"What accounting?" Ollie asked again.

"I've been trying to chase down all her money. I spoke to her brother in Germany half an hour ago . . ."

"The one whose wife dumped him," Ollie said, nodding. He was already on his second slice of pizza. "The one who sent the wedding band."

"That's the one. He told me she got paid two hundred grand for picking up some dope in Mexico."

"We're in the wrong racket," Ollie said.

"Plus a ten-grand tip."

"Dope dealers are tipping people nowadays, huh?"

"The way I figure it, she kept the ten grand aside for petty cash. Struthers stole whatever was left of it."

"Eight thousand bucks," Meyer said.

He was wondering how many calories were in the slice of pizza he now picked off the tray. Ollie seemed to have no such problems.

"Popped two hundred grand into her safe deposit box," Carella said, "and then slowly transferred it into two separate checking accounts and a savings account."

"Placement and layering," Meyer said.

"Smurfing," Ollie agreed, and picked up a third slice of pizza.

"All accounted for," Carella said. "And, incidentally, all good money. What's left of it."

"Who says?"

"A lady at the bank."

"Reliable?"

"Maybe."

Ollie raised a skeptical eyebrow.

"But for the moment, let's say the two hundred grand is *not* counterfeit, okay?" Carella said.

"Okay. Two hundred large in nice clean money."

"That leaves only the *ten* grand she got as a tip."

"*Only?*" Ollie said. "That's bigger than the weekly collection from Riverhead."

Cops were always joking about payoffs from Riverhead or Calm's Point being short or being late or withheld for one reason or another. Some of the cops weren't joking. Meyer figured Ollie for an honest cop, though. Only a cop with a clear conscience could eat the way Ollie did.

He watched him as he washed down the third slice of pizza with a huge swallow of beer, thought What the hell, and bit ferociously into his own pizza wedge. With his right hand, Ollie signaled to the waitress for another pie. With his left hand, he was reaching for a fourth slice. Meyer wondered what he would look like if he had three hands.

"A ten-grand tip from the boys in Mexico," Carella said. "Which Cass keeps around the house to use for incidentals while she's distributing the *big* money in her various accounts. Okay. Struthers breaks in, finds eight thousand—or maybe more—sitting in a shoe box or wherever, and swipes it. He tries to spend one of the hundreds, but gets nailed by the Secret Service, who tell him they're investigating a kidnapping . . ."

"Bullshit," Ollie said.

"I agree. In any case, they return the bills and send him on his way."

"Why?"

"Good question. Now here's what's troubling me . . ."

Ollie bit into the fourth slice of pizza. Chewing, he looked across the table at Carella. Meyer was looking at him, too.

"Struthers tried to cash another bill earlier today. Which makes me think he originally swiped more than the eight G's. But never mind. We take the bill to the bank, lady there thinks it's a phony—something called a super-bill the Iranians are running off on presses they . . ."

"Bullshit," Ollie said again.

"I'm not so sure. But forget the Iranians for a minute, okay? Maybe that *is* bullshit, who knows? Let's just say, for now, that the bill *is* phony. Let's say every *one* of those hundred-dollar bills Cass Ridley got as a tip were phony. Ten thousand bucks in fake hundreds. Can we say that for a moment?"

Meyer was frowning.

"What?" Carella asked.

"If that ten grand was fake . . ."

"Right."

"And Struthers stole it . . ."

"Or what was left of it."

"And the Secret Service checked it out . . ."

"Yes."

"How come they didn't recognize it as fake?"

"That's just what's troubling me," Carella said, and nodded, and bit into his cold slice of pizza.

"I must be missing something," Ollie said.

"If the Secret Service had its hands on eight thousand bucks in bad money," Carella said, "why didn't they just confiscate it? Why'd they return it to Struthers?"

"I'll bite," Ollie said, and bit into another slice of pizza. The waitress was arriving with the fresh one. He ordered another round of beers from her. Now, two-fisted and ham-handed, he began lifting slices of pizza from both trays, some hot, some cold, all disappearing with remarkable rapidity into his briskly energetic mouth. "Why *did* they return the money to him?"

"All I can figure is they didn't," Carella said.

"You just said . . ."

"They returned eight thousand dollars to him, yes, but it wasn't the eight thousand they'd taken from him earlier. They returned *good* money to him. Even the lady at the bank said it was good."

"Why would they do that?"

"Because they didn't want anybody making waves down the line. Take his money from him, he might start trouble later on, who knows? Might even come squawking to *us,* who knows?"

"An ex-con?" Ollie said.

"Who knows? But give him back eight grand in *real* bills . . ."

"They probably got a slush fund," Meyer said. "Same as us."

"I'll bet. They pull eight large from it, send Struthers on his way, nice to know you, kid, don't bother us anymore."

Ollie looked at him.

"Too fucking deep for me," he said.

"Don't you see?" Carella said. "Why would two blond hitters carrying a bottle of champagne go up to a lone woman's apartment on a bullshit birthday story, stick an ice pick in her head, waltz her over to the park, strip her naked, and toss her into the lion's den where she gets eaten beyond all recognition? Why did they want her to disappear?"

"Why?" Ollie asked.

"Because she stumbled into something down there in Eagle Branch, Texas."

"Eagle Branch?" Ollie said, and stopped chewing.

"What is it?" Carella said at once.

"My publisher has a sales rep lives down there."

"Your publisher?"

"Yeah, I'm writing a book, didn't I tell you?"

Carella glanced at Meyer.

"I happened by chance on a publisher looking for a good thriller," Ollie said. "So when I'm not practicing piano, I work on the book. The countdown has *begun!*" he announced dramatically, and popped another slice of pizza into his mouth.

"You happened upon a publisher by chance," Carella said. "With a sales rep who lives . . ."

"I caught a guy stuffed in a garbage can on Christmas Eve," Ollie explained. "Bullet at the back of his head. Looked like a drug hit to me, but turned out he's an honest-to-God sales rep. Wadsworth and Dodds. That's the name of the publishing house he worked for."

"Ollie," Carella said. "Eagle Branch is where Cass Ridley hooked up with the two guys who sent her to Mexico."

"Well, I *know* that, Steve-a-rino."

"Eagle Branch is where this all *started.*"

"Well, why do you think I mentioned it?"

"Are you saying you've got a linked homicide?"

"I'm not saying that at all. I'm saying I caught a stiff who worked for a publishing house that has a sales rep who lives in Eagle Branch, Texas. Is what I'm saying."

"What's his name, this guy in Texas?"

"Randolph Biggs."

"The Texas Ranger," Carella said to Meyer.

"No, he's a sales rep," Ollie said.

"Your stiff didn't happen to be carrying any phony hundred-dollar bills, did he?" Meyer asked.

"Well, I don't know if they're phony or not," Ollie said, "but you're welcome to look at them. I already turned them over to the Property Clerk's Office."

They signed for and checked out the seven $100 bills Detective Oliver Wendell Weeks had recovered from Jerome Hoskins' wallet and deposited for security with the Property Clerk's Office. At ten minutes to ten that night, when the last FBI pouch left for Washington, D.C., the money was on the plane, together with an urgent note to the Federal Reserve, asking for an immediate authenticity pop.

The bills and the response from the Fed were waiting on Carella's desk when he got to work early the next morning, the twenty-eighth day of December.

The money was real.

9.

It really upset Nikmaddu Zarzour to be treated like a terrorist. Even if he looked like one. Even if he was one. Which, in fact, he happened to be.

The problems started the moment he transferred from Air France's flight 613 from Damascus to Paris, onto their connecting flight 006 to the United States. He was wearing a black linen suit, a white shirt without a tie, and a little red fez of the sort favored by Turkish gentlemen though he was neither Turkish nor a gentleman. On the Syrian leg of the flight, he was merely another Arab, his complexion the color of desert sand, his black mustache neatly trimmed, a single gold tooth occasionally glinting in the upper left hand corner of his mouth. But the moment he transferred planes in Paris he became someone whose shabby-looking suitcase and clothes called him to the attention of the security guard who was boarding the 3:15 P.M. flight to the States. It never occurred to the guard that if Nikmaddu were truly a terrorist—which, in fact, he was—he would have been carrying a Louis Vuitton suitcase or something less likely to call attention to his appearance. The guard riffled through his meager belongings, and then questioned—and confiscated—the little box of fresh figs Nikmaddu said he was taking to the U.S. for his maiden aunt. The guard did not suspect that the battered and scarred brown leather suitcase contained a false bottom. He could not have imagined that close to two million dollars in U.S. currency was neatly layered along the bottom of the suitcase; X-ray machines do not pick up paper.

And, of course, there was the same hassle coming through Customs and Immigration here on the eastern shores of the munificent United States of America, even though his passport was in order, even though he showed them a visa, little did it matter to them. He looked like a terrorist, ergo he *was* a terrorist. Which, in fact, he was. But it rankled.

Now . . .

At last.

"*Uhlan wa-Sahian.*" Welcome.

"*Ahlan Bikum,*" Nikmaddu said.

The proper reply, in plural because he was talking to three of them. He had never met any of them before. The men introduced themselves now. One of them, the obvious leader, sported a tiny uptilted mustache that made him look as if he were smiling. He had been trained in Afghanistan, was said to have links with the Egyptian Islamic Jihad.

"*Ismi Mahmoud Gharib,*" he said. My name is Mahmoud Gharib.

The second man had the harsh, leathery look of a

desert camel driver, deep creases on his brown face,
thick veins standing out on the backs of his strong
hands. He told Nikmaddu his name was Akbar. He
had the unsettling grin of a shark, all teeth and no
sincerity. He was their demolitions expert.

The man who introduced himself as Jassim had
the look of a pit viper, small and dark and pock-
marked. His handshake was remarkably strong, his
fingernails encrusted with a deep dark residue, perhaps the traces of explosive powders or oils. He was
the one who would go in with the bomb.

One who smiles only with his mustache,
Nikmaddu thought, another who smiles with false
teeth, and a third—with dirty fingernails—who
does not smile at all.

"So you're here at last," the third one said. Jassim.

"Il-Hamdu-Allah," Nikmaddu answered. Thanks
be to God.

"Was it a pleasant flight?" Akbar asked. All false
glittering smile and bright dark eyes.

Nikmaddu shrugged.

"Did you bring the money?" Mahmoud asked.
Mustache smiling. A direct question. Without the
money, there would be no explosives. Without
the money, there would be no preparations. Without
the money, there would be no escape routes afterward, no safe passages home. Without the money,
there would be nothing.

"I brought the money," Nikmaddu said.

And now they could discuss the business at hand.

. . .

The apartment they were meeting in was rented by Mahmoud himself. He was already three months in arrears, another reason for him having asked so soon about the money, his bloodsucking Jew landlord threatening eviction on an almost daily basis. The apartment was in a four-story walkup in a section of the city called Majesta after Her Majesty, the late lamented virgin queen of England, when these United States were still colonies. Once upon a time, Majesta was inhabited by Irish immigrants. Then it became Italian. Then it became Puerto Rican. Now it was populated largely by immigrants—many of them illegal—from third-world nations in the Middle East. The men sat sipping strong Turkish coffee as they looked out past the swirling snow to the towers of the Majesta Bridge in the misty distance. Jassim would have loved to wire that bridge with explosives, but Mahmoud was of a more conservative bent.

It was Mahmoud's opinion that all successful terrorist acts were premised on what had happened in Algiers almost half a century ago. It was there that the Arab struggle for independence from France began in 1954, culminating in July of 1962, when the Democratic and Popular Government of Algeria was formed. It was during those eight years that terrorism discovered its claws and its fangs. It was then that women wearing long dresses as prescribed in the Koran—*O prophet, tell your wives, your daughters, and the wives of the believers that they shall lengthen their garments. Thus, they will be recognized and avoid being insulted*—wearing as well the *hijab* that covered all of the face except the eyes, and the *khimar* that covered their bosoms, strolled unrecognized into grocery stores or onto buses, carrying shopping bags full of high explosives which they conveniently left behind while they went home to their families.

The world of terrorism—Mahmoud now told Nikmaddu—had expanded too greatly. The leaders were thinking too big. Their plans were too grandiose. Why bomb a World Trade Center in New York or a Federal Building in Oklahoma City or a U.S. Embassy in Nairobi or Dar es Salaam? Why bring down an airplane over Lockerbie or La-Guardia? Events such as these only created intense scrutiny and enormous animosity. Why not settle instead for leaving a small bomb in a cinema? Or a railroad station? Why not compromise instead for leaving a satchel with explosives under a sixth row orchestra seat at Clarendon Hall on the night Svi Cohen would be playing Beethoven's "Spring" sonata in F Major, or his "Kreutzer" in A Minor, or whichever other tune the Big Jew chose to perform on his accursed Zionist fiddle?

"Why not commit *tiny* acts of terrorism that will allow them to realize we can strike anywhere, anytime we choose?" Mahmoud asked.

"Clarendon Hall is not so tiny," Akbar said, grinning.

"You understand my point," Mahmoud said reasonably to Nikmaddu.

"I understand your point," Nikmaddu answered reasonably.

He was enjoying the coffee. He was not so sure he was enjoying the terrorist beliefs of a half-lira philosopher like the man with the comic mustache here. Nikmaddu himself had worked with Osama bin Laden on the Dhahran bombing attack in which nineteen U.S. servicemen were killed. It was his own belief that only *major* attacks of terrorism would leave any impression at all on the forces of evil polluting the Arab world. Only desperate measures would provoke wholesale departures. The withdrawal of all U.S. and western forces from Moslem countries in general and from the Arabian Peninsula in particular was the stated goal of *al Quaida.* Killing all Americans, including civilians, everywhere in the world was merely a means toward this end. But Nikmaddu was nothing if not a faithful servant of God. Someone higher up had ordered the Clarendon Hall bombing. He was here merely to serve.

They sat sipping coffee.

"Tell me the plan," Nikmaddu said.

The owner of Diamondback Books was named Jotham Davis. He was in his early forties, Ollie guessed, a black man with an entirely bald and very shiny head. He was wearing black jeans, black loafers, and a black turtleneck sweater. A gold chain hung around his neck, dangling to somewhere in the middle of his narrow chest. He told them that in the Bible, Jotham was the youngest of Gideon's seventy sons. He told them things were quiet after Christmas. He told them fifty percent of a bookstore's sales were in the three months before Christmas. He told them if a bookstore didn't make it at Christmastime, it might as well fold. Ollie thought he was full of shit. That was because Ollie figured a Negro couldn't possibly know anything about selling books.

It was now almost twelve noon on the twenty-eighth day of December, three days before New Year's Eve, six minutes or so before lunch time. Ollie was always aware of the clock, but only because it announced mealtimes. He and Carella had been in the shop for almost ten minutes now, listening to this bald jackass telling them about the book business when all they wanted was information about Jerome Hoskins who'd been shot at the back of the head and stuffed in a garbage can four days ago.

"You sell many books from Wadsworth and Dodds?" Ollie asked. "In the three months before Christmas?" He was thinking these people would probably be his publishers once he finished his book, so he wanted to know how well their books sold.

"Not too many," Jotham said. "They publish mostly technical stuff, you know."

"What do you mean, technical?" Carella asked.

"Engineering stuff, architectural. Like that."

"How about thrillers?" Ollie asked.

"Haven't seen any thrillers from them," Jotham said.

"They told me they do some thrillers."

"Maybe so. I just haven't seen any."

"Did their salesman mention any thrillers to you?"

"No, I don't recall him mentioning any thrillers."

"Man named Jerome Hoskins? He never mentioned any thrillers to you?"

"No, I don't think so."

"When's the last time he came by?" Carella asked.

"Must've been in September? Maybe October. Sometime around then. That's when most of the reps come around. Right after they have their sales conferences."

"Was he in here last week?" Ollie asked.

"Nossir."

"Two days before Christmas, to be exact."

"Nossir, he definitely was not in here two days before Christmas."

"You read newspapers?" Ollie asked.

"I do."

"You watch television?"

"I do."

"Read or see anything about Hoskins in the past few days?"

"No, I didn't. What happened to him?"

"How do you know anything happened to him?" Carella asked.

Jotham gave him a look that said Man, when you were born and raised in this neighborhood and two cops come calling on you one fine morning, and start asking questions about the last time a sales rep was in here, you know damn well they ain't here to buy no book about electrical engineering.

"Thanks for your time," Carella said.

Not three blocks away from the bookstore, Wiggy the Lid was talking to the bartender at the Starlight Bar, where he'd met one of the blondes who'd cold-cocked him on Christmas night.

"I never seed her before that night," the bartender said.

"Just walked in out of the blue, is that it, John?"

"That's what it was, Mr. Wiggins."

"She ever been in here before?"

"Don't recollect seeing her."

"Or another blonde looked just like her?"

"I'd've remembered somebody looked like that," John said.

"Neither one of them come in here, ast did a man named Wiggy Wiggins frequent this place?"

"No, neither one of 'em, Mr. Wiggins."

"Man named Wiggy the Lid? Did either one of 'em come in here, ax for me by that name?"

"Nobody come in here axin for you by no name at all."

"Cause I think she come in lookin for me, John."

"I wouldn't know about that."

"I think she knew I'd be here, come in here lookin for me specific."

John the bartender clucked his tongue in sympathy.

"Found out somehow that I drop in here every now and then, come in here to *get* me, John."

John the bartender clucked his tongue again.

"You didn't happen to see me get in that limo with her, did you?"

"Well, yes, I was watchin thu the winder."

Wiggy opened his eyes wide.

"You didn't happen to see the license plate, did you?"

John the bartender grinned from ear to ear.

In the next three bookshops on the list Ollie had obtained from Wadsworth and Dodds, the two detectives learned a few things about the publishing business in general and his prospective publisher in particular.

"A sales rep'll make fifty to seventy K a year," the first of the booksellers told them. His name was Oscar Haynes. He asked them to call him Oz. Ollie figured him for a fag because he was wearing a purple shirt.

"To cover the U.S., you've got to hire, what, twenty to thirty reps?" Oz said. "That comes to big bucks. Frankly, I don't see how a small firm like W&D can afford that kind of coverage."

"They've only got five reps," Ollie said.

"Even so, that comes to two hundred and fifty K minimum," Oz said. "That's a lot of bread."

In the second bookstore, they learned from a bookseller whose last name was African and unpronounceable—he asked them to call him Ali—that most publishers have a two-season list, and it was therefore not unusual for Jerome Hoskins to make calls here only twice a year. "Unless a house has a big bestseller, where there'll be reorders, a rep has no reason to come by again. W&D has never had a bestseller in its history, take it from me."

"Never?" Ollie said, dismayed.

"Not that I know of. You want my opinion, W&D publishes books nobody wants to read."

In the third and last of the bookshops, they learned that a firm the size of Wadsworth and Dodds usually employs a distribution company to peddle its books. "A distributor will handle sales for a hundred or so small companies," the bookseller told them. His name was David. He was black, too, and he was wearing a pink shirt. Ollie figured him for another fag. Ollie was beginning to think the entire industry was populated with faggot Negro booksellers. "I'm surprised W&D has its own reps, really," David said.

"Did Jerome Hoskins stop by here on the twenty-third?" Carella asked.

"If he did, it had to be after five o'clock. That's when I closed."

"When's the last time you saw him?" Ollie asked.

"September sometime. October. Around then."

"Ever see him with any other W&D reps?"

"Nope."

"Man named Randolph Biggs? Ever meet him? From Texas?"

"Nope."

It was time for lunch and all they'd learned about Hoskins was that he hadn't visited any of his bookshop customers on the twenty-third. Which meant he'd been up here for some other reason. Some other reason that had got him shot in the head and dumped in a garbage can.

"Total fucking loss," Ollie said.

"Not entirely," Carella said. "We now know Wadsworth and Dodds is a two-bit publisher that never had a bestseller in its history."

"Who gives a shit?" Ollie said. Actually, he was heartbroken; he'd been hoping his first novel would sell millions of copies.

"But they hired five sales reps, anyway," Carella said. "At fifty to seventy grand a pop. To peddle a list of books nobody wants to read."

"Let's go eat," Ollie said.

• • •

Since the ability to fix tickets for traffic violations was essential to Wiggy the Lid's business, one of the people on his payroll was a sergeant in the Motor Vehicles Bureau. He called the man—whose name was Evan Grimes—at one o'clock that afternoon, and asked if he could trace a car for him, and then gave him the license plate number John the bartender had seen through the window of the Starlight on Christmas night. Grimes got back to him ten minutes later. He told him that the car was registered to a company called West Side Limousine, and he gave Wiggy an address and a telephone number he could call. He also advised Wiggy not to call him at work again and hung up abruptly, which was tantamount to a gladiator thumbing his nose at the emperor. Wiggy called him back, at work, an instant later.

"Let me splain the rules of the game, shithead," he said.

Grimes listened.

Carefully.

Then he personally called the city's Taxi and Limousine Commission and asked if a trip sheet had been filed by West Side Limo for a pickup at the Starlight Bar on St. Sebastian and Boyle around one A.M. on December twenty-sixth. "License plate would've been WU 3200," Grimes said, "I don't have the car number." The guy at T&L asked him to wait while he checked, and then came back on the line some five minutes later.

"I think I got what you want," he told Grimes.

"But I don't have it as the Starlight Bar. I've got it as 1271 St. Sebastian."

"What time would that have been?"

"Ten past one."

"That'd be it. Who ordered the car?"

"Company named Wadsworth and Dodds. You need an address?"

"Please," Grimes said.

Which is how, within minutes of each other that Thursday afternoon, three people converged on the old landmark building off Headley Square.

One of them was Wiggy Wiggins himself.

The other two were Detectives Steve Carella and Ollie Weeks.

Actually, they rode up in the elevator together.

Wiggy knew these two dudes were cops the minute they stepped into the car. He could smell cops from a hundred miles away. Even if he hadn't seen the butt of a nine-millimeter pistol showing under the fat one's jacket, he'd have spotted him for plainclothes. The other one, tall and slender, had Chinese eyes that didn't hide the look of awareness about him, as if he was expecting a crime to erupt around him any minute and was getting ready for it to happen. The fat one was saying that was the worse pastrami sandwich he'd ever had in his life. Half of it was on his jacket, from the looks of it, mustard stains on one of the lapels, ketchup stains on the other. Wiggy looked up at the ceiling.

The elevator operator was a pimply-faced white kid wearing a brown uniform with gold braid. "Fourth floor," he said, as the elevator ground to a halt. He slid open the door and looked over his shoulder at all three of them. The two cops—Wiggy was sure they were—stepped out into a large waiting room with framed posters of books lining the walls. Wiggy hesitated.

"Sir?" the elevator operator said. "This is the fourth floor."

In the next ten seconds, Wiggy did some quick calculations. Two blondes had forced him to give up the money he'd taken from Frank Holt before shooting him dead and stuffing him in a garbage can. Now two cops were here at the place that had hired the limo for the two blondes. Was it possible the cops were also looking for the blondes? If so, how long would it be before they linked Wiggy himself to the murder of Frank Holt?

"I think I made a mistake here," he said to the elevator operator.

"Hi, Charmaine," the fat cop said to the fat broad behind the reception desk.

"Take me back to the lobby," Wiggy said.

The elevator operator shrugged and started to pull the door shut.

The tall, slender cop turned and took a look at Wiggy just as the closing door blocked him from view.

· · ·

The man who introduced himself as the publisher here at Wadsworth and Dodds was wearing a brown suit, darker brown shoes, a corn-colored shirt, and a green bow tie sprinkled with gold polka dots. He had snow white hair, and he told Carella his name was Richard Halloway. He remembered Ollie as Detective Watts, a misapprehension Ollie quickly corrected.

"It's *Weeks,* sir," he said. "Detective Oliver *Weeks.*"

"Yes, of course, how stupid of me," Halloway said. "Sit down, gentlemen, please. Some coffee?"

"I could use a cup," Ollie said.

"Detective Carella?"

"Yes, please."

Halloway lifted the receiver on his phone, pressed a button on the base, and asked someone to bring in some coffee. He put down the receiver, turned to the detectives, smiled, and said, "So. What brings you back here, Detective Weeks?"

"We're still trying to figure out what Jerry Hoskins was doing up in Diamondback on December twenty-third," Ollie said. "According to his customers, he wasn't there to see any of them."

"It is peculiar, isn't it?" Halloway said.

"A couple of the booksellers seemed surprised you had sales reps at all," Carella said.

"Oh? Did they?"

"Seemed to think a firm this size might do better with a distributor."

"We've considered that, of course. But then we wouldn't get the personal service we now enjoy."

"Five sales reps altogether," Carella said.

"Yes."

"One of them in Texas, is that right?"

Before Halloway could answer, a knock sounded on the door, and the receptionist came in with a tray on which there was a pot of coffee, three cups and saucers, a pitcher of milk, and a bowl containing an assortment of white, pink, and blue packets.

"Ah, thank you, Charmaine," Halloway said.

Charmaine put the tray down on the coffee table in front of the sofa.

"You wouldn't have any cookies or anything, would you, Charmaine?" Ollie asked.

"Well . . . uh . . ."

"See if we have any cookies," Halloway said.

"Yes, sir," she said, and went out.

Ollie was already pouring.

"How do you take this?" he asked.

"Black for me," Halloway said.

"A little milk, one sugar," Carella said.

He was watching Halloway. A good three or four minutes had passed since he'd asked about the sales rep in Texas, more than enough time for Halloway to frame an answer. Halloway seemed to be engrossed in Ollie's short order technique. Ollie was opening a packet of sugar now, pouring it into Carella's cup. He handed it to him, and then carried Halloway's black coffee to the desk. Charmaine came in with a platter of Fig Newtons, just as Ollie sat on the couch beside Carella again.

"Thank you, Charmaine," he said.

Charmaine smiled at him and went out.

"Your rep in Texas," Carella said.

"Yes."

"He lives in Eagle Branch, is that right?"

"Yes, Eagle Branch."

"You listed his name as Randolph Biggs . . ."

"Yes, that's his name."

"Would this be a side job for him?"

"A side job?"

"A second job. He wouldn't have another job, would he?"

"Not that I know of. Another job? No. Why would he have another job? Working for us keeps him busy enough, I'm sure."

"He wouldn't be a Texas Ranger, would he?"

Halloway burst out laughing.

"Forgive me," he said, "a Texas *Ranger?* I hardly think so."

"Have you ever met him?"

"Of course I've met him."

"Did Jerry Hoskins know him?" Ollie asked.

"Yes, I'm sure they knew each other. I'm sure they were at sales conferences together."

"Twice a year, is that right?" Carella asked.

"Yes. In the spring and the fall."

"Would they have seen each other this year?"

"I feel certain."

"This spring? This fall?"

"Yes, I'm sure."

"Where, Mr. Halloway?"

"Why, here. We had both conferences at the Century Hotel."

"You didn't have your conferences in Texas, did you?"

"No."

"Eagle Branch, Texas?"

"No."

"So they couldn't have met down there, could they?"

"Hardly."

"When's the last time you yourself saw Mr. Biggs?"

"When he was up here in September. For our last sales conference."

"Do you talk to him often?"

"Every now and then."

"Will you be talking to him anytime soon?"

"I would imagine."

"Tell him we were asking for him, will you?"

"I'll be sure to."

There seemed nothing further to say.

Carella was wondering if they had enough on Biggs to justify an arrest warrant and extradition from Texas. Ollie was thinking he would like to ask this little white-haired son of a bitch if he knew that Biggs had introduced Cassandra Ridley to his friend Frank Holt, who'd paid her two hundred thousand dollars to fly dope up from Mexico. He wanted to ask him if maybe Biggs had a *third* job besides sales rep and Texas Ranger, and could that third job possibly be smuggling drugs? He wanted to suggest that if one of Halloway's sales reps was fucking with drugs down in Mexico then maybe *another* of his reps was doing the same thing up in Diamondback, which was maybe what had got him killed. Ollie wanted to scare the shit out of Halloway, was what he wanted. Sometimes, if you scared them hard enough, they jumped the wrong way.

The silence lengthened.

"Well," Carella said, "thanks for your time. We appreciate it."

"And the delightful repast," Ollie said, and stuffed some Fig Newtons into his jacket pocket.

They were walking out of the Headley Building, toward the square across the street with its statue of William George Douglas Rae, the gentleman scholar who had captivated the heart of the city with his grace, his charm, and his sparkling wit, when Ollie said, "What do you think? Is the flyboy's word enough for an arrest warrant?"

"What flyboy?"

"Cass Ridley's brother in Germany."

"Depends on what judge we get."

"You think Halloway's in on this?"

"In on what?"

"On whatever the fuck it *is.*"

"If he is, we've got him thinking."

"We shoulda scared him more."

"I think we scared him enough," Carella said.

But Halloway's bad day was just beginning.

The detectives didn't notice Walter Wiggins cross the street and head toward the Headley Building the moment he spotted them coming out onto the sidewalk. Nor did they notice the two Hispanic-looking men who crossed the little park in the square and walked toward the building, reaching it at just about the same time Wiggy did. The two men were Francisco Octavio Ortiz and Cesar Villada, and they had just arrived from Mexico this morning.

They got into the elevator with Wiggy, and all three men told the operator they wanted the fourth floor. The two Mexicans gave Wiggy a glance and then turned away. To Wiggy, they looked like spic hit men. He was beginning to regret having come here altogether. First two bulls in the elevator and now two big hitters. "Fourth floor," the elevator operator said, and yanked open the door. Wiggy was looking out at the same reception room he'd seen half an hour ago, same fat white chick behind the desk. The two Latinos stepped out of the elevator ahead of him, no fuckin manners. They walked to the desk, Wiggy right behind them.

"We're looking for a man who works here named Jerome Hoskins," one of them said.

It came out, "We lookin for a man worrs here name Jerr-o Hosk."

"Frank Holt," the other one said.

The last name came out "Hote."

Which was clear enough to Wiggy, who all at once began to think these two Spanish-American gentlemen were not two hitters but were instead two detectives from the Eight-Eight, investigating the murder of Frank Holt. He almost bolted for the elevator.

"I can't understand what you're saying," the receptionist said, squinting.

"What's *your* name?" the first man asked.

He made it sound like a threat, even though it came out with a Spanish accent as thick as guacamole.

"Charmaine," she said.

"You know a man name Randoff Beegs?" he said. "In Texas?"

"Eagle Branch," the other one said.

Wiggy was trying to remember if Frank Holt had told him he'd come up from Eagle Branch, Texas. All he could recall was him saying the hundred keys of cocaine had come up from Guenerando, Mexico. He wondered now if Guenerando was anywhere near Eagle Branch. He tried to appear as if he was not listening to the conversation between these two possible dicks and the fat chick behind the desk, but he was standing only three feet behind them, and it was impossible to appear small and insignificant when he weighed two hundred and ten pounds and stood an even six feet tall. He wondered if he should go sit on the bench against the wall, but then he'd miss this fascinating conversation about the man he'd shot in the head. So he stood where he was and pretended not to be eavesdropping. He would have whistled to show how nonchalant he was, but he thought that might only attract attention to him.

"What was that name again?" Charmaine asked. "In Texas?"

"Randolph Biggs," the first man said.

It still came out "Randoff Beegs."

"Oh. Yes," she said, decoding the accent at last. "Let me see if our sales manager is free." She lifted the receiver on her phone, pressed a button in its base, asked, "Whom shall I say is here?" and raised her eyes expectantly.

"Francisco Ortiz," one of the men said.

"Cesar Villada," the other one said.

Wiggy noticed that they did not flash gold badges or identify themselves as detectives. Maybe they were associated with Mr. Holt in some other way. Maybe they were from Eagle Branch, Texas. Maybe they were good old buddies of Frank Holt's, here to inquire how come he was now dead. In which case, Wiggy *still* felt he ought to get out of here fast.

"Miss Andersen," Charmaine said, "there are two gentlemen here inquiring about Mr. Biggs." She listened, nodded, looked up at the two men again. "May I say what firm you're with?" she asked.

"Villada and Ortiz," Ortiz said.

"Villada and Ortiz," Charmaine said. She listened again. "Is that a bookstore?" she asked.

"Yes, it's a bookstore," Villada said.

"In Eagle Branch," Ortiz said. "Texas," he said. "Villada and Ortiz, Booksellers."

Charmaine relayed the information, listened again, put the phone receiver back on its cradle, rose, and said, "I'll show you in." She turned to Wiggy as she came around the desk, said, "I'll be with you in a moment, sir, won't you have a seat?" and walked off with the two men Wiggy now knew owned a bookstore in Eagle Branch, Texas, which sounded like total bullshit to him.

He went over to the wall on the left of the elevator doors, and sat on the bench there. He looked around the room at the posters hanging on the walls. He'd never heard of any of the books. In a minute or so, Charmaine came back. Instead of going to her desk, though, she walked over to where he was waiting, and sat beside him on the bench.

"So," she said, and smiled. "How can I help you, sir?"

"On Christmas night," Wiggy said, "somebody up here phoned for a limo. I want to talk to whoever that might've been."

"That's very fanciful," Charmaine said, and smiled coquettishly. "Are you a writer?"

"No, I'm a drug dealer," Wiggy said, and grinned like a shark.

"I'll bet," Charmaine said.

"I run a posse up in Diamondback," he said.

"Oh, sure," she said.

"Who do I talk to about this limo was called for?"

"If *anyone* called for a limo, it would've been Douglas Good, our publicity director. But no one was here on Christmas night. We closed on Christmas Eve at three in the afternoon, and didn't open again till the following Tuesday. But I'll see if Mr. Good will talk to you."

"Just tell him Mr. *Bad* is here," Wiggy said, and grinned again.

Karen Andersen was telling the two Mexicans that Randolph Biggs did indeed work for them, and so had Jerry Hoskins. But she hadn't seen Randy since their sales conference in September, and Jerry had been the victim of a fatal shooting on Christmas Eve. Was there anything she could do for the gentlemen?

The gentlemen explained to her—in halting English which she nonetheless understood—that Jerry Hoskins, who until recently they had known only as Frank Holt, had purchased from them a hundred keys of excellent cocaine . . .

"I beg your pardon," Karen said, looking astonished.

. . . for which they had been paid in hundred-dollar bills . . .

"Gentlemen, I'm sorry," she said, "but . . ."

"Yes, we're sorry, too," Villada said.

"Because the money was bad," Ortiz said.

• • •

Douglas Good was a black man who did not appreciate brothers who looked or sounded like Walter Wiggins.

"Two girls named Sheryl and Toni," Wiggins was telling him.

"Yes?" Douglas said.

"West Side Limo," Wiggins said. "The Starlight Bar."

"Mr. Wiggins . . ."

"Somebody here called a limo from West Side to take two girls named Sheryl and Toni uptown to a bar named the Starlight on St. Sab's and Boyle on Christmas night," Wiggins said. "St. Sebastian's," he explained.

"Somebody from Wadsworth and *Dodds* called a limo . . ."

"Is the information I have."

". . . for two girls named Sheryl and Toni?"

"That's they names. The ladies owe me some money, bro."

Douglas didn't like black men who looked or sounded like Walter Wiggins to call him "bro."

"Mr. Wiggins," he said, "we don't have any women named Sheryl and Toni working for us."

"Two very tall blond ladies," Wiggins said.

"I'm sorry."

"This was a limo from West Side," Wiggins explained again, patiently. "Black Lincoln Town Car with a chauffeur same color as the car. The blonde named Toni was sittin in it, and she picked up me and the blonde named Sheryl outside the Starlight and drove me to my office on Decatur Av, where they relieved me of a certain amount of money, at gun point, on Christmas night."

"No one was here on Christmas night," Douglas said.

"The Taxi and Limousine Commission seems to believe otherwise, bro."

"The Taxi and Limousine Commission made a mistake," Douglas said.

"I don't think so," Wiggins said.

"Let me ask Mr. Halloway to come in," Douglas said.

"Who's Mr. Halloway?"

"Our publisher."

He went to the desk phone, picked up the receiver, and hit Halloway's extension button.

"Halloway."

"Richard, it's Douglas."

"Yes, Douglas."

"I have a man with me who thinks we sent a limo up to Diamondback on Christmas night. His name is Walter Wiggins."

"He should've left well enough alone," Halloway said.

"I thought you might like to meet him."

"I'll be right in," Halloway said.

Douglas put the receiver back on the cradle, smiled at Wiggins, and said, "He's on his way."

• • •

Karen Andersen was still trying to bluff her way out of this.

"Bad money?" she said.

"Counterfeit," Ortiz said. "We wass paid with queer money."

"One million seven hun'red t'ousan dollars of it," Villada said.

Karen smiled.

"We don't think it's so funny, Miss," Ortiz said.

"In any case," Karen said, "Jerry Hoskins is dead."

"In any case," Ortiz said, "so is Randolph Biggs."

Karen looked at them.

"He met with an electrical accident in Piedras Rosas, Mexico," Villada said, and nodded.

"We want our money," Ortiz said.

"Gentlemen, I have absolutely *no* idea what you're talking about," Karen said.

"We are talking about one million seven hun'red t'ousan dollars two people who worr for you company focked us out of in Mehico," Villada said.

Or something like that.

Which Karen Andersen all at once understood clearly because Ortiz suddenly seemed to be holding a gun in his hand.

Douglas Good didn't want to say anything further to Mr. Wiggins here until Halloway joined them.

Wiggins had obviously done a little research, first locating West Side's name and next tracing them back to the offices here. Douglas figured the man was here to get his money back, which wasn't his money at all since he should have paid it to Jerry Hoskins after the cocaine had been turned over. Wiggins's oversight had resulted in a visit from "The Weird Sisters," as Sheryl and Toni were affectionately called even though they were not related. W&D's oversight—or rather Halloway's—had been in not dispatching the man the moment the money was in their hands. Halloway had ruled out such an action, partially because he had no real evidence that Wiggins had been responsible for the murder of one of their best people, secondly because black-white relationships were touchy enough in Diamondback without giving the drug people up there a reason to distrust future commerce with Whitey. In any case, Wiggins should have left well enough alone. Instead, here he was, the fool.

"You know why I'm here, don't you?" Wiggins asked, and smiled wisely.

"I have no idea," Douglas said.

"No, huh? Then why'd you ax your boss to come in?"

Douglas had called Halloway because he was the only person sanctioned to order Wiggins's death—as he should have done on Christmas night. If Wiggins had anything incriminating to say, he wanted Halloway to hear it first hand. So that maybe he'd give the goddamn correct orders this time around.

"I'm here for my money," Wiggins said.

Big surprise, Douglas thought, and Halloway walked in without knocking. "Hello, Mr. Wiggins," he said, extending his hand. "Nice to meet you." The men shook hands. Their eyes met. Douglas figured Wiggins should have known in that single meeting of eyes that he was a dead man. But maybe he was stupid.

"Are you authorized to make a payout?" he asked Halloway. "Cause what I need fum you is one million nine hundred thousand dollars in cash."

In all her years with W&D, Karen Andersen had never before looked down the barrel of a gun or into the eyes of a person who would have no qualms about pulling the trigger of that gun. She wondered briefly what Halloway would do in similar circumstances. She had seen him perform admirably in comparably challenging situations, but those had been when they were in bed together, and always during the window of opportunity Viagra presented. She was surprised now to discover that she was not at all frightened. Calmly, coolly, she said, "Please don't force me to call the police."

Villada laughed.

Karen reached for the phone on her desk, intending not to call the police but to summon Halloway for help. Ortiz slammed the butt of his revolver down on her hand. She pulled it back, winced, held the throbbing fingers to her breasts. Her lip was quivering, but she did not scream.

"We'll be back," Ortiz said. There was blood on the butt of the pistol. He yanked a tissue from the box on Karen's desk, wiped the butt clean, and tossed the stained tissue into an ashtray. "Get the fockin money," he said. *"Real* money this time, *comprende?"*

"Or we'll kill every fockin one of you who works here," Villada said.

Not if we kill you first, Karen thought.

"I have no idea what money you mean," Halloway said.

"The money your two blond ladies took from me," Wiggins said.

"I don't know which ladies you mean."

"Sheryl and Toni. With the long legs and the AK-47."

"We have no such employees. Mr. Wiggins," Halloway said, slowly and distinctly, "you are making a terrible mistake here."

Their eyes met again.

This time Wiggins read the meaning in them.

Which was perhaps why he drew a pistol from a holster under his jacket. He pointed the gun first at Halloway, and then swung it around toward Douglas, as if to emphasize that his enmity was large enough to include both of them. The gun looked like a snub-nosed .38. Douglas didn't think the man was foolish enough to kill them here in their own offices, especially since he was here to negotiate the return of money he felt was his. But who knew with these street thugs?

Halloway had been in hairier situations than this one. Not for nothing was he in charge here. He looked at the gun in Wiggins's hand, and then raised his eyes to meet Wiggins's again. His eyes seemed to say *This is only about money, friend. Do you really want to die for it?* But would Wiggins have pulled a gun on them if he didn't realize he was already a dead man?

"You don't want to do this," Halloway said.

"I've done it before," Wiggins said.

"Not with the consequences this would bring."

Douglas knew this was bullshit. If Wiggins had in fact killed Jerry Hoskins, there had been no consequences at all. Wiggins must have realized this, too. He had blown one of them away, and the only thing that had happened was The Wierd Sisters coming to call. Douglas wondered if, in retrospect, Halloway was thinking he should have given the termination order back then on Christmas night. A bit late now, though.

"Tell you what," Wiggins said. "I realize you don't have that kind of money juss layin aroun in cash. But go get it, okay? I'll come see you sometime soon," he said, and backed away toward the door.

Sometime soon, you'll be dead, Douglas thought.
Bro.

Wiggins stepped out into the hallway.

The three men reached the elevator at about the
same time. One of the two Mexicans pressed the
bell button set in the wall.

"How'd it go?" Wiggy asked them.

"Fockin people still owe us money," Ortiz said.

Which was how a rather strange triumvirate was
founded.

It was still Thursday on what was shaping up to be
the longest day of the year, never mind what the al-
manac said. Sitting at his desk at a quarter to five
that evening, the squadroom almost deserted,
Carella tried to make some sense of this bewilder-
ing case that seemed to focus entirely on money,
real or largely imagined. The imagined cash appeared to originate in Iran, where billions of dollars
in so-called super-bills were being printed on intaglio presses with plates provided by the good old
U.S. of A., talk about payback time.

Carella knew some things for certain. The rest he
could only guess at. He knew that Cass Ridley had
made four trips to Mexico with a certain amount of
money she'd exchanged for some kind of controlled
substance, and had been paid $200,000 in cash for
her efforts. This money was real, if the lady at First

Federal could be trusted, whatever her name was. But Cass Ridley had also been given a ten-grand tip by the pair of Mexicans involved in the transaction, whoever *they* were, and *that* money was fake. Poor Will Struthers, trying to spend the cash he'd pilfered, had twice been nailed passing phony hundreds. According to the lady at First Federal, Antonia Lugosi or something, twenty billion dollars in counterfeit hundreds were floating around out there, enough bogus bills to concern the Treasury Department, who had relieved Struthers of the phonies he'd stolen and given him real cash in exchange—but that was only a guess. Belandres! Antonia *Belandres!* Hence the Lugosi association, for *Bela* Lugosi, the best Dracula there ever was, the mind worked in curious ways its wonders to reveal.

Carella wished with all his heart that this case would reveal itself as clearly to him as Lucy's throat had been revealed to the count all those years back when Carella first saw the black-and-white film on television, the count's head descending, his lips drawing back, the fangs bared, Carella had almost wet his pants.

The money in Jerry Hoskins' wallet was real, too. No question about that, the Federal Reserve had run it through their machines, the hundred-dollar bills were genuine. But Jerry Hoskins had worked for Wadsworth and Dodds, and the man who'd set up the flying arrangement with Cass Ridley also worked for W&D, though there seemed to be some confusion about whether or not Randolph Biggs was *also* a Texas Ranger, which Carella sincerely doubted—but that, too, was a guess.

Lots of guesswork here, no hard facts.

He wondered what time it was in Texas.

He looked up at the wall clock, opened the bottom drawer of his desk, took out his massive directory of law enforcement agencies, found a listing for the Texas Department of Public Safety headquarters in Austin, figured somebody would be there no matter *what* time it was, and dialed the number. He told the woman who answered the phone what he was looking for, was connected to a sergeant named Dewayne Ralston, repeated everything again, and was asked to "Hang on, Detective." He hung on. Some five minutes later, Ralston came back onto the line.

"Nobody in the Ranger Division named Randolph Biggs," he said. "You landed yourself an imposter, Detective."

"While I've got you on the line," Carella said, "could you check for a criminal record?"

"Don't go away," Ralston said.

Carella didn't go away. Across the room, he could see Kling at his desk, hunched over a computer. Cotton Hawes was just coming through the railing that divided the squadroom from the corridor outside. Telephones were ringing. In one corner of the room, the squad's meager Christmas tree blinked holiday cheer to the street outside. From the Clerical Office down the hall, he could smell the aroma of coffee brewing. This was a very familiar place to him. He felt suddenly sad and could not have explained why.

"You still there?" Ralston asked.

"Still here."

"No record on a Randolph Biggs, B-I-G-G-S. But if this is the same dude, he turned up dead in Piedras Rosas two days ago. Found him floating in a tub of water with a plugged-in cattle prod. Death by electrocution. Apparent suicide."

"That makes two," Carella said.

"Pardon?"

"One of his colleagues was murdered up here on Christmas Eve."

"Looks like you got your hands full," Ralston said.

"Looks that way," Carella said.

The phone on Ollie Weeks's desk rang some five minutes later.

"Weeks," he said.

"You handlin that murder happened last week?" a man's voice asked.

"Which murder would that be?" Ollie asked.

Up here in the Eight-Eight, there were 10,247 murders every day of the year.

"The newspaper said he was Jerry Hoskins," the man said. "To me, he was Frank Holt."

"Who's this?" Ollie asked at once.

"Nev' mine who's this," the man said. "I know who killed him."

Ollie pulled a pad into place.

"Tell me your name," he said.

"Is they a reward?"

"Maybe. I can't deal with you unless you tell me your name."

"Tito Gomez," the man said.

"Can you come up here in half an hour?"

"I rather meet you someplace else."

"Sure. Where?"

"The Eight' Street footpath into Grover. Fourth bench in."

Ollie looked up at the wall clock.

"Make it a quarter to six," he said.

"See you," Tito said, and hung up.

Ollie hit the files.

It did not take Wiggy and the two Mexicans long to discover that what they had in common was a hundred keys of cocaine. It also appeared they had each been stiffed by a company that purported to publish books, but which instead seemed to be involved in the transport and sale of controlled substances. They did not yet know they were fucking with something much bigger here. For the time being their shared grievances were enough to provide motivation for what they planned to do sometime tomorrow.

They were discussing all this over beers in a bar on Grover Avenue, not too distant from Grover Park, where Ollie and Gomez would be meeting twenty minutes from now. In many ways, the big bad city was just a small town.

"I can't get over these people payin you queer

money for your goods," Wiggy was saying. "Which by the way was very high quality shit, I have to tell you."

"Gracias, señor," Ortiz said, pride of product glowing in his eyes.

"Which is a shame," Wiggy said, "them stiffing you that way. But I have to tell you the money *I* paid *them* was hundred-percent genuine American currency, and I want it back cause they sent two blondes to take it away from me."

This was not entirely true. Wiggy had never paid a single penny to Hoskins or Holt or whoever he was. He had shot him in the head instead.

"They stole *your* money, too?" Ortiz asked incredulously.

"For damn sure."

Neither was this entirely true. They had, in fact, taken the money from his safe, but this was not stealing from him. This was collecting money rightfully owed them for the hundred keys of cocaine they'd delivered as promised.

"So they are stealing from *all* of us," Villada said.

"Basic thieves is what they are," Wiggy said.

"Like us," Ortiz said, and all three men burst out laughing.

"So what we're gonna do tomorrow . . ." Wiggy said.

At first, it looked as if there was nothing on him but a marijuana violation two years ago. But at the time

of the bust, Tito Gomez—whose street name was
Tigo—had worked for a place named King Auto
Body, and this rang a bell with Ollie. So he cross-
checked the files and lo and behold, there it was. A
massive conspiracy arrest some six months back.
Ollie went to his desk and phoned Carella.

"Steve," he said, "I got a call from somebody
says he knows who killed Hoskins. I'm meeting
him in Grover Park ten minutes from now. You want
to join us?"

"Where in Grover?" Carella asked.

"We go up there together," Wiggy said. "We tell
them give us the fuckin money you owe us or you
all dead men. Your million-seven. My million-
nine."

Nobody owed Wiggy anything. But he already
believed himself the true owner of the million-nine
the blondes had taken in rightful payment for the
drugs he'd purchased.

"Fockin crooks," Villada said, shaking his head.

Ortiz was shaking his head, too. But only because
he didn't like the plan. His reasoning was simple.
Threats and warnings were one thing. Reality was
another. In his broken English, he explained that
between yesterday and today, nobody up at
Wadsworth and Dodds could have gathered together the million-seven his partner had demanded,
much less the million-nine their new associate was

seeking. That came to a total of three-million-six . . .

"Which ees a ho lot of money," Ortiz explained.

Wiggy was thinking there was once a time in his life when two dollars for a water pistol seemed like a whole lot of money.

Tito Gomez was sitting on the fourth bench into the park when Carella got there at ten minutes to six that Thursday night. The two seemed to be hitting it off extremely well. Gomez was smoking a cigarette and listening to Ollie intently as he concluded what was apparently a joke because Gomez burst out laughing just as Carella approached.

"Hey, Steve!" Ollie called. "You know the one about the guy who puts a condom on his piano?"

"Yes," Carella said.

He sat on the bench beside Gomez, the two detectives flanking him like mismatched bookends. "This the man you were telling me about?" he asked Ollie.

"This is him," Ollie said. "Tito Gomez. Otherwise known as Tigo. Meet Detective Carella, Tigo."

Tigo nodded.

"So I understand you want to talk to us about something," Carella said.

"Yeah, but I ain't got all day here. You got any more detectives you need to call?" he asked Ollie.

"No, this is all of us," Ollie said affably. "He says

he knows who killed Jerry Hoskins, ain't that interesting? He wants to know if there's a reward."

"We can maybe come up with a little something,"
Carella said.

"What do you mean *maybe?*"

"We can talk to the commissioner, see what this
case means to him."

He was thinking with counterfeit super-bills
somehow involved, the commissioner might be able
to come up with a little something.

"What I have in mind is fifty thousand dollars,"
Tigo said.

"That's a lot of money, Tigo."

"But that's what makes the world go round, no?"
Tigo said, and grinned. "Money, money, money."

"Well, that all depends on the value of the information you have for us, eh, *amigo?*" Ollie said, still
affably.

Tigo didn't like to be called *"amigo."* His father
was from Puerto Rico, true enough, but his mother
was black, and he was proud of his heritage on her
side of the family. As pleasantly as he could—these
were, after all, cops he was dealing with—he said,
"I don't speak Spanish, *amigo,"* which was a lie, but
which seemed to make his point.

"Oh, sorry," Ollie said, "I didn't realize. So tell us
why you wanted to see us."

"There was this buy on Decatur Av?" Tigo said,
making it sound like a question. "Guy runs a posse
from a crib on the whole second floor there,
knocked out the walls of three apartments? He

brings up dope from Mexico, Colombia, Peru, sells it in ten-kilo lots for forty, fifty a pop, whatever the traffic will bear. I've been workin for him almost two years now, you'd think he'd start talkin bout makin me a partner, but no. He's still got me on salary . . ."

So that's why he's ratting him out, Carella thought.

". . . treats me like a fuckin courier, don't get me started. I used to make more money driving the truck. I used to drive a tow truck for this auto body shop on Mason."

"What's this guy's name?" Carella said.

"First tell me how much the commissioner's gonna okay on this," Tigo said.

"Well, we haven't talked to him yet," Ollie said affably. "We have to *go* to him with something, you see. We tell him there's this guy *maybe* has information, he'll say go take a walk, fellas."

"Can you at least tell us when this buy went down?" Carella asked.

"Sure," Tigo said. "Four, five days ago."

"When exactly?"

"What's today?"

"The twenty-eighth."

"So it must've been . . . let me see." He began counting back on his fingers. "Last Saturday night? When was that? Christmas Eve?"

"No, the twenty-third," Ollie said.

"So that's when it was. Like I said. Four, five days ago."

"Where?" Carella asked.

"I told you, this crib on Decatur. It's these three apartments, this person we're talking about knocked out the . . ."

"What's the address?"

"1280 Decatur."

"Were you there when the buy went down?"

"Yeah. This dude was waitin in the front room while we tested the shit. He was supposed to get a mill-nine for the hundred keys."

"What was his name?"

"Frank Holt. But his picture in the paper said he was Jerry Hoskins. The same guy, right?"

"The same guy," Carella said. "Tell us what happened."

"This is where the bus stops," Tigo said. "Go talk to the commissioner."

"Suppose we go to 1280 Decatur instead, talk to whoever's got the second floor there, tell him his trusted employee just ratted him out?" Carella said.

"Now, now, Steve," Ollie said affably. "The man hasn't ratted out anyone yet, have you, Tigo?"

"Not till I see the green."

"You just told us you participated in a drug deal, do you realize that?" Carella said. He was thinking this was an odd reversal of roles, him playing Bad Cop to Ollie's Good.

"Gee, did I?" Tigo said. "Are you wired, Detective? If not, who's your witness? Another cop? A bullshit bust, and you know it."

"I can tell you right now, nobody's giving you

fifty thousand dollars so we can nail a two-bit drug dealer in Diamondback."

"Even if it's murder?"

"Even if he raped the Mayor's mother."

"How much *are* you prepared to give me?"

Sounding like a fucking lawyer all at once.

"You tell us you witnessed a murder, you give us all the details, you agree to testify at trial, we can maybe scrape up two or three . . ."

"Goodbye, gentlemen," Tigo said, and got off the bench.

"Sit down, punk," Ollie said.

Tigo looked surprised.

"I *said* sit the fuck *down.*"

Tigo sat.

"Let me tell you what you're gonna do for us," Ollie said.

"Okay, I got a better idea," Wiggy was telling the two Mexicans. "We go in heavy, all three of us. Semi-automatics under our overcoats. We hold the mother-fuckers hostage."

Villada looked at Ortiz.

"We go in early tomorrow morning. They got the whole fourth floor, ain't nobody but us gonna know we're in there holdin guns on them. We stay there till they come up with the cash."

"The banks will be closed till Tuesday," Ortiz said.

"It's the long weekend," Villada said, nodding agreement.

"Man, they stole a mill-nine from me, you think they put that in a *bank?* These people are thieves, man. They got that money *stashed* someplace, is what. All we got to do is ask that white-haired fuck to take us to wherever it is."

"What about *our* money?" Ortiz asked.

"We'll get that, too, don't worry," Wiggy said. "One thing I know for sure, you stick a piece in some dude's face, he's gonna give you every fuckin nickel he has."

Actually, Wiggy didn't give a rat's ass about their money. Far as he was concerned, they could eat tacos and beans the rest of they fuckin lives. All he needed them for was the extra muscle they brought to the gig. He was already figuring they would be the ones who stayed behind to watch the others while him and Halloway went to retrieve the money that was rightfully his.

Ortiz was ahead of him.

"Who goes for the money?" he asked.

"Halloway. Their boss."

"Who goes *with* him?"

"Any one of us," Wiggy said.

"I think it should be either me or Cesar," Ortiz said.

"Sure, whoever," Wiggy said, and grinned.

• • •

Tigo said No, he would not go in with no wire on him.

Ollie said either he wore the wire or they would bust his ass for the Fire Lane Scam.

"What the fuck is the Fire Lane Scam?" Tigo asked.

"You drove the tow truck, remember?" Ollie said affably. In fact, he was actually smiling.

"What's the Fire Lane Scam?" Carella asked.

"What I done when Tigo called me," Ollie said, "was see what we had on him in the files. Aside from a bullshit marijuana violation two years ago . . ."

"I was acquitted."

"I told you. Bullshit. In fact, I was just about to tell Detective Carella here that there didn't seem to be anything else on you. So I figured you were clean."

"I am."

"Except for participating in a drug deal last Saturday night," Carella said.

"You got only my word for that," Tigo said, making a joke. In fact, he grinned at them as if expecting them to laugh.

Ollie didn't laugh, but he grinned back.

"Your record said you were employed by King Auto Body when you were busted for the weed," Ollie said. "So I cross-checked and found out why that name sounded familiar. I found a big, big arrest six months ago, Tigo. The Fire Lane Scam. For which Joey King—no relation to Larry—is doing a five-and-dime at Castleview. You know what I'm talking about now, Tigo?"

"No, I don't."

"You were driving a tow truck for him, right?"

"That's right. I went out on calls for dead batteries, flat tires, lockouts, like that."

"You also went out on calls for Berry Appliances, who were in on the scam with Joey."

"I never heard of anything called Berry Appliances."

"George and Michael Berry," Ollie said. "They used to sell washing machines, refrigerators, stoves, all that shit. A shop on Twelfth and Moore, you remember it?"

"No."

"Had a little alley running alongside the shop, remember the alley?"

"No."

"What it was," Ollie explained to Carella, "George Berry went to the Fire Department and greased a few palms—they all went down together, by the way. Joey King, George and his brother, and the two Fire Department assholes who signed papers declaring the alley a so-called fire lane. They're all exercising in the yard upstate."

"Ho-hum," Tigo said.

"Yeah, ho-hum," Ollie said, and turned back to Carella again. "What it was, George and his brother posted these signs on the walls of the alley saying it was a fire lane, and you couldn't park there, or your car would be towed if you did. Guy comes back, finds his car towed, he reads the small print on the bottom of the sign, it tells him he can recover the car at King's Auto Body Shop on Mason Avenue. What Tigo here did was make a sweep of the alley every few hours, tow any car parked there. There were always five, six cars in the alley, nobody paid any attention to the signs. Tigo picked up the cars, towed them over to King's. When the owner came to collect his car, Joey told him it would cost a hundred bucks to release it. You towed maybe twenty cars a night, didn't you, Tigo? People in this city have no fuckin respect for the law. 'No Parking' signs all over the alley, 'Fire Lane,' they just ignored them. A hundred bucks a car, that's two thousand bucks these guys were splitting every night of the week. That's like fourteen grand a week, how much do we make, Steve?"

"Not that much," Carella said.

"Not even in a good week," Ollie said. "I keep tellin you, we're in the wrong business."

"Where'd you get all this shit?" Tigo said, shaking his head as if in disbelief.

"It's all in the record. You were driving the tow truck. But you told the D.A. you were just a salaried employee who didn't know anything wrong was going on, and they believed you. You were just a kid, they had bigger fish to fry. But guess what Joey King told me?"

"You talked to *Joey?*"

"Yeah, gee, I did. I figured I might need insurance if you got all pissy on me. So I called Castle-view just before I left the squadroom, had a nice lit-tle chat with him. He told me they were paying you twenty bucks for every car you brought in. Three, four hundred bucks a night. Something like two grand a week. You were in on the deal, Tigo."

"I was a salaried employee. Go look at my social security records."

"Salary *plus,* Tigo. You were part of a conspiracy. You should be up there at Castleview with them."

"But I ain't," Tigo said.

"Ah, but you could be. Joey seems to think early parole sounds very nice indeed."

Tigo looked at him.

"He's ready to rat you out, friend, ah yes."

"You're full of shit," Tigo said.

"Well, maybe so," Ollie said affably.

"Tigo," Carella said, "I think he's got us."

10.

Charmaine looked up when the three of them came out of the elevator. The moment the doors closed behind them, guns came out from under their coats. She was reaching for a button on her desk when Wiggy said, "Don't, Fatso." This hurt. A moment later he slapped her across the face to let her know he was serious. This hurt even more. One of the Mexicans was already rushing down the long corridor flanked with posters of books nobody ever heard of. Wiggy went directly into Halloway's office.

He was hunched over his computer keyboard, his jacket draped over the back of his chair, his bow tie hanging unknotted and loose around his neck, the top button of his shirt unbuttoned, his sleeves rolled up. He jerked his head around the moment Wiggy burst into the room, and then immediately stabbed at one of the keys on the computer. Four key strokes would have allowed him to escape the program and the machine: the Windows key to the right of the space bar, the Up arrow, the Enter key, and the Enter key again. Once the computer was shut down, no one would be able to boot it again without the proper password. Halloway managed to hit the Windows key, and was about to tap the Up arrow when Wiggy said, "Don't, Whitey." Halloway hesitated. For a moment, it seemed he might complete the action, anyway. Just tap the remaining three keys, and shut down the computer, effectively locking it.

But the gun in Wiggy's hand was very big and rather ugly.

There were eight employees altogether, all of them seated around the long conference table now. Richard Halloway sat at the head of the table, as befitted his status as publisher. David Good from Publicity sat on his left, Karen Andersen from Sales on his right. There was an editor named Michael Garrity, and another editor named Henry Daggert. There was Charmaine, the fat receptionist, and someone named George Young from the stock room, and someone else named Betty Alweiss from the Art Department. Eight of them in all. They all looked frightened.

Wiggy and the two Mexicans leaned against three of the walls, weapons in their hands. Wiggy was holding a Cobray M11-9 he had purchased last night for five hundred dollars from a man named Little Nicholas in Diamondback. Villada and Ortiz were each carrying Mark XIX Desert Eagle pistols. The clock on the conference room wall read twenty minutes to ten. They had caught everyone by surprise, and now they were about to lay their demands on the table.

The Mexicans had decided to let Wiggy do all the talking. Ortiz had objected to this at first, on the grounds that his English was impeccable. Villada had convinced him at last. The men leaned against the walls nonchalantly. Their weapons—dangling casually in their hands—looked almost non-threatening. The three of them figured they had nothing to worry about here with these bookish types. Little did they know.

"Now, this here's the story," Wiggy said. "Our grievance is a mill-seven for my frens here, and a mill-nine for me. We don't know where you keep your stash, but one of you's gonna go with one of us to get the cash an' bring it back here. Then we'll all be on our way, and you alls can go home to enjoy the ress of the holiday. Do I make myself clear?"

"We don't have that kind of money," Halloway said.

"We're bettin you do," Wiggy said. "We're bettin you'll go get it before . . ."

He looked up at the clock.

"Before six o'clock tonight. That's eight hours from now, more or less. Cause for every hour we sit here without goin for the money, we're gonna hafta shoot one of you. Eight hours, eight people. By six

o'clock, you all be dead less'n we has our money.
Do I make myself clear now?"

The room was silent.

"I'll have to make some calls," Halloway said.

"We'll be listening," Wiggy said.

The Mexicans were smiling.

Wiggy figured he had made himself clear.

The men of the 87th Detective Squad couldn't seem
to keep their minds on business at their weekly
Friday-morning, think-tank meeting. Carella was
trying to tell them what he and Ollie had learned
from Tito "Tigo" Gomez. He was trying to tell them
that if Tigo could be trusted, a dope dealer named
Walter "Wiggy" Wiggins was responsible for the
murder of Jerome "Jerry" Hoskins, alias Frank
Holt . . .

"Was that in this precinct?" Lieutenant Byrnes
asked.

"No, but the murdered woman was."

"What murdered woman?" Andy Parker asked.

He was dressed for undercover work today,
which meant he hadn't shaved, and he was wearing
jeans and a black turtleneck sweater and a brown
leather jacket and motorcycle boots. He thought he
looked like an upscale drug dealer. Actually, he
looked like a slob.

"The woman who got eaten by lions," Meyer
said.

"Ha-ha, very funny," Parker said.

"This happened a week ago, where have you been?" Brown said.

"She got stabbed with an ice pick first," Carella explained.

"What's Hoskins got to do with her?" Byrnes asked impatiently. He was thinking if any of this had happened in some other precinct, he'd be glad to get it off his plate.

"He paid her to pick up some dope in Mexico," Meyer said.

"Which he later sold to this Wiggy character," Carella said.

"Who paid *him* with a bullet in the head."

"Here in the Eight-Seven?"

"No, the Eight-Eight. Fat Ollie caught it."

"So let him keep it."

"He also caught one-fifth of the Ridley case."

"Who's Ridley?" Parker asked.

"The lady who got eaten by lions," Kling said.

"Ha-ha, very funny," Parker said.

"How can you catch one-fifth of a case?" Willis asked.

"Her leg," Meyer said.

"Am I supposed to be following this?" Parker asked.

"Nobody else is," Byrnes said. "Why should you be an exception?"

"The point is," Carella said, somewhat edgily, "we're sending Gomez in with a wire."

"Why?" Brown asked.

"Cause we've maybe got a line on the perp in a homicide."

"This Wiggy character?"

"Right. Who maybe killed Jerry Hoskins, who for sure hired Cass Ridley to go to Mexico for him."

"And *we* caught the Ridley case, is what you're saying."

"Four-fifths of her."

"Why's this so important, anyway?" Parker asked, and looked around the room, and shrugged, and said, "Don't anybody want a bagel?" and went to help himself from the tray on Byrnes's desk.

"There's funny money involved," Carella said.

"So let the Secret Service worry," Byrnes said.

"They *are* worrying," Carella said. "They grabbed eight grand in queer bills from a two-bit burglar and gave him real currency in return."

"The lunatics have taken over the asylum," Hawes said.

"I don't like complicated cases," Parker said.

"Neither do I," Byrnes said.

"Well, that's truly unfortunate," Carella said, "but I didn't ask to *catch* this one, either."

"What the hell's wrong with *you* this morning?" Parker asked.

"I'm trying to make some sense of this goddamn case, that's all, and you guys are . . ."

"Relax, okay? Have a bagel."

"There's dope involved here," Carella said, gathering steam, "and counterfeit money, and the Secret Service, and Christ knows what . . ."

"So let our new President handle it," Parker said.

"Sure."

"Our beloved flounder," Willis said.

"Let *him* ask the Secret Service what's going on here," Brown said.

"Sure."

"Next motorcade he's in," Hawes said, "he can wave out of his limo and ask them what they know about a lady got eaten by lions."

"Go on, Steve, have a bagel," Parker said.

"I don't want a bagel," Carella said.

"You know who woulda made a better President than the one we got now?" Hawes said.

"Who?" Kling asked.

"Martin Sheen."

"The guy on *The West Wing,* you're right!"

"He'd call the Secret Service on the carpet, tell them to quit handing out good money for bad."

"No, you know who'd do that? If he was President?" Willis said.

"Who?" Kling asked.

"Harrison Ford."

"Air Force One!"

"President James Marshall!"

"Oh, yeah!" Brown said. "He was maybe the *best* President we ever had. Remember what he said? 'Peace ain't merely the absence of conflict, but the presence of justice.' Man, that's fancy talking."

"Remember what the *bad* guy said?" Willis asked.

"Who cares what bad guys say?" Parker said, and took another bagel from the tray.

"He said, 'You murdered a hundred thousand Iraqis to save a nickel a gallon on gas. Don't lecture me on the rules of war.' *That's* fancy talking, man."

"That was Bush he was talking about," Kling said.

"No, that was President James Marshall," Willis said.

"Yeah, but that was *Bush* who started the Gulf War."

"You want to know who was an even *better* President than Harrison Ford?" Hawes said.

"Who?"

"Michael Douglas."

"Oh, *yeah.*"

"He was maybe the best President we ever had. You see that movie, Steve?"

"No," Carella said curtly.

"Have a bagel, sourpuss," Parker said.

"*The American President.* That was the movie. Michael Douglas was President Andrew Shepherd."

"You remember who his aide was?" Kling asked.

"No, who?"

"Martin Sheen! Who is now *President!*"

"President Josiah Bartlet!"

"President *Jed* Bartlet."

"What goes around, comes around."

"What's *his* aide's name?"

"Who cares?" Parker asked.

"He might be President one day."

"Fredric March was a good President, too," Byrnes suggested.

"Who's Fredric March?" Kling asked.

"Seven Days in May."

"Never heard of it."

"Or Henry Fonda," Byrnes said. "In *Fail-Safe.*"

"That was the same movie, wasn't it?" Brown asked.

"It only *seemed* like the same movie," Hawes said.

"Who's Henry Fonda?" Kling asked.

"How about Kevin Kline?" Willis asked.

"Yes, he was a very good President," Meyer said solemnly.

"He was also this guy who *looked* like the President."

"Dave."

"That was the name of the movie. *Dave.*"

"It was also the name of the lookalike. Dave Kovic."

"Because the *real* President had a stroke while fucking his secretary. I saw that movie," Parker said. "This sexy broad."

"Yeah," Willis said, remembering.

"Yeah," Brown said, nodding.

They all had another bagel.

"But you know who was the *best* actor?" Meyer asked. "Who ever played the President?"

"Who?" Kling said.

"Ronald Reagan."

"Oh yes," Kling said.

"Yes," Hawes agreed.

"Unquestionably," Byrnes said.

What's the use? Carella thought, and took a bagel from the tray.

The call from Carella's sister came at a little before ten that Friday morning. The surveillance equipment from the Tech Unit had already arrived. Across the room, Meyer Meyer was helping Fat Ollie Weeks tape the battery-powered recorder to Tito Gomez's chest.

"Who's gonna be on the other end of this?" Tigo asked.

"Nobody," Ollie said. "It ain't a transmitter, it's a recorder."

"Then who's gonna come save my ass if Wiggy tips?"

"Don't worry about it," Meyer said.

"I worry," Tigo said.

On the telephone, Angela was asking Carella if he could come to Mama's house tonight after work.

"Why?" Carella said.

"We want to talk to you."

"We're talking right now," Carella said.

"You're at work and so am I."

"What do you want to talk about?"

"We'll tell you when you get here."

"I'm working a homicide, I may not get out of here till late," he said.

"That's okay, we'll wait."

"What is it, Angela?"

"A surprise," she said.

"I'm a cop," he said. "I hate surprises."

"I'm leaving early today. Can you get to River-head by five?"

"Only if I'm out of here by four."

"Whenever," she said. "I'll see you later."

He put the receiver back on its base and walked across the room to where Tigo was complaining that the tapes were too tight.

"You don't want the gadget rattling around, do you?" Ollie asked.

"I don't want the gadget, period," Tigo said.

"It'll save you a lot of time upstate," Meyer said.

"If he says anything."

"That's your job," Carella said. "To get him talking."

"He's not so fuckin dumb, you know. I start talkin about that night, he's gonna wonder why."

"Make it sound casual," Meyer suggested.

"Sure. Hey, Wiggy, remember the night you shot that dude in the back of his head and dropped him in a garbage can? Boy, that was fun, wasn't it?"

"Do it over a few drinks," Carella suggested.

"Sure. Have another beer, Wiggy. Remember the night you shot that dude in the back of . . ."

"Just play it cool," Meyer said. "Don't even think about the wire. Make believe you're two guys shootin the breeze."

"Sure."

"The mike's right here," Ollie said. "It looks like a button on your shirt."

"Suppose he *spots* the fuckin thing?"

"He won't."

"But *if* he does."

"Don't worry, he won't be thinking about a wire."

"What if he *starts* thinking about a wire? This man can become very violent. He is not called Wiggy the Lid for no reason."

"Just tell him you work for a record company," Meyer said.

"Tell him you're a talent scout for Motown," Ollie said. "Tuck your shirt in your pants."

Tigo tucked in his shirt.

He turned to face the cops.

"How do I look?" he asked.

He looked extremely worried.

"You look great," Meyer said.

Kling came over from across the room.

"You're wearing a wire, right?" he said.

"Yeah," Tigo said. "Why?"

"I never would've guessed," Kling said.

Halloway told them he would have to call their treasurer. Wiggy asked what his name was.

"Her," Halloway said. "Her name is Susan."

Susan was a code word. The moment whoever answered the phone heard the name "Susan," he or she would know there was trouble.

"Make sure you talk to her and her alone," Wiggy said. "Give me the number. I'll dial it."

The clock on the wall read ten minutes past ten.

Halloway wrote the number on a slip of paper. Wiggy looked at it as he dialed. The instant he heard it ringing on the other end, he handed the receiver to Halloway and picked up an extension phone. The phone rang once, twice . . .

"Hello?"

A woman's voice.

"Susan?" Halloway said.

"Yes?"

"This is Dick Halloway. Happy New Year."

"Thank you, Dick," she said. "Same to you."

His use of the familiar diminutive told her he was not alone. If Karen Andersen had announced herself as Karey, or David Good as Davey, it would have meant the same thing. By repeating the diminutive, the woman on the other end of the line was telling Halloway she understood he had company.

"Did you try to reach me yesterday?" she asked.

"Yes, I called around three," he said.

He was telling her there were three people there with him.

"Sorry I missed you. How can I help?"

"We need some cash," he said.

"How much?" she asked.

To Wiggy, listening on the extension, this all sounded legitimate so far.

"Are you sitting down?" Halloway asked, and smiled.

Wiggy smiled, too.

So did the Mexicans.

Everyone was smiling at Halloway's witticism.

"That much, huh?" Susan said.

Her name wasn't Susan, but that's who Wiggy thought she was. He also thought this was going along splendidly so far. He didn't have the slightest notion that he and his two pals were being set up.

"Three-million-six," Halloway said.

"Oh dear," Susan said.

"Indeed," Halloway said, and rolled his eyes heavenward.

Wiggy nodded encouragement. You're doing fine so far, his nod said.

"Where do you want it?" Susan asked.

Wiggy motioned for Halloway to cover the mouthpiece with his hand.

"Tell her you'll come there for it," he whispered.

"I'll come there for it, Sue."

Warning her again that he had company, three in number, remember? Trouble, Sue. Or Suzie. Big trouble here. Come help us, Suze.

"How soon can you get it together?" he asked.

"How soon will you need it?"

"As soon as possible, Sue."

"How does one o'clock sound?"

Halloway looked at Wiggy. Wiggy nodded.

"One o'clock sounds fine," Halloway said.

"Allow yourself a half-hour to get here," Susan said.

This meant he could expect help at twelve-thirty.

"I'll have to make three or four calls, Dick."

She was telling him she'd be sending three or four people.

"And, Dick . . . ?"

"Yes, Sue?"

"They're doing some work out front, lots of heavy machinery all over the place. Come in the back way, will you?"

"See you in a bit," he said.

She had told him they'd be heavily armed. She had told him they'd come up the emergency staircase at the rear of the Headley Building. She had so much as told him that Walter Wiggins and his Mexican associates were already as good as dead.

The hands on the wall clock now read a quarter past ten.

"Charmaine?" Wiggy said. "Why don't you make us all some coffee?"

Will Struthers didn't call the bank until ten-twenty that morning. As a former bank employee himself, he knew there was always an early-morning rush of customers, and he suspected Antonia Belandres would have been particularly busy until now, it being the start of the big New Year's Eve weekend and all.

"Miss Belandres," she said.

The "Miss" pleased Will. It meant a) she was single, and b) she wasn't one of these damn feminists who called themselves "Ms." and aspired to pee in men's rooms.

"Hello, Miss Belandres," he said, "this is Will Struthers."

"Lieutenant Struthers!" she said, sounding enormously surprised. "How *are* you?"

"Fine, thank you," Will said, not bothering to correct her. "And you?"

"Busy, busy, busy," she said. "We close at noon today, and it's been bedlam."

"I know just how it is," Will said.

"I know you do," she said. "So tell me, are you looking forward to the new year?"

"Actually, I never have liked New Year's Eve," he said. "It always seems like a big disappointment to me. I don't know why."

"I feel exactly the same way."

"You do?"

"Yes. I've been to small parties and big ones, I've stayed home and I've gone to night clubs, and it's always the same thing. A big buildup to an even bigger letdown."

"Gee," he said.

"Yes," she said.

There was a short silence.

"Miss Belandres . . ." he said.

"Antonia," she said.

"Antonia," he said. "I know this is short notice . . ."

Silence again. He could hear her breathing on the other end of the line.

"But I was . . . ah . . . wondering . . ."

"Yes, Lieutenant?"

"If you don't . . . ah . . . have any other plans . . ."

"Yes?"

"Do you think you might care to have dinner with me tonight?"

"Why, I think that would be lovely," she said.

"Good," he said at once. "Good. Does seven o'clock sound convenient to you?"

"Seven o'clock sounds lovely."

"Do you like Italian food?"

"I love Italian food."

"Seven o'clock then, good," he said. "Good. Where shall I pick you up?"

"It's 347 South Shelby, apartment 12C."

"I'll be there at seven on the dorothy," he said.

"I'll be waiting," she said.

He was thinking, Antonia, you and me are going to be millionaires.

"This is Clarendon Hall," Mahmoud said.

Nikmaddu wished the man's little mustache didn't make him look as if he were constantly smiling. This was a serious matter here.

"Jassim will be sitting here, in row F in the center section."

Jassim of the dirty fingernails and no smile nodded. He was familiar with the seating plan, knew exactly what he was to do tomorrow night.

"Seat number 101 on the aisle," Mahmoud said.

Nikmaddu looked at the plan more closely.

"If we're lucky," Mahmoud said, "the explosion will carry to the stage. If not, we will have made our point, anyway."

"Killing the Jew is not the point, you understand," Akbar said. The desert camel driver, deep creases on his brown face, thick veins on the backs of his strong hands. Their demolitions expert. "We are teaching them that we can strike anywhere, anytime. We are telling them that they are completely vulnerable. Unless they wish to strip-search every American entering a theater, a movie house, a concert hall, a restaurant, a coffee shop, a supermarket, anywhere. They are at our mercy, is what we will be proving to them tomorrow night."

"Still, getting the Jew would be a bonus," Jassim said.

"But not a *priority*," Akbar insisted. "If we get the Jew, fine. If not, many others will die. Our point will be made."

"To die for Allah would be an honor," Jassim said. He was the one going in with the bomb. By rights, he should have the last word. But Akbar had fashioned the bomb and the timing device.

"Akbar is right," Nikmaddu said. "It will be better if no sacrifice were involved this time." He was referring to the suicide bombing of the United States destroyer in Yemen. "We must let them know we are professionals, not fanatics."

Jassim took this as a personal affront. He gave Nikmaddu what he hoped was a disdainful look, and then lighted a cigarette.

"When will this happen?" Nikmaddu asked.

"After the intermission," Akbar said.

"Precisely when?" Nikmaddu asked.

"The Jew is the guest artist in the second half of the evening. We now know he will be playing Mendelssohn's violin concerto in E Minor. The bomb will be set to go off sometime during the first movement."

"When, precisely, during the first movement?"

"It is difficult to time the music precisely," Akbar said. "The first movement is about twelve and a half minutes long, depending."

"Depending on what?"

"The performer, the conductor—artistic license. But it will rarely run much longer than that. In any event, the bomb will be set to go off at nine-thirty."

"At *precisely* nine-thirty?"

"Precisely, yes. It will explode toward the end of the first movement, trust me."

Nikmaddu was beginning to realize that although this man looked as if he belonged in a tent on the desert, he was perhaps more intelligent than any of the others.

"What do you mean by movement?" Jassim

asked. The stupidest of the lot. And the one with the most responsibility. The one who would go in with the bomb. "What does movement mean?"

"The Mendelssohn concerto has three movements," Akbar explained.

"But what is a movement?"

"It's not important that you know," Akbar said. "You will place the bomb and leave the hall. The rest is up to Allah."

"Will Jassim have enough time to get back to his seat, leave the bomb, and make his departure?" Nikmaddu asked.

"A good point," Mahmoud said. "Have you timed all this?"

"I have been to six concerts this season," Akbar said. "And hated them all. I know exactly how long it takes to get from the street to the lobby, and from there back to the seat in row F. Without rushing, Jassim should be out of there before the bomb explodes."

"At nine-thirty precisely," Nikmaddu said, seeking confirmation yet another time.

"Yes, at nine-thirty precisely," Akbar said. "A fitting climax to the first movement."

The men laughed. All but Jassim, who found nothing humorous in any of this.

"What kind of bomb are you using?" Nikmaddu asked.

"A simple pipe bomb. Two of them actually. Taped together and packed with black powder, nails, and screws. Similar to the one in Atlanta four years ago."

"And the timer?"

"A battery-powered clock."

"How will he carry it in?" Nikmaddu asked.

"In a handbag," Akbar said.

"I'll be carrying a *handbag?*" Jassim said.

"A *man's* handbag. Europeans carry them all the time. Besides, I've taken one into the hall on six different occasions now. There is no security check. Women go in with handbags, even shopping bags, men carry briefcases. They are very sure of themselves, these Americans."

"That will all change tomorrow night," Nikmaddu said.

"Yes, it will," Akbar said.

"*Inshallah,*" Mahmoud said.

"*Inshallah,*" the others said in unison.

Man seemed to have disappeared from the face of the earth.

First place Tigo tried was the crib on Decatur. Thomas—who on the night of the murder had been chatting with Mr. Jerry Hoskins, alias Frank Holt, while Tigo and Wiggy tested the dope in the other room—was watching television when Tigo waltzed in.

"Hey, man," he said.

"Whut'choo watchin?" Tigo asked.

This was ten to eleven in the morning, man was sittin here watching television.

"I don't even know," Thomas said. "Suppin with Sylvester Stallone."

Tigo watched the screen for a moment.

Sylvester Stallone was dangling from a rope.

"Where's Wiggy?" he asked.

"You got me, man."

"You seed him today?"

"Nope."

"When'd you get here?"

"Bout an hour ago."

"He wasn't here?"

"Nope."

"He come back, you tell him I'm lookin for him, okay?"

"Peace, brother," Thomas said.

My ass, Tigo thought.

Next place he tried was Wiggy's barber. This was a man named Roland, who cut mighty fine hair and also took in numbers on the side. Or vice versa. Tigo figured Wiggy might be here gettin a trim, New Year's Eve comin up and all. He could use a trim hisself, matter of fact. Roland said he hadn't seen hide nor hair—

"You get it?" he asked.

—of Wiggy since a week ago today when he last cut the man's hair.

"Try L&G," he suggested.

L&G was short for Lewis and Gregory, who were

two brothers owned a haberdashery on Chase Street. Both brothers were there when Tigo arrived at eleven that Friday. The shop was packed with people returning ties, and shirts and shit they'd got for Christmas and had no use for. Greg told him he hadn't seen Wiggy since before Thanksgiving, was the man all right? He usually came in here and splurged two, three times a year. Tigo told him Wiggy was fine, just'd been busy was all. Greg said, "Tell him I said happy new year, hear?"

"I'll tell him," Tigo said.

He was wondering had Wiggy vanished from sight?

This business, vanishing from sight was always a distinct possibility.

He tried a bar called the Starlight, which was already doing very good business at a quarter past eleven, two days before New Year's Eve. Tigo could just imagine what the place would be like on the big night itself. But John the bartender told him he'd seen Mr. Wiggins on Christmas night, when he was sittin here at the bar hittin on a blonde who'd come in out the cold, and again just yesterday aroun this time.

"Is that so?" Tigo asked. "A blonde?"

It was too bad the tape recorder wasn't turned on because first it missed a hair joke from Wiggy's barber, and now it just missed a thickening of the plot with Wiggy working a blonde on Christmas night. He told John if Mr. Wiggins came in again to tell

him he was lookin for him, okay, and then—so it
shouldn't be a total loss—he tossed off a shot of
Dewar's before he went out into the cold again.

It was beginning to snow.

No snow for Christmas, but now it was coming
down to beat all hell.

Tigo looked at his watch. It was twenty minutes
past eleven. He didn't know where to go next.

He tried the pool hall on Culver and Third, but
nobody there had seen Wiggy, and then he tried The
Corset Lady on South Fifth, which was run by a
foxy chick named Aleda who made very fine ladies'
underwears and who used to go with Wiggy, but not
for six months or so now, but she hadn't seen him
and didn't *care* to see him, thanks. Then he tried the
First Bap on St. Sab's because believe it or not Walter Wiggins was a religious man who went to
church every Sunday, but the Reverend Gabriel
Foster hadn't seen him since, in fact, last Sunday,
had anything happened to him? Foster was always
looking for something that had happened to anybody in the black community, some cause he could
champion on his radio show, some put-upon black
he could go march to City Hall about. Tigo was beginning to think maybe something *had* happened to
Wiggy. This business, things happened.

He finally tried a man named Little Nicholas,
who did business out the back of a laundromat he
owned and operated on Lyons and South Thirty-
fifth. Little Nicholas was about five-feet, eight-
inches tall and Tigo guessed he weighed something

like three, four hundred pounds. What Little Nicholas did was sell guns. He told Tigo that Wiggy had been in there late last night, and had purchased a beautiful submachine gun called the Cobray M11-9, would Tigo be interested in seeing some very fine banned weapons and silencers that had come in from all over the nation only yesterday? Tigo asked had he seed Wiggy anytime *today?* Little Nicholas said No, he hadn't had the pleasure.

It was a quarter to twelve.

The snow was coming down pretty hard now.

Tigo wondered where the fuck Wiggy could be.

Wiggy was sitting at Halloway's computer up at W&D. One of the Mexicans—he guessed it was Ortiz—came out of the conference room where they were holding the staff, and asked him shouldn't he be going for the money soon? They had already decided, after some sound reasoning from Wiggy, that he should be the one who went for the cash, in case there was any language problem, not that he meant to be disparaging. He looked up at the wall clock now. It was only twelve noon, and Halloway's accountant had advised them to allow a half-hour to get there for their one o'clock appointment, which meant there was still plenty of time before him and Halloway had to go out into what looked like a full-fledged blizzard.

"I got time yet," he told Ortiz, or Villada, or whoever the hell he was. *Whoever* he was, Wiggy planned never to see him or his partner ever again the minute he got his hands on that money. *Adios, amigos,* it was very nice knowing you.

Meanwhile, there was some very interesting information on the W&D computer.

Carella and Meyer were having lunch in a diner on Culver and Eighth, not far from the station house. Meyer was eating a salad and drinking iced tea. Carella was eating a hamburger and fries. Meyer told him that just two days ago, his wife had told him they should go buy him some clothes for the new year.

"She said we'd have to go to a shop for *large* men, was what she called it. I said, 'Why do we have to go to a large men's shop?' She said, 'Because we won't find anything to fit you in a regular men's store.' I said, 'Hey, come on, Sarah, I can buy clothes off the rack at any store in town! Large men's shops are for men who are *obese.*' So she looks me dead in the eye and says, 'Well?' "

"Sarah said that, huh?"

"Sarah."

"Said you were fat, in effect."

"Obese."

"In effect."

"Do you think I'm obese?"

"No. Ollie Weeks is obese," Carella said, and popped a fry into his mouth. "You're what I'd call chubby."

"Chubby! That's *worse* than obese!"

"Well . . . plump maybe."

"Keep going. How's your damn hamburger?"

"Terrific."

"The fries?"

"Splendid."

"You forgot stout."

"Stout's a good one, too."

"You ever have a weight problem?"

"Never. I've always been svelte."

"I've always been borderline."

"Borderline what?"

"Obese!" Meyer said, and both men burst out laughing.

The laughter trailed.

"I've got other problems, though," Carella said.

"Yeah?"

"Yeah."

Meyer looked at him. Carella's face, his eyes were suddenly very serious.

"Tell me," Meyer said.

"You think I've changed?" Carella asked.

"How do you mean?"

"I don't know. Am I different?"

"You seem the same to me."

"Teddy says I've changed since my father got killed. She says I never cried for him. She says I never cried for Danny, either, Danny Gimp. I don't even remember if I did. She says I've been drinking too much, she says . . ."

"Ah, shit, Steve, you haven't, have you?"

"No. I don't think so. I hope not. It's just . . .."

"What?"

"Ah, Jesus."

"What, Steve? Tell me."

"I think I'm scared."

"Come on. You're not scared."

"I think I am. Teddy's afraid I might eat my own gun one day. I'll tell you the truth . . .."

"Don't even say it."

Both men fell silent.

Carella was looking down at his hands.

"I think I'm scared," he said again. "Really, Meyer."

"Come on, scared. Of what?"

"Dying," Carella said. "I'm afraid I'll get killed."

"We're all afraid we'll get killed."

"I came so close, Meyer."

"We've all come close, one time or another. O'Brien comes close every day of his life."

"O'Brien's a hard luck cop. And he never had a lion sitting on his chest."

"So what are you scared of? Another lion sitting on your chest? Come on, Steve."

"He almost had my head in his mouth, I could feel his breath on my face, I could smell his breath. Another minute, he'd have closed his jaws on me. I never came that close to dying before."

"And you'll never come that close again. What do you think this is, the African plains? Come on. This is a *city*, Steve. You don't run into lions on the streets here."

"I dream about that lion every night, Meyer. Every fucking night, I see that lion in my dreams. I wake up sweating, Meyer, shaking. I'm scared it'll happen again. And next time . . ."

"It's okay to be scared," Meyer said.

"Not if you're a cop."

"We're all scared."

"Cops shouldn't . . ."

"Not only cops. Everybody. We're all scared, Steve. If you meet another lion, just look him in the eye. Stare him down."

Carella's hands were trembling.

"Come on," Meyer said. He slid out of the booth, came around the table, sat beside his friend, and put his arm around his shoulder. "Come on, Steve."

Tito Gomez walked in just then.

"How tender," he said.

"Go fuck yourself," Meyer explained.

"Nice talk. I can't find Wiggy. I don't know where he is. What now?"

Wiggy was still at Halloway's computer.

There was a folder named MOTHER, which he couldn't open because whenever he double-clicked on it, he was told to enter a password. But when he double-clicked on a folder called WITCHES AND DRAGONS—which he thought at first might be some kind of a game—it opened to his touch, and he found a whole list of files with names like ADA and NETTIE and DIANA and EM and TESSIE and

RONI and BELA and GINA. Was W&D in the
business of tracking hurricanes, or had he lucked
into Halloway's personal little black book of cuties,
oh you sly old dog, you! Or were these the names of
writers the company published? But then why use
first names? And even some nicknames?

Intrigued now, Wiggy double-clicked on the file
labeled TESSIE because that was the name of the
first girl he'd ever talked into licking Frick and
Frack, a thirteen-year-old high yaller beauty fresh
up from the South with her grandma. There wasn't
nothing in that file about girls, mellow or otherwise.
What was in there was information about the West
Side Limousine Corporation, which it would appear was a subsidiary of Wadsworth and Dodds
here, and which made all kinds of trips to and from
the city's two airports and the one across the river in
the next state, not to mention a trip to Diamondback
on Christmas night.

He began wondering why a file about a limou-
sine company would be called TESSIE, and then
he realized that there were two S's in the words
WEST SIDE, and also a T, and—lo and behold—an
I and an E! So what you had here was little old
TESSIE all curled up in the back seat of a WEST
SIDE limo!

He double-clicked on the file labeled EM.

What was in there was an itemized list of drug
deals that made Wiggy's little operation in Diamondback look like somebody selling lemonade by
the side of the road. Dates, places, number of kilos

purchased, dollars paid for them. He wasn't surprised that the list existed; everybody kept records *someplace,* man. In fact, his own transactions uptown were recorded on a computer disc called HAPPY DAYS that could only be opened with the password WW2, which stood not for World War II, but instead for his initials and the month of his—it suddenly occurred to him that WITCHES AND DRAGONS stood for Wadsworth and Dodds.

What he was looking at here was a record of drug buys the book publishers had made in Mexico over the past two years. And suddenly he realized that the name EM was buried in the word MEXICO, same as TESSIE was buried in WEST SIDE, was in fact the first two letters of that word, reversed, and he began wondering how many of the *other* girls' names in the WITCHES AND DRAGONS folder were buried in larger words, hiding there, so to speak, lurking there in the dark for somebody smart like Wiggy to find.

He kept opening file after file.

When finally he double-clicked on the file named DIANA, his eyes opened wide.

He was reading all about Diamondback, which was where he conducted business, the uptown ghetto where Jerry Hoskins alias Frank Holt had come calling with a hundred keys of prime cocaine purchased in Mexico.

DIAMONDBACK.

Little ole white girl DIANA hiding up there in the blackest of black holes.

The magnitude of his discovery made him suddenly want to pee.

Grabbing the Cobray from where it was resting on the floor at his feet, he went down the hall to the men's room at the rear of the office complex.

At that very moment, The Weird Sisters and two very tall, very broad black men were entering the Headley Building through the back door in an alley that was posted with NO PARKING—FIRE LANE signs. This time around, Sheryl and Toni—whose real names were Anna and Mary Jo—were *each* carrying guns with silencers affixed to the muzzles.

So were the black men.

Wiggy didn't hear any shooting because the weapons were wearing silencers.

All he heard was screaming.

The screaming wasn't coming from the two Mexicans, who were dead within minutes after the assassins entered the conference room. Instead, they were coming from Charmaine the receptionist, and Betty Alweiss from the Art Department. Karen Andersen wasn't screaming. She was learning how to be as cold-bloodedly unemotional as her boss and sometime lover.

"There's a third one," Halloway said.

By that time, Wiggy was down the fire stairs and out of the building.

• • •

The Weird Sisters unashamedly stripped the Mexicans naked and wrapped them in tarpaulin. Their two black associates carried the bodies down the fire stairs, hoisted them into the back of a white ML320 Mercedes-Benz, and transported them to a garbage dump on Sands Spit, not far from the airport. It was Halloway's surmise that the Mexicans would never be identified and therefore would never be missed.

At about four-thirty that afternoon—just as Carella was leaving the squadroom—Anna and Mary Jo went up to Diamondback to look for Walter Wiggins. This time, their orders were to kill him.

Carella got to his mother's house in Riverhead at a little past six that evening. He recognized his sister's car in the driveway outside the house, and parked just behind it. His mother's Christmas tree glowed behind the windows fronting the house. At least a foot of snow covered the walk to the front door, and it was still coming down. He climbed the low flat steps, pressed the button set in the door jamb, and heard familiar chimes sounding inside the house. He waited. Falling flakes covered his hair and the shoulders of his overcoat. He was about to ring again when the door opened.

"Hey," his mother said, and hugged him. "You should wear a hat."

"I know," he said. "You told me."

"From when you were six," she said.

"Three," he corrected.

"Come in. Angela's already here."

"I saw her car."

"Come in."

He followed his mother into the house. This was where he'd grown up. This was what he'd called home during his childhood, his adolescence, and his early manhood. Home. It seemed strange to him now, smaller, somehow cheerless. He wondered if that was because his father no longer lived here. Angela was sitting at the big dining room table, drinking a glass of red wine. Another glass of wine was on the table, just opposite her. He remembered when they were kids and used to hide together under this very table. He remembered Sunday afternoons here in his parents' house, the penny-ante poker games, he and Angela hiding under the dining room table. He remembered his sister once breaking his head with the clasp on a pocketbook she'd swung at him in anger. He couldn't remember now what had so enraged her. Something he'd said jokingly. He'd loved her to death when they were kids. He still did. She kissed him on the cheek in greeting.

"How's the traffic?" she asked.

"Pretty bad. The roads are getting slick."

"Steve, some wine?" his mother asked. "Something stronger?"

"A little wine, yes," he said. "Thanks."

He sat alongside Angela. Outside the window, the snow was coming down heavily. He didn't live

very far from here, but the roads were already bad.
He was beginning to regret not having gone straight
home from the office. His mother brought him his
glass of wine, and went to sit opposite him and Angela at the table. They all lifted their glasses.

"*Salute*," his mother said in Italian.

"Cheers," Carella said.

"Health," Angela said.

They drank.

"So," Angela said.

"So," his mother said.

They were both smiling.

Carella looked across the table at his mother. He
turned to look at his sister.

"What?" he said.

"We're getting married together," Angela said.

"A double wedding," his mother said.

"Me and Henry, Mama and . . ."

"I don't want to hear this," Carella said.

He was already standing, surprised to find himself on his feet, wondering when he'd got up. Was it
when they'd both started smiling? Was it then that
the feeling of impending dread had lurched from
his heart into his throat?

"Sit down," his mother said.

"No, Mom. I'm sorry, but . . ."

"Sit down, Steve."

"No. I don't want to hear about you getting married so soon after . . ."

"Your father's been dead almost . . ."

"I don't want to *hear* it!" Carella shouted, and

whirled on his sister. "And I don't want to hear about you marrying the man who . . ."

"What the hell is wrong with you?" Angela asked.

"Oh no," he said. "Oh no, you don't."

"Have you lost your . . . ?"

"Never mind what's wrong with *me!* What's wrong with you? Have you both forgotten Papa already? How can you sit here in *his* house . . ."

"Papa is dead, Steve."

"Oh, is he? Gee, no kidding. What do you think this is about here? What are we talking about here? What are you both planning to do if not spit on Papa's . . ."

"Don't you *dare!*" his mother said.

"Oh, for Christ's sake, Mom, stop behaving like a schoolgirl. And you stop encouraging her!" he shouted, whirling on Angela. "You want to marry that jackass, at least have the decency to leave her out of it."

Angela was shaking her head.

"Sure, shake your head," he said. "I'm wrong, right? She meets a Wop fresh off the boat . . ."

"Not in my house," his mother said. "Never use that word in my house."

"Oh, forgive me, what is he? A Yankee Doodle Dandy?"

"I think that lion scrambled your brains," Angela said.

"And never mind the fucking *lion!*" he shouted.

"Not in my *house!*" his mother said, and slapped him.

He looked at her.

"I'm sorry," she said.

"Sure."

Angela suddenly began crying.

"All we wanted was your blessing," she said.

"Well, you didn't get it," he said. "If you can both forget Papa so easily, I can't. Goodnight, Mom. Thanks for the wine."

He turned and was starting for the door when his mother said, "I'm not a schoolgirl, Steve."

He continued going for the door.

"I love him and I'm going to marry him," she said.

His hand was on the doorknob.

"Whether you like it or not," she said.

"Goodnight," he said again, and opened the door, and walked out into the fiercely falling snow.

The tape recorder was going.

Tigo couldn't believe what he was hearing. Nor did he *want* to be hearing what he was hearing. He wanted to get this conversation back to the reason he was wearing a wire to begin with. He wanted Wiggy to start talking about December twenty-third.

He wondered suddenly if this was all bullshit Wiggy was giving him here. Did Wiggy maybe *know* he was wired? Was he maybe making up a good story so the fuzz would get off the scent? It sure was a peculiar story he was telling here. Almost made Tigo forget why he was here. Almost made Tigo sorry he had finally found the man.

"You really think all this is true, huh?" he asked. "Cause to me . . ."

"Man, I was lookin straight into they computer! I seed all this stuff with my own eyes!"

"It just sounds, you know, like science-fiction, you know?" Tigo said. "This file named Mothah you can't open cause you need a password, an all this money floatin aroun, and these dope deals here an there, and these people causin trouble all over the world, an tryin'a fuck us right here in Diamon'back, I mean, man, it sounds like suppin you'd see in a *movie,* you know what I'm sayin, man?"

"It'd make a *good* movie, that's for damn sure," Wiggy said, "but it's *true,* man! I got it from they *computer!*"

"That don't mean it couldn't of been garbage in there," Tigo said, and shrugged.

"The point is, whut we gonna do about it, Tigo? I mean, these guys are messin with our *people!*"

Tigo had never particularly felt that any of these people they sold dope to were necessarily *related* to him in any way. Maybe *Wiggy* thought of they customers as his "people" but Tigo didn't share the sentiment. To tell the truth, if they was money to be made recycling dope here in the hood, Tigo didn't care *who* sold them the dope to begin with or where the proceeds of the sale were going. In fact, the only thing he wanted to do right this minute was talk about what he'd come here to talk about so he could go back to the police and collect his reward. He planned to retire from the dope business—

He didn't yet realize how close his retirement was.

—soon as he got his hands on however much money the commissioner gave him for this valuable stuff he was about to tape. So he didn't need to know about any *conspiracy* Wiggy had tapped into through somebody's computer. Nor did he want to *do* anything about any such conspiracy, even if it did exist, which he strongly doubted because Wiggy's story sounded like so much jive to him. So—subtly and not wishing to appear too aggressive or inquisitive—he asked, "How'd it feel killing that dude on Christmas Eve?"

"I think we should go to the police," Wiggy said, "tell *them* the story."

And suddenly, he shoved himself out of his chair and went marching straight for the telephone.

Carella was on his way home when the cell phone in his car rang. Ollie Weeks was on the other end.

"Guess what?" he said.

"Surprise me," Carella said.

"I just got a call from Walter Wiggins."

"What?"

"Ah yes."

"The man Gomez is supposed to be taping?"

"The very same."

"The man who maybe shot and killed Jerry Hoskins?"

"That's the one."

"Is he confessing?"

"I don't think so. But he wants to talk to us."

"What about?"

"Some kind of big conspiracy."

"Uh-huh," Carella said.

"I'm on my way to 1280 Decatur. You want to meet me?"

Carella looked at the dashboard clock.

"Give me half an hour," he said.

Antonia Belandres was very impressed that Will had managed to find his way here in all this snow. He jokingly told her he used to drive a dog sled team in Alaska, which somehow she took to be the truth, and was even more impressed. He now had two lies to account for. He hoped he did not lose her when he told her he was not a police lieutenant, and had never been to Alaska in his life.

There wasn't a single cab in sight when they came downstairs from her apartment. He had deliberately picked an Italian restaurant not too distant from where she lived on South Shelby, but it was really coming down and he apologized for asking her to walk the six blocks, but he was afraid they might lose their reservation.

"Don't be silly, Lieutenant," she said. "I *love* walking."

Lieutenant, he thought. Boy.

As it was, he needn't have worried about the reservation. The restaurant was almost empty. In fact, the owner fawned over them as if they were the Mayor and his wife who'd braved the storm to come here. He offered them a bottle of wine on the house, and then reeled off the specials for the night, all of which sounded delicious. Antonia ordered the *osso buco.* Will ordered the veal Milanese, which turned out to be breaded veal cutlets, oh well.

"By the way," he said, when they had each drunk a glass of wine and Will was pouring again, "I'm not a police lieutenant. In fact, I'm not even a cop."

"Oh?" she said.

"That's right," he said. "Here's to golden days and purple nights," and clinked his glass against hers.

"Where'd you learn that toast?" she asked. "Golden days and purple nights."

"Singapore."

"Me, too."

"So here's *to* them," he said.

"Here's *to* them," she said. "Golden days and purple nights."

They drank.

"Then what were you doing with all those detectives?" she asked. "If you're not a cop."

"I was sort of with them," Will said.

"If you're not a cop, what are you?"

"Actually, a burglar," he said.

"Really?"

"Yeah," he said, and shrugged.

"Did they arrest you for burglary? Was that it?"

"Not exactly."

"Then what?"

"They thought I passed a phony hundred-dollar bill."

"Was that the super-bill they asked me to examine?"

"I guess so. It sure looked real to me. I think that's why they let me go."

"What do you mean?"

"Well, I think it fooled *them,* too. I mean, if *they* couldn't tell it was fake, how was I supposed to know?"

"Well, you did work in a bank once."

"Yeah, but I never saw a super-bill in my life. They told me they could've charged me with a class-A mis, but this was Christmas, what the hell. They let me go."

"So as I understand this . . ."

"That's right . . ."

". . . you're a common thief."

"Well, I'm a burglar. That's not so common."

Antonia laughed. Will figured this was a good sign.

"Also, I have some plans that ain't so common neither," he said.

"Oh? What plans?"

"I'll tell you later," he said.

Antonia was thinking the plans he was talking about had to do with sex. He was referring to possibly taking her to bed later on tonight. After dinner. While the storm raged outside. Which wasn't a bad idea at all. Except that he was a common thief. Well, a burglar.

"What makes a burglar so special?" she asked.

"Well, first of all, we're like doctors."

"I see. Doctors."

"Yes. Our motto is 'Do no harm.' In fact, we go out of our way to keep from harming people. We see a light burning in an apartment, we think there's somebody in there, we'll avoid it like the plague."

"Why is that?"

"I just told you. We don't want some old lady screaming so we'll have to hurt her. Do no harm. Also, the rap is bigger. If you hurt somebody while you're inside a dwelling, or even if you're just carrying a gun. It goes up from Burg Two to Burg One. That's a difference of ten years, when it comes to sentencing."

"You sound very familiar with all this," Antonia said.

"Oh sure," he said. "Well, I've been doing it for a long time now."

She was wondering why she was still sitting here. The man had just told her he was a burglar, a *thief.*

"I thought you said you worked in a bank," she said.

"Long time ago," he said. "I was just a kid when I went out on the Rim."

"But you never saw a super-bill," she said.

"Never."

"I'm surprised. Plenty of them in Southeast Asia."

"Plenty of them *everywhere,* from what you said."

"Where'd you get the one you tried to cash?"

"I stole it."

"Why am I not surprised?" she said, and rolled her eyes.

"That's okay. Not many people get to dine with burglars."

"Lucky me," she said, and rolled her eyes again.

"That might turn out to be the case," he said.

She still thought he was talking about taking her to bed later on. Which she still thought might not be such a bad idea.

"You know that woman who got eaten by lions in Grover Park?" he said. "The zoo there? Did you see that on television?"

"No," she said. "But I read about it in the newspaper."

"That was who I stole the money from."

"Oh my, you're famous," she said.

"Well, *she* was, I guess. It's not everybody gets eaten by lions."

"What do you suppose she was doing in the lion's cage?"

"I have no idea. I only talked to the lady once in my entire life."

"You didn't have anything to do with . . ."

"No, hey, *no,"* he said, "I'm a burglar!"

"Yes," she said. "So I'm beginning to understand."

Their food arrived. She was thoughtfully silent for a while. Then she said, "So, if you were me, what would you do here?"

"What do you mean?"

"Would *you* go to bed with you, knowing you're a burglar? Or would you eat your dinner and go home like a nice little girl?"

"You could do both," Will suggested.

Tigo Gomez was getting very nervous.

Wiggy had just told him that the man who was on his way here was the very same person who'd strapped this tape recorder to his chest—"That's just great," Tigo said—none other than Detective Oliver Wendell Weeks of the Eighty-eighth Detective Squad.

"You maybe seed him aroun the streets," Wiggy said. "Fat Ollie Weeks. He's this big fat guy."

No kidding, Tigo thought.

The problem was that Wiggy thought he'd be doing a favor for the police, when all *they* wanted to do was send him up for Murder One. The further problem was that Tigo couldn't warn the man how dangerous this fat hump was because then he'd have to reveal that he himself had visited the police to ask for a favor of his own by way of a cash reward, and they'd wired him tight as Dick's hatband, which is why he was sitting here this very minute, still attempting to get information he could use as a bargaining tool when the Law arrived and the shit hit the fan.

"You goan tell him you a drug dealer?" he asked.

"No, I don't have to tell him that."

"Then how come you *know* these people are sellin dope up here?"

"I coulda heard."

"How you coulda heard, Wigg? You goan tell the fuzz this man Hoskins come up here Christmas-time, sold you a hundred keys of coke to distribute to li'l kiddies in the streets?"

"No. But I could . . ."

"You goan tell 'em you shot this man Hoskins back of the head an dropped him in a garbage can? You goan do that, Wigg?"

"I'm sayin it don't seem right, what these moth-ahs are doin to our people."

"They's evil folk in this world," Tigo said, "it *is* a shame."

He was thinking Jerry Hoskins may have brought that shit up from Mexico and sold it to Wiggy, but Wiggy was the one passin it down the line till it got to his "people" in the streets. And he *still* hadn't said one damn word about the Christmas Eve murder. Tigo was about to prod him again, get this show on the road here, nem mine feelin sorry for all the drug addicts in this sorry world of ours, when Wiggy said, "You know what the name Nettie stans for?"

"Nettie, you say?"

"N-E-T-T-I-E," Wiggy said, spelling it out for him. "You know what word that name is hidin' in?"

"No, I has to admit I do not," Tigo said.

"Counterfeit. That's the word. You search that word, you find Nettie lurkin in there. You double-click on her name, you transported straight to Net-tieland. You want to hear this, man, or you want to stay ignorant the ress of your life?"

Tigo did not want to hear anything but how Wiggy had killed Hoskins—but neither did he wish to remain ignorant the rest of his life. He nodded wearily, and listened as Wiggy began telling him all about his adventures in Nettieland. Gradually, he began to lean closer. Gradually, his eyes opened wide. He was listening intently, his attention completely captured, when all at once he heard footsteps pounding in the hallway outside. He turned toward the front door. An instant later, he heard the sound of rapid gunfire, and all at once the door flew off its hinges.

At that very moment, Steve Carella was turning his car into Decatur Avenue, never once realizing he was about to meet another lion.

Tigo was running for the window even before the two blond ladies burst into the room. Somewhere behind him Wiggy screamed in pain. Tigo dove through the glass head first, came through onto the fire escape in a cascade of shattering shards, heard more firing from inside the apartment.

"The window!" one of the women yelled, but he was already on his feet and charging down the ladder. The iron rungs were crusted with snow, slippery underfoot. He almost lost his balance, almost went over the rail, but continued running, sliding, slipping, almost flying down those steps while above him the blondes were on automatic, bullets kicking up snow everywhere around him, clanging against the iron of the fire escape. He jumped the dozen feet or so to the ground, began broken-field running across the back yard, the blondes still firing, and was climbing the fence between this yard and the next one over, when they finally found the range. He heard wood splintering everywhere around him, and then felt slugs ripping across his back as he came over the top of the fence. Another slug ripped through his right hand. He dropped to the ground, zig-zagged toward the alleyway alongside the building, tucking his bloody hand in against his body, cradling it, blood leaking onto the white snow from his hand and his chest as he ran.

The storm had kept most people off the street.

He stumbled out of the alleyway, fell, got to his feet again.

He turned to look behind him, fell again, and began crawling toward the streetlamp on the corner. He was lying there under the lamp for perhaps two or three minutes when a tall hatless man came running around the corner. Tigo did not know whether the shots had attracted him or whether there'd been some other disturbance in the hood. He only knew he was glad to see him. The man knelt beside him. Tigo recognized him at once.

"You know who did this to you?" Carella asked.

Tigo nodded.

"Who, Tigo? Can you tell me?"

Carella's lion had just followed Tigo's trail of blood up the alleyway.

"Mother," Tigo said.

"Your *mother* shot . . . ?"

"Nettie," Tigo said.

"Is that your mother's name?"

Carella's lion was just running out of the alleyway behind them.

"Diana," Tigo said.

"I don't under . . ."

But Tito Gomez was already dead.

And Carella's lion was almost upon him.

He turned just in time to see someone dressed entirely in black, carrying what was unmistakably an AK-47.

If you meet another lion, just look him in the eye. Stare him down.

This lion wasn't a male.

There was merely a surprised instant that robbed Carella's eye of steely intent and lessened the speed of his gun hand, but that was all it took to give the blonde the advantage she needed. He registered three things in the tick of a heart beat. A car pulling into the street. The blonde angling the weapon toward his head. A man getting out of the car.

The blonde was about to squeeze the trigger when Fat Ollie Weeks shot her in the back, dropping her in her tracks.

"That's two, Steve," he told Carella, and grinned into the flying snow.

11.

Will guessed this was why he'd never been to bed with a hooker.

You went to bed with somebody who you had to pay, she put on her clothes directly afterward, said, "Thanks, I had a nice time," and went home. He guessed. But with a woman like Antonia Belandres, you sat here on a Saturday morning, drinking orange juice and coffee, and eating the chocolate croissants he'd gone down to the bakery to get, and it was . . . well . . . intimate. You could have sex with a hooker, but he didn't guess you could get intimate with one.

Antonia was wearing nothing but a little silky peignoir she'd taken from her bedroom closet. Will was wearing the slacks and shirt he'd put on when he went downstairs for the croissants. It was a little past ten-thirty. The snow had stopped and the sun was shining. In the street outside, everything looked clean and white and sparkling. He told Antonia that maybe they should go for a walk later on, if she thought she might like that. She told him she might like that a lot. He smiled and nodded. She smiled and nodded back.

He didn't tell her his plan until they were in her bed together again, and then only after they'd made love yet another time. She was cuddled in his arms, the blanket pulled up over their shoulders, frost still limning the window across the room, sunlight striking the glass.

"I know how we can both become millionaires," he said.

"Yes, how?" she said.

Black hair fanned out on the pillow. Brown eyes opened wide. Wearing no makeup. Her face looking as expectant as a child's on Christmas Day.

"We use the bills."

"What bills?" she asked.

"The super-bills."

"Use them?" she asked. "How do you mean?"

"You said you send any suspect bills to the Federal Reserve."

"Yes?"

"That's what you told the detectives."

"That's right. That's what we do."

"Somebody brings in a bill that looks phony . . ."

"Right, we send it to the Fed."

"You confiscate the bill, is that right?"

"That's right."

"Do you give the person a genuine bill in exchange?"

Which was just what the Treasury Department

had done with the eight grand they'd taken from him. But he didn't know that.

"Of course not," she said. "That would be the same as condoning counterfeiting."

"Do you give the person a receipt for the bill?"

"Not if we know for certain it's counterfeit," she said. "In that case, we simply take the bill out of circulation."

"Even if the person didn't know it was counterfeit?"

"Too bad for him."

"How about if you're not *sure* it's counterfeit? If it's one of those terrific bills you have to send to the Fed?"

"Then we give the customer a receipt for it, yes."

"And if the Fed decides it's phony?"

"It never comes back to us. They take it out of circulation, and notify us. We in turn notify the customer, and that's that."

"What if they say it's real?"

"They return it to us, we notify the customer, and he comes to pick it up. No harm done all around."

"Okay, what if you *don't* send a suspect bill to the Fed? What if you just take it from the customer, give him a receipt for it . . . and keep it."

"Keep it?"

"Yes. And then two weeks later . . . or however long it usually takes the Fed to get back to you . . ."

"It varies."

"Two weeks, three weeks, whatever, you call the customer and tell him Sorry, your bill was phony and the Fed has confiscated it. Goodbye, sir, and good luck."

Antonia looked at him.

"That would be stealing," she said.

"Yes," he said. "But it wouldn't be stealing *real* money."

Antonia was still looking at him.

"It would be stealing *counterfeit* money," he said.

"What's the difference?" she said. "I fail to see the difference."

"That's exactly my point. If nobody can *tell* the difference, we can use tons of fake money just as if it's real money. We can use fake money to pay for anything we buy."

Which was just what Jerry Hoskins had tried to do with the Mexicans. But Will didn't know this, either.

"It still seems like stealing to me," Antonia said.

"Ain't nothing wrong with stealing," Will said, and kissed her again.

"Do you like violin music?" she asked.

Fat Ollie was eating.

He was also listening.

For him, he was eating lightly. That is to say, he

was eating a baloney sandwich on rye with butter and mustard, and a sour pickle, and a potato knish, and a banana, and he was drinking coffee while he and Carella listened to the tape they'd retrieved from the recorder Tigo Gomez was wearing when the unidentified blonde—now in the hospital, and *still* unidentified—shot and killed him. Carella was eating a tuna and tomato sandwich on white, and drinking a glass of milk. The two detectives were in the interrogation room at the Eight-Seven, where Ollie seemed to be spending a lot of time lately, now that he was responsible for Carella's life two times over. Carella devoutly wished he would not save his life a third time, otherwise he might become a permanent fixture up here.

Ollie much preferred eating to listening to tapes.

The trouble with police tapes was that they were very rarely interesting. If you went to see a movie or watched a television show, or even if you were desperate and decided to read a book, there was usually a story you could follow. Listening to a tape was the same as hearing people talking, except that when you were in a room with people and they were babbling away, you didn't always recognize how boring it was. Listening to a tape, you were always aware of the fact that you were hoping these people would *say* something you could use against them. Usually, there was one person wearing the wire and the other person or persons present were totally unaware that they were being recorded. So they rambled on about anything under the sun, while you sat there with your thumb up your ass waiting for some kind of plot development. Even though Ollie did not much enjoy reading books, he knew all about plot development now that he'd started writing his thriller, which to tell the truth he'd found much easier than learning the first three bars of "Night and Day." In fact, he couldn't understand why the guys who wrote such shit got paid so much money for it.

The interesting thing about the tape Gomez had recorded was that Wiggins hadn't shot him at once. Because anyone listening to it—as Ollie and Carella were listening to it now—had to recognize from minute one that Tigo was on a fishing expedition and that what he was fishing for was an admission of murder. But Wiggins had something else on his mind, and as the detectives listened and ate— Ollie's banana was particularly tasty with a baloney sandwich smothered in mustard—they began to become more and more interested in what Wiggins was saying than in Gomez's inept attempts to wring a confession from him.

Since Gomez's voice was the only one they'd heard before now, they cleverly detected which of the two speakers was the one wearing the wire and doing the fishing, which easily enabled them to assign the other voice to Wiggins. And since both detectives were used to *reading* transcripts of tapes, they automatically began *listening* that way, labeling each voice as it came from the recorder. They were frankly getting bored stiff with Tigo's clumsy interrogation, expecting Wiggy to yell "The fuck you *doin,* man?" and shoot the silly jackass dead, when all at once Wiggy began talking about the computers he'd tapped into up at Wadsworth and Dodds. Ollie wondered what the man had been doing up there at his future publishing house, but Wiggy wasn't about to explain that. Instead, he began talking about what he'd found on the computers. Ollie looked at Carella. Carella shrugged.

WIGGY: All these files labeled with girls' names.

TIGO: Whut you mean names?

WIGGY: Rina and Bela and Ada and Gina and Tessie, and here's the one really got me . . . Diana.

TIGO: Like Princess Di?

WIGGY: Yeah, but it's Diamondback. It's code for Diamondback.

TIGO: How you know that, Wigg?

WIGGY: It was on the PC. Man left it wide open for me when I showed him the ugly. D-I-A-N-A. Right there in the name Diamondback, juss mixed up and turned all aroun, is all.

TIGO: If the man put a code in there, why he want to go *splain* it to you?

WIGGY: Nobody splained it to me, man. I doped it out all by myself. Same as how B-E-L-A is for Lebanon. And G-I-N-A is for Nicaragua.

TIGO: Why they want to do that for, Wigg?

WIGGY: To hide what they *doin* in those places. Man, don't get me wrong. I don't give a shit bout the mischief they into anyplace else. But when they buyin dope in Mexico and sellin it up here in Diamondback . . .

TIGO: We selling dope here, too, Wigg.

WIGGY: It ain't the same thing, man. They sellin dope up here for altogether different reasons. Man, they shittin on us black folk is what they doin.

TIGO: I just don't know, Wigg. I mean . . .

WIGGY: What is it you don't know? I just *tole* you what's happening, what is it you don't unnerstan?

There was a long silence on the tape. Ollie peeled another banana. He looked at Carella again. Carella shrugged again.

TIGO: You really think all this is true, huh? Cause to me . . .

WIGGY: Man, I was lookin straight in they computer! I seed all this stuff with my own eyes!

TIGO: It just sounds, you know, like science-

fiction, you know? This file named
Mothah you can't open cause you need a
password, an all this money floatin
aroun, and these people causin trouble
all over the world, an tryin'a fuck us
right here in Diamon'back, I mean,
man, it sounds like suppin you'd see in
a *movie,* you know what I'm sayin,
man?

WIGGY: It'd make a *good* movie, that's for damn
sure, but it's *true,* man! I got it from they
computer!

TIGO: That don't mean it couldn't of been
garbage in there.

WIGGY: The point is, whut we gonna *do* about it,
Tigo? I mean, these guys are messin
with our *people!*

There was another long silence.
"What the hell's he talkin about?" Ollie asked.
"Shhh," Carella said.

WIGGY: I think we should go to the police, tell
them the story.

"Good idea," Ollie said to the tape.
There was the sound of a phone being dialed.
"He's calling me," Ollie said.
"I figured."
They listened to Wiggy's end of the conversation.
Ollie opened a bag of potato chips. Carella finished

his glass of milk. There was the sound of the phone receiver clicking onto the cradle. Ollie dipped into the bag of chips.

WIGGY: Weeks is on the way.
TIGO: That's just great.
WIGGY: You maybe seed him aroun the streets. Fat Ollie Weeks. He's this big fat guy.

"Hey, watch it," Ollie said.

TIGO: You goan tell him you a drug dealer?
WIGGY: No, I don't have to tell him that.
TIGO: Then how come you *know* these people are sellin dope up here?
WIGGY: I coulda heard.
TIGO: *How* you coulda heard, Wigg? You goan tell the fuzz this man Hoskins come up here Christmastime, sold you a hundred keys of coke to distribute to li'l kiddies in the streets?

"Here we go," Ollie said.
"Shhh," Carella said again.

WIGGY: No. But I could . . .
TIGO: You goan tell him you shot this man Hoskins back of the head an dropped him in a garbage can? You goan do that, Wigg?

"Go for it, man," Ollie said.

WIGGY: I'm sayin' it don't seem right, what these mothahs are doin to our people.

TIGO: They's evil folk in this world, it *is* a shame.

WIGGY: You know what the name Nettie stans for?

TIGO: Nettie, you say?

WIGGY: N-E-T-T-I-E. You know what word that name is hidin' in?

TIGO: No, I has to admit I do not.

WIGGY: Counterfeit. That's the word. You search that word, you find Nettie lurkin in there. You double-click on her name, you transported straight to Nettie-land. You want to hear this, man, or you want to stay ignorant the ress of your life?

"This is all bullshit," Ollie said.

"Let's hear what the man . . ."

"He's hallucinatin," Ollie said.

"For Christ's *sake!*" Carella said, and snapped off the recorder, and shot Ollie a look. Ollie dug into the bag of chips again. Carella hit the rewind button. Ollie looked offended.

WIGGY: . . . hear this, man, or you want to stay ignorant the ress of your life? What these mothahs doin, they buyin fake money in I-ran. Hunnerd-dollar bills. So good you want to lick 'em right off the page. They buy 'em at a fifty-percent discount. That means they pays half a century for a C-note, they ahead of the game by fifty already, you dig, man?

TIGO: I'm listening.

WIGGY: They takes this fake money to Mexico, where they buy high quality shit with it. You member what that white dude was sellin us aroun Christmastime?

TIGO: The one you shot and thowed in the garbage can?

WIGGY: The hunnerd keys we tested, you member it?

TIGO: I member you shootin him. Why'd you kill that man, Wigg?

WIGGY: Point I'm makin is them hunnerd keys was purchased with funny money, man. They gettin *twice* the dope they should be gettin cause they payin for it with bills coss 'em ony *half* what they face value is. You see the scam they got goin here, man?

TIGO: Wish we'da thought of it, Wigg.

WIGGY: But *we* ain't gettin no fifty-percent payback here in Diamondback, man! We payin the full an honorable price for the shit. And they takin the big profit they make up here an usin it for financin all they activities all over the world, you know what I'm sayin? Man, we payin 'em good money, an they usin it to start some revolution in *Africa* some-place!

TIGO: Who you mean by *they,* man? Who's *they?*

WIGGY: I don't *know* who they is. But I'll bet you any amount of money it's right there in that folder marked *Mothah*. You fine the password to that folder, man, you on the way to trackin down *zackly* who these people are.

TIGO: Why you so keen on knowin that, man?

WIGGY: What's the matter with you, Teeg, you some kind of fool? They fuckin us six ways from the middle! You close Nettie and you double-click on Diana, you know what you fine in that Diamond-back file? You fine what the plan is for *us,* man. You see what they *really* doin up here, you see how this thing comes full circle.

TIGO: What is it they doin, Wigg? I'm sorry, but I don't see what . . .

WIGGY: They buildin a community of *dope* fiends, man. They keepin the nigger in his place so he can't work, he can't vote, he can't do a fuckin thing but shoot H in his arm or sniff coke up his nose! They turnin us into fuckin slaves all over again.

TIGO: Man, Wiggy.

WIGGY: Yeah, man, is right. That's why I called that fat hump cop. They got to know what's goin on here, Teeg. Somebody got to put a stop to it.

TIGO: One thing I don't get, Wigg.

WIGGY: What's that?

TIGO: These dudes in I-ran? The ones gettin paid *real* money for the fake stuff?

WIGGY: Who gives a shit about them, man? You unnerstan what I'm *sayin* here?

TIGO: I was juss wonderin what they *do* with that money, that's all.

The shots exploding from the recorder startled both detectives. Ollie actually dropped the bag of potato chips. Screams erupted over the ugly stutter of automatic gunfire. A woman's voice shouted, "The window!" There was the sound of glass breaking. Heavy breathing. More shots. Footsteps clanging on metal. The breathing harsher now. Yet more shots. More footsteps pounding. And then Carella's own voice came from the machine.

CARELLA: You know who did this to you? Who, Tigo? Can you tell me?

TIGO: Mother.
CARELLA: Your *mother* shot . . . ?
TIGO: Nettie.
CARELLA: Is that your mother's name?
TIGO: Diana.
CARELLA: I don't under . . .

There was more shooting.
Heavy breathing.

OLLIE: That's two, Steve.

"Who the fuck is Mother?" Ollie asked.

From where Svi Cohen stood center stage, he could see the vast enclosing arms of Clarendon Hall, from the orchestra level soaring upward to the first and second tiers, and the dress circle, and the front and rear balconies. A giant of a man himself, he felt dwarfed by the golden sweep of the most prestigious concert hall in the United States. It was here that Jascha Heifetz, a seventeen-year-old Russian violinist, made his explosive American debut in 1917. It was here—not a decade later—that a ten-year-old prodigy named Yehudi Menuhin stunned the world of classical music with a violin style that combined the elegance of Kreisler, the sonority of Elman, and the technique of Heifetz himself. Here, too, on this very stage, the great Russian pianist Svetlana Dyalovich had made her American debut. Svi stood staring out at the red-carpeted space, overwhelmed.

"So how does it look to you?" Arthur Rankin asked, beaming.

Rankin was the Philharmonic's conductor, a man in his sixties, a man who'd been playing violin since he was four years old and conducting since he was thirty, but in the presence of this thirty-seven-year-old genius from Tel Aviv, he was virtually awe-stricken.

"Wait till you hear the sound," he said.

"I can imagine," Svi said.

The orchestra was beginning to tune up.

Tonight's program would start with "La Gazza Ladra"—the "Thieving Magpie" overture from Rossini's *The Barber of Seville*. They would then play Mozart's no. 40 in G Minor to conclude the first half of the evening. There would be a twelve-minute intermission, and then Svi Cohen would take the stage. The orchestra had been rehearsing all of the pieces for the past week now, but this was the first time they would be playing the Mendelssohn E Minor with the Israeli violinist.

Rankin tapped his baton for silence.

"Gentlemen?" he said. "May I introduce our honored guest?"

• • •

The plan was a simple one.

They had been trained to believe that all good plans were simple ones.

Part of the seed money had been spent for false identity papers created for them by a master forger who'd been trained in Bucharest and who now lived in a small town upstate, where he sold antiques as a sideline. Passports, green cards, driver's licenses, social security cards, credit cards—all that anyone might need to move freely around the United States, or indeed around the world. From the stock of a Cadillac dealership in the state across the river, Nikmaddu—using the assumed name on his new driver's license—had purchased outright a black DeVille sedan. The car would be used in the attack tonight, and then driven to Florida, where it would be disposed of before all four men parted company. Akbar, Mahmoud, and Jassim would board separate flights to Zurich, Paris, and Frankfurt, and would then disperse to the far corners of the Arab world. Nikmaddu would leave first for Chicago, and then San Francisco, and finally Los Angeles. The attack here in this city would have put only a small dent in the cash he'd carried from home. Activities elsewhere in the United States required money, too. Money was what made the world of terrorism—or, as he preferred to call it, liberation—go round. Money was both the engine and the fuel.

At seven-forty-five tonight Akbar, wearing a chauffeur's uniform, would drive the Cadillac—

They called this luxurious car a Caddy, the Americans. They also used this word to describe the menial who carried a golfer's clubs. A strange country.

He would drive the Caddy, then, to the front door of Clarendon Hall. Jassim, barbered and bathed and manicured and groomed, well-tailored in a black business suit, carrying a man's handbag purchased at Gucci on Hall Avenue, would present his ticket and enter the hall. If he was asked to open the bag, which was highly unlikely, they would find in it only a package of cigarettes, a gold and enamel cigarette lighter also purchased at Gucci, a Coach leather wallet, and a paperback copy of *Catcher in the Rye*. It was not until later that Jassim would re-enter the hall carrying the armed bomb.

"Where will you be during the first part of the concert?" Nikmaddu asked.

Akbar, who had assembled the bomb, and who would be responsible for arming it before Jassim went back in, said, "I'll be parked just across the street."

"Wouldn't it be better to park directly outside?"

"It is forbidden to park in front of the hall. Or, in fact, anywhere on that side of the street. Most of the limo drivers park across the way or around the corner. Jassim knows where I'll be. We've run this through many times already."

Mahmoud looked at him skeptically.

"Half the taxicab and limousine drivers in this city are from the Middle East," Akbar said. "I will not arouse any suspicion. I will sit behind the wheel quietly, minding my own business, smoking a cigarette and waiting for my fat Jew employer to come out of the hall. Jassim and I will find each other, don't worry."

"You've got only twelve minutes to find each other," Mahmoud reminded them.

"I'll be watching for him to come out," Akbar said. "We'll have more than enough time, believe me."

"What time does the concert start?" Nikmaddu asked.

"It's supposed to begin at eight. Experience has taught me that it always starts some five or ten minutes later."

"And the intermission is when?"

"The Rossini overture can take anywhere between nine and eleven minutes and the Mozart symphony between twenty-five and thirty-five. On average, I would expect the first half of the concert to run some forty minutes. The intermission should start at around nine or a little bit after."

"Can you not be more precise?" Nikmaddu asked.

"I'm sorry," Akbar said. "Western music is not always precise. In any case, I'll arm the bomb when Jassim returns to the limousine. I'll place it in his bag, and he'll go back into the hall. You'd be surprised how long a time twelve minutes is."

"I hope so. I wouldn't want the bomb to explode while he's still outside on the sidewalk."

"No, that can't possibly happen. The intermission will end, let's say, at nine-fifteen. They will allow at most five minutes for everyone to get settled again. Let's say the Jew comes on stage at nine-twenty. The bomb will be set to explode at nine-thirty. Jassim will be long gone by then."

"Inshallah," Mahmoud said.

"Inshallah," the others repeated.

The men fell silent.

"The weather is supposed to be clear and cold tonight," Nikmaddu said at last.

"Good," Mahmoud said. "Then our drive to Florida should be trouble free."

"Someday, I would love to spend some time in Florida," Akbar said, almost wistfully.

The blonde Ollie had shot in the back was in a room on the sixth floor of Hoch Memorial. A male police officer was stationed outside the door to the room. The clock on the wall behind him read twelve-forty P.M. The blonde had plastic tubes trailing out of her nose. The blonde had lines running into her arm. Neither Carella nor Ollie felt the slightest bit of pity or compassion for her on this cold December afternoon at the end of the year.

"Want to tell us who you are?" Carella asked.

"I don't have to tell you anything," she said. "You're making a grave mistake here."

"You're the one who made the grave mistake," Ollie said.

"Three of them," Carella said.

The blonde smiled.

"What's your name?" he asked.

"I don't have to tell you that."

"You killed two civilians and tried to kill a police officer. Do you know what kind of trouble you're in here?"

"I'm not in any trouble at all."

"Two counts of Murder Two . . ."

"Another count of Attempted . . ."

"On our block, that's pretty serious," Ollie said.

"On my block, it's routine," she said.

"And where's that, Miss?"

"What's your name, Miss?"

"Where do you live?"

"How come you weren't carrying any identification?"

The blonde smiled again.

"You think this is pretty funny, don't you?" Ollie said. "Trying to kill a police officer."

"How about a police officer shooting me in the back?" she said. "Do you think *that's* funny?"

"Not as funny as it might have been if I'd killed you," Ollie said. "That really would've been comical."

"You think so, huh? Just wait, Mister."

"For what?" Ollie said.

"Just wait."

"What it is, you see, we don't like cops getting shot in this city."

"Then cops in this city should keep their noses out of other people's business."

"Which people are you talking about?"

"People with more important matters on their minds than two piss-ant dope dealers."

"Oh?" Carella said.

"Oh?" Ollie said.

"You knew they were dealing, huh?"

The blonde smiled.

"What else did you know about them?"

She shook her head.

"Did you know one of them killed a man named Jerry Hoskins?"

She kept smiling, shaking her head.

"Ever hear that name?"

"Jerry Hoskins?"

"Got himself shot on Christmas Eve by one of the guys *you* shot last night? Think there might be a connection?"

"Stop blowing smoke up my skirt," she said.

"Jerry Hoskins? Frank Holt?" Ollie said.

"One and the same person," Carella said.

"Sold Wiggins a hundred keys of coke on Christmas Eve . . ."

"Got paid for it with a bullet at the back of his head. Ever hear of him?"

"Jerry Hoskins?"

"Frank Holt?"

The blonde said nothing.

"Ever hear of a woman named Cass Ridley?" Ollie said.

"Cassandra Ridley?" Carella said.

"Flew a hundred keys of shit out of Mexico for Jerry Hoskins. Ever hear of *her?*"

"I'm not saying anything until my people contact you."

"Oh? Your people? Who are these people?"

"You'll find out."

"You got friends in high places?" Ollie asked.

"The Mayor's office?"

"The Governor's mansion?"

"The White House?"

"Go ahead, laugh," she said.

"Nobody's laughing," Ollie said. "What it looks like is you knew Walter Wiggins was dealing drugs, and maybe you also knew Hoskins was in the same business . . ."

"Keep blowing smoke," she said.

"Did you also know Cass Ridley, who flew the shit up from Mexico?"

"Did you happen to take a bottle of champagne to her apartment?"

"Did you and another fine lady walk her over to the zoo?"

"You and another blond lady?"

"Both of you wearing black?"

"We got a doorman just *itching* to identify you."

"Keep blowing, I'm beginning to enjoy it."

"I wonder how you'll enjoy your date with the D.A."

"You've got a date with my people," she said. "But you don't seem to . . ."

"We're dying to meet them," Carella said.

"Tell us who they are, we'll go pay them a visit."

"Maybe they can explain how come you killed Wiggins who killed Hoskins who hired Ridley to fly dope for him."

"Maybe they can explain how Ridley ended up in that lion's cage," Ollie said.

"No ID on her," Carella said.

"Maybe your people can explain all that."

"Maybe my people can have you both walking beats tomorrow morning."

"Oooo," Carella said. "A threat, Ollie."

"Oooo," Ollie said.

There was nothing he liked better than a perp trying to pull rank. Especially when the perp had tried to gun down a cop.

"You think these important people you know'll come riding to the rescue, is that it?" he said.

"You don't know what you're messing with here."

"Gee, I thought we were messing with an Attempted Murder One and a pair of Murder Twos."

"You'd never make it to trial. They'll step on you like a bug."

"Who? Your important people in high places?"

The blonde smiled.

Ollie just loved it when they smiled.

"If your friends take you out of here, they'll be harboring a fugitive," he said. "That's called Hindering Prosecution in the first degree, Section 205.65 of the Penal Law. Want to hear it?"

"Shove it up your ass," the blonde said.

"Nice talk on the lady," Ollie said. "Hindering prosecution is rendering criminal assistance to a person who's committed a class-A felony. Murder Two is a class-A felony. So's Attempted Murder One. If your friends whisk you out of here, they'll be staring at a seven-year max in the slammer. Maybe that's why they're not here yet, huh?"

"All in good time," the blonde said.

"Oh sure, I hear them thundering down the hallway right this minute."

The blonde actually cocked her head toward the door.

"But maybe not," Ollie said. "Ballistics is checking the slugs that killed the two dealers. If they match the ones we test-fire from that cannon you were carrying . . ."

"Save it. I'm not interested."

"Well, let me tell you what else we've got," Carella said. "It might change your mind."

"I got shot last night. I'm tired. Goodbye, Mr. Detective."

"We've got one of the guys you killed wearing a wire. We've got the other guy you killed *talking* on that wire. Saying a lot of interesting things about a company called Wadsworth and Dodds, ever hear of them?"

"No."

"W&D?"

"No."

"Witches and Dragons?" Carella said. "Is that a glimmer I see in your eye? How about Mother? Do you know who Mother is?"

The blonde said nothing.

"Ever see that name on a W&D computer?"

The blonde was still silent.

"Ever hear that name anyplace?"

"Why don't you go home, Mr. Detective?"

"People keep telling me to go home," Carella said to Ollie.

"Maybe you should," Ollie said.

"Yeah, but gee, I'd like to finish this, you know?"

"So finish it."

"Here's where we're coming from, Miss," Carella said, turning back to the bed. "A person is guilty of Murder in the First Degree when the intended victim is a police officer who at the time of the killing is engaged in the course of performing his official duties, quote, unquote, Section 125.27 of the state's Penal Law. You tried to kill a police officer last night, honey. *Me. Would* have killed me, in fact, if another police officer—Detective Oliver Wendell Weeks here—hadn't expediently intervened. That makes the crime *Attempt* to Commit Murder, which in this case is an A-1 felony. Add to that the *actual* murders of both Tito Alberico Gomez and Walter Kennedy Wiggins, and you're looking at twenty-five years to life, three times over. That comes to seventy-five years in the slammer. You'll be a hundred years old when you get out."

"A hundred and five," the blonde said.

"That's if we don't get a positive ID from the doorman."

"What doorman?"

"The one who let you in Cass Ridley's apartment building. Where you stuck an ice pick in her forehead. You can add another twenty-five for that one."

"You think so? *I* think I'll be out of here before you jerks leave the building."

"You got shot when?" Ollie said. "Seven, seven-thirty last night? You know what time it is now? Almost one o'clock the next day. Has anyone been here to see you? Has anyone even called you? Where's the cavalry, sweetheart? They're riding into the sunset, that's where they are, and leaving you to take the fall. But, hey, be loyal. Seventy-five years behind bars may seem better to you than anything we've got to offer."

The blonde was looking at him.

Ollie figured he had her attention.

"Want to hear it?"

"No. I want to go to sleep."

"Okay, go to sleep. I guess we'll have to charge her on all three counts, Steve."

"Maybe four if we get lucky with the doorman," Carella said. "Too bad she can't help us get our search warrant, huh?"

"A crying shame," Ollie said.

"Well, what are you gonna do?" Carella said, and shrugged. "Let's go home."

"So long, Miss," Ollie said, and both detectives started out of the room.

"What do you mean?" the blonde asked.

They turned back to the bed.

"About a search warrant?" she said.

"Let me be honest with you, okay?" Ollie said, which was the last thing he wished to be with her. "We know you won't admit you're a hitter for W&D because that would make this Murder for Hire, and that means the Valium cocktail if you're convicted."

"The death penalty," Carella explained. "Lethal injection."

"I hear it's actually pleasant," Ollie said, and smiled. "But we know you won't admit that somebody *paid* you for offing the redhead and the two Negroes, so all we've really got for sure are the pair of Twos and the One-Ten. Which is enough to put you away for seventy-five, I might remind you, ah yes, if that's the route you choose to take."

"Or," Carella said.

"Or," Ollie agreed, and nodded.

"Or *what?* Let me hear it."

"To the point, I like that in a woman," Ollie said. "Do you know what's on any of the W&D computers?"

"Let's say I *can* know what's on them if I *need* to know what's on them."

"Let's say you *need* to know what's on them if you want to deal here," Ollie said.

"But of course we can't speak for the D.A.," Carella said.

"Of course not. But *if* the lady wants to deal, she would have to tell us she knows what's on those computers."

"You're both so full of shit," she said. "Tell me what you want me to say."

"We want you to say that evidence of a crime exists on W&D's computers."

"What crime?"

"From what we understand, the Criminal Sale of Controlled Substances."

"In the first degree," Carella said.

"Section 220.43."

"An A-1 felony."

"Twenty-five to life upstate."

"Heavy," Carella said.

"That's the crime," Ollie said. "From what we understand."

"And how do you happen to understand this?"

"A good question," Ollie said. "We've got a tape, remember?"

"We want you to listen to that tape," Carella said.

"Tell us it's accurate . . ."

". . . so we can get a search warrant on probable cause."

"Reliable information from a cooperative witness and all that," Ollie said.

"*If* I cooperate," the blonde said.

"Well, that's entirely up to you, m'little chick-adee, ah yes."

"What do I get in return?"

"We'll drop the One-Ten," Ollie said. "That okay with you, Steve? I mean, you're the one she tried to kill."

"That's fine with me, if it's okay with the D.A."

"Yeah, well, it's not fine with me," the blonde said.

"Then you tell us."

"Drop everything."

"We can't do that."

"Oh, yes you can. I walk, you get the big boys."

"Well, maybe we can reduce the murder counts to manslaughter."

"Well, maybe I don't think that's good enough, either, okay?"

"Two counts of Manslaughter One? That's *very* good," Ollie said. "And we'll drop the Attempted, don't forget."

"Sorry, boys."

"Somewhere between five and twenty-five on each?" Carella said. "That's a good deal. Don't you think that's a good deal, Ollie?"

"I do indeed. What do you say, Miss?"

"I say I want five, not twenty-five."

Carella pretended to be thinking this over. He looked at Ollie. Ollie sighed.

"Okay, five," Carella said.

"And you run the sentences concurrently," the blonde said.

"No, we can't do that," Carella said. "That'd come to only two and a half on each hit."

"Come on, honey, be realistic," Ollie said.

"The guys who got whacked were a pair of shits," the blonde said. "I did society a favor."

"Still, just five *concurrently?*" Carella said.

"For a *double hit?*" Ollie said.

"That's all they're worth," the blonde said.

"Let me call the D.A.," Carella said. "Play the tape for her, Ollie."

12.

They interrogated Richard Halloway at ten minutes to five that Saturday afternoon. He was wearing gray flannel slacks, a blue blazer, a blue button-down shirt, and a green bow tie printed with little red prancing deer. He had waived his right to an attorney, and so there were only four people in the interrogation room—Halloway himself, Detectives Carella and Weeks, and Detective-Lieutenant Byrnes—all of them sitting around the long cigarette-scarred table, drinking coffee. Halloway seemed completely relaxed and supremely self-assured.

"Mr. Halloway," Carella said, "when we entered the offices of Wadsworth and Dodds this afternoon at three-thirty, were you packing to move?"

"Is it a crime to move one's offices?" Halloway asked.

"Only if you're moving to conceal evidence of a crime."

"I see. And what crime was I supposed to have been concealing?"

"We have a warrant to open your computers, Mr. Halloway."

"So open them," Halloway said, and smiled, and added, "If you can."

"Oh, we will."

"Good luck."

"We think we might find some interesting stuff on your database."

"If you find sales figures interesting."

"Tell me about that database, okay?"

"Sure. Which book?"

"A folder called Witches and Dragons."

"I'm not familiar with that title. How about *Diagnostic and Statistical Manual of . . . ?*"

"How about a file named Diana?"

"Don't know that title, either."

"Or Em. Interesting file, Em. Seems to list all the drug deals your firm has made in Mexico over the past two years. Dates, locations, number of kilos, purchase prices, etcetera, etcetera, the whole megillah."

"I'm more familiar with *Practical Classroom Chemistry* by Guthrie Frane. I know we have a file on that."

"Do you have a file called Nettie?"

"Not to my knowledge."

"The Feds might be interested in that one. We think Nettie stands for 'counterfeiting.' We think you've been buying counterfeit money in Iran and using it to finance your various drug transactions."

"My, my, all this crime in such a small publishing house."

"We think your database will provide evidence of those crimes. And other interesting activities."

"Assuming, of course, that you can get into our computers."

"I think we can."

"Well, you can certainly try."

"Our nerds are very determined."

"I'm sure they are," Halloway said, and finished his coffee, and stood up, and smiled. "Well, I have things to do," he said, "as I'm sure you do, too. So let's not waste any more time here, hmm? I know you believe . . ."

"You're under arrest here, Mr. Halloway," Byrnes said. "Please don't forget that."

"Perhaps *you* should forget exactly that," Halloway said. "Believe me, you're not going to pick up any marbles this time. Not this time, boys. So, if there's nothing further . . ."

"Sit down," Byrnes said.

Halloway smiled. But he sat.

"We're charging you with the criminal sale of controlled substances in the first degree," Byrnes said. "That's Section 220.43 of the Penal Law, an A-1 felony punishable by a term of twenty-five years to life. We've got twenty-four hours to arraign you before McNabb-Mallory kicks in. That means you'll be before a criminal court judge early tomorrow morning. We'll ask for sky-high bail, you're an international drug dealer. If he goes along with that, we'll have six days to crack your goddamn computers and present our case to a grand jury. Any questions?"

Halloway was still smiling.

"Let me give you some advice," he said. "You should have listened to the Secret Service when they told you to back off, but you didn't. So here we are, at an awkward juncture that could have been avoided. I certainly shouldn't be here, but neither should you. Which is why I'm suggesting you listen to me now." He looked at his watch. "When I walk out of here in five minutes, you will forget you ever saw me, you will forget a woman named Cass Ridley met a horrible fate in the zoo's Lion Habitat, you will forget . . ."

"What are you, a hypnotist?" Ollie said.

"Allow me to finish, Detective Weeks. I am advising you to put all of this behind you. Forget Jerry Hoskins was murdered, forget that two black drug dealers in Diamondback were subsequently killed, forget everything that's happened since December twenty-third, forget you ever woke *up* that morning. There are bad people in this world, boys. Pursuing this any further . . ."

"People like you," Carella said, nodding.

"No, you've got it backwards. I'm one of the *good* guys. I'm talking about people who are *terrorists*. People who consider us the Great Satan. People who wish us nothing but harm. These people all believe in the same cause. And that cause is to drive Americans out of the Arab world."

His tone had changed all at once, his voice sounding suddenly portentous and, to tell the truth, somewhat frightening.

"There's a vast network of individual terrorist cells out there," he said, "take my word for it. Three or four dedicated individuals in each cell, that's all it takes to do considerable mischief. Anonymous little *gangs,* if you will, who get their orders and their financing from the top, and then use their own judgment in executing those orders. Makes it enormously difficult to zero in on them, no less stop them. Why do you think those two men who bombed the *Cole* still can't be traced back to bin Laden? Why do you think . . . ?"

"What's any of this got to do with you buying and selling dope?" Ollie said.

"No one has yet produced any evidence to that effect," Halloway said. "Once I walk through that door . . ."

"You're not walking through any door," Byrnes said. "You're going straight to a detention cell downstairs."

"That would be inadvisable."

"Who the fuck do you think you are?" Ollie asked. "The CIA?"

Halloway smiled.

"Cause you want my opinion, there *ain't* no CIA. Any outfit so fuckin stupid has got to be a cover for our *real* intelligence agency."

"I'll have to remember that one," Halloway said, and actually laughed. "No CIA, that's very funny. On the other hand, *you* might wish to consider the possibility that the CIA, *if* it exists, has adopted the same techniques as the people they're fighting. If there *is* a CIA—and perhaps you're right, perhaps there isn't—but on the slight offchance that there *might* be, then perhaps they've splintered into hundreds of little *counter*-terrorist cells all over the globe. Little self-reliant units that take orders from the top and carry them out autonomously. Authorized roving bands of brothers, you might say—sisters, too, if you wish to be politically correct. Legitimate loose cannons. And if this is actually so, then perhaps you stepped . . ."

"Authorized by *who?*" Ollie said.

"Well, if there *is* a CIA, then the authorization comes directly from the President or the National Security Council, doesn't it?" He smiled again. Looked at his watch again. "Let's say you stepped in the way of a rolling cannon on a tilting deck, boys. You stumbled into something far more vital to the interests of the United States than a bunch of dumb flatfoots, believe me. You should have known enough to step aside, boys. Instead, you stepped in shit. Wipe off your shoes and go home."

"Somebody else telling us to go home," Carella said.

"I'm telling you it's possible to get chewed to shreds by lions," Halloway said.

"He's saying don't go in the lion's cage tonight," Ollie said.

"For the lions are ferocious and they bite," Carella said.

"Well, Mr. Halloway," Byrnes said, and stabbed at a button on his intercom, "I appreciate your advice, truly. But you see we might feel derelict in our duty if we just let you walk out of here. So with the permission of the President and the National . . ."

"Sir?" a voice said.

"I'll need an officer to take a prisoner down," Byrnes said.

"I'll send someone forthwith, sir."

"Thanks," Byrnes said, and clicked off.

"I want to warn you again not to do this," Halloway said. "Don't open a can of peas that might explode in your face. Don't threaten our very existence, our sacred undertaking, our . . ."

"Gee, sacred," Ollie said.

"Because if you do, if you destroy everything we've been trying to accomplish, if you open our files to public scrut . . ."

"I thought your computers were sacred, too," Ollie said.

The door to Byrnes's office opened.

"Sir?" a uniformed officer said.

"Maggie, find a cell downstairs for this gentleman, will you?" He turned to Halloway. "Do we have to cuff you?" he asked.

"Only lions bite," Halloway said, and smiled

thinly. "You'll never even get me arraigned, I promise you. You've got to be kidding here. The Commissioner will come down on you so hard you'll wish you lived on Mars. You think we'll let a Mickey Mouse detective squad in the asshole of the universe jeopardize everything we've been working for? Who'd stop those bastards *then,* can you tell me? Who'd stop them from poisoning our reservoirs or blowing up our trains? Who'd stop them from planting bombs in day care centers or baseball parks? Who'd stop them from destroying this land of ours? This *world* of ours? This *free* world of ours? You? Are you the ones who'll save us? Don't make me laugh! You should get on your hands and knees and praise God we exist! Because if it weren't for us, there'd be nobody! Nobody at all! They'd make it impossible to walk the streets! They'd blow up your babies in their cribs! Without us, who the hell on earth would even *try* to stop them? I'm asking you. *Who?"*

Will Struthers helped Antonia out of the taxi in front of Clarendon Hall and looked up at the falling snow. The snow added a somewhat festive air to the evening. In a city of strangers, people were actually smiling at each other as they entered the old limestone building. Will looked up at the television monitors spaced high on the walls everywhere around the lobby, all of them showing the stage inside. "For the benefit of latecomers," Antonia explained, which Will didn't quite understand, but he followed her as she handed their tickets to a man standing at one of the entrance doors to the hall itself. Together, they stepped into the vast space, all red and gold and magnificent, glittering like an outsized Christmas present left by Santa himself. Will had never seen anything so splendiferous in his life. Not even in Texas.

The short, slight man who stepped out of the black Cadillac DeVille was wearing a black overcoat with a mink collar. The trousers of a black suit showed below the bottom edge of the coat. He was wearing a black homburg and highly polished black shoes. Hanging from a strap over his left shoulder was a man's black leather handbag. The hat, the coat's collar, the coat's shoulders became immediately dusted with falling snow. The tinted glass window of the limo slid down silently. The man leaned into it and gave the driver some instructions in English. The driver answered in English and then the window slid up again, and the limo pulled away from the curb.

Standing in the falling snow on the sidewalk outside Clarendon Hall, Jassim Saiyed reached into the handbag, removed from it a package of Marlboro cigarettes, shook one free, and lighted it. He glanced at his wristwatch. It was fifteen minutes to eight. Puffing calmly on his cigarette, Jassim watched the crowd of smiling Americans entering the building.

They took their seats in row G, seven rows back from the stage, numbers 2 and 4 on the aisle.

"Good, huh?" Antonia said, grinning. "One of my best customers plays oboe with the orchestra. This was his Christmas present to me."

Will was thinking that when he and Antonia became millionaires, they would come to places like this all the time, never mind free handouts from anybody. There was a sense of excitement and anticipation in this opulent place, resounding now with the repeated sounds of strings and horns tuning up. Leafing through the program, he noticed that one of the pieces they'd be playing tonight was something called "La Gazza Ladra," which he saw was translated as "The Thieving Magpie."

He showed this to Antonia, and then whispered, "I hope this isn't anything personal."

Antonia laughed.

A hush fell over the audience.

The concert was about to begin.

Jassim looked at his wristwatch.

If Akbar's calculations were correct, the intermission would begin at approximately nine o'clock. Jassim would go up the aisle, and out into the lobby, and hence into the street, where Akbar would be waiting in the Cadillac. He would arm the bomb's timing device, and Jassim would come back into the hall, and take his seat again. Several moments later, after the Jew had started playing, Jassim would rise again from his seat, apparently on his way to the men's room, leaving behind him his hat, his coat, and the bag containing the bomb. At precisely nine-thirty, the bomb would explode.

Jassim wondered why he felt so calm.

Will was bored to death.

The kind of music he liked best was what he heard back home in Texas. Songs about cowboys. Songs about women with broken hearts. Songs about true-blue hound dogs. The orchestra up on the stage there sounded like it was practicing.

He could hardly wait for the intermission.

Terror was the only thought on Jassim's mind.

Strike terror into their hearts.

Deliver fatal blows all over the world.

He rose the moment the lights came up, placed his coat and his hat on the seat, and began walking swiftly toward the back of the hall. His watch read exactly three minutes past nine. He wanted to be back in his seat again by nine-fifteen, when the intermission would end. The aisle was thronged with concert-goers making their way to the rest rooms or the street outside. Patiently, Jassim milled along with them, but his heart was pounding inside his chest. He tried not to look at his watch again until he reached the lobby outside.

Nine-oh-six.

He raced through the lobby and out onto the sidewalk.

He looked across the street.

The Cadillac was parked exactly where Akbar said it would be.

But a policeman in a black rain slicker was standing outside the door on the driver's side.

There was in the lobby a palpable air of anticipation. The first part of the concert had been agreeable enough, but this glittery crowd was not here for the Rossini or the Mozart. In fact, they were not even here for the Mendelssohn. They were here for the man who would be playing the Mendelssohn. The chatter was about Christmas gifts received and exchanged, and plans for tomorrow night's celebration, and the weather and the market and the latest war abroad, but the people here in the lobby or smoking in the falling snow on the sidewalk outside were merely trying to conceal their excitement over the imminent appearance of the Israeli violinist. Like children careful not to wish for sunshine for fear it might rain upon their circus, they dared not even breathe his name lest he vanish somehow in a puff of smoke, disappointing their expectations.

The policeman stood leaning into the open window on the driver's side of the Cadillac, a massive man in a slippery black coat, the snow falling everywhere around him. Akbar was handing documents to him. The policeman was examining the documents. Akbar was smiling at him politely. The snow kept falling.

Jassim looked at his watch.

The television monitors spaced around the lobby showed only an empty stage now, its lights dimmed. Will kept hoping they'd show a football game or something.

"Are you enjoying it so far?" Antonia asked.

"Oh yes indeed," he said.

So far, it was putting him to sleep.

"So far, I love it," he said.

"Just wait," she said. "The real fireworks won't begin till the Israeli starts playing."

The policeman did not walk away from the Cadillac until fourteen minutes past nine. Dodging heavy traffic on the street, Jassim ran across to it, and yanked open the rear door on the curb side. Slamming into the car, he whispered, "What happened? What did he want?"

"Profiling!" Akbar shouted.

"What?"

"Profiling, *profiling,* never mind, give me the fucking *bag!"*

Jassim handed him the bag. He looked at his watch and then glanced immediately over his shoulder through the rear window. The intermission would end in less than a minute; the sidewalk outside Clarendon Hall was rapidly clearing. In the front seat, Akbar was working on the timing device. Jassim could hear his heavy breathing, could see perspiration beading on his forehead, could hear as well the ticking of the clock to which Akbar was wiring the detonator. He waited. His palms were sweating. He looked back over his shoulder again. The sidewalk was clear now. He caught his breath. Waited. Kept waiting. The windows of the car were beginning to fog with their exhaled breaths. It seemed to Jassim that he could hear the beating of his own heart in the steamy darkness of the vehicle. At last, he heard a faint click. The bomb was armed, the timer and detonator wires securely fastened to the two taped pipes. Akbar eased the device into the bag. He closed the flap, snapped the bag shut.

Jassim looked at his watch.

The time was twenty minutes past nine.

The intermission had ended five minutes ago.

But he still had ten minutes to get back to his

seat, plant the bomb, and get out of the hall before it
went off. He stepped out onto the sidewalk and ran
across the street to the lobby entrance doors. The
lobby was empty. The huge ornate brass clock over
the center entrance doors read nine-twenty-one.
There was violin music coming from within the
hall. The second part of the concert had already
begun. On all the television monitors circling the
lobby, a miniature Svi Cohen was standing before
the orchestra, violin under his chin, head bent as if
in prayer, deeply engrossed in his playing. Jassim
noticed that the Jew held the fiddle in his unclean
hand. He was reaching for the brass handle on the
door nearest him when a man wearing a gray uniform said, "I'm sorry, sir."

Jassim turned to him, puzzled.

"I can't let you in until the first movement is
over."

Jassim blinked.

"It started three minutes ago, sir. I'm sorry, those
are my orders."

The time was nine-twenty-two.

The Mendelssohn concerto had started at nine-
nineteen, and the bomb was set to detonate at nine-
thirty.

Will was wondering how long he'd have to sit here.
He was thinking that maybe him and Antonia could
go for a bite to eat after this fiddle player did his

thing, there seemed to be a nice Italian restaurant right across the avenue.

He was also wondering if anybody had ever tried to steal instruments from this place. Was there a room where they stored tubas and trombones and such? Or did all those musicians up there have their own instruments? He guessed maybe they did. Besides, he had to stop thinking like a thief. If Antonia went along with his scheme, he would never in his lifetime have to commit another burglary.

But, man, was *this* boring!

Jassim looked at his watch again.

It was now nine-twenty-four.

The first movement of Mendelssohn's accursed violin concerto was about twelve and a half minutes long. The Jew had started playing it at nineteen minutes past nine, which meant he would end the first movement at a bit past nine-thirty-one, perhaps later, nine-thirty-three, even nine-thirty-four, depending on how much artistic license he took with the piece. Jassim could not wait until any of those times because the bomb was set to go off at nine-thirty, which meant that unless he went into the hall, it would explode right here in the lobby in six minutes.

He took a deep breath.

"Hey!" the guard shouted, but he was too late.

Jassim had thrown open one of the doors and was

already running down the aisle on the right hand side of the hall.

Will turned to look up the aisle when he heard somebody screaming. The person screaming was a short dark man carrying a handbag, holding it by the straps and beginning to twirl it over his head as he ran toward the stage, screaming. Will didn't know what the man was screaming because it was in a foreign language, but whatever it was, there was enormous rage in the words. As the man rapidly approached the stage where the Israeli was playing, he almost looked like an undersized David twirling a slingshot to hurl a stone at a giant Goliath.

Will got to his feet the moment he realized this was close to what the little man intended.

"Hey! What the hell you doing?" he shouted, and threw himself at the man, intending to tackle him, but missing by a hair. He stumbled forward, off balance, as the man stopped some three feet from the stage and shouted something else in the same foreign language.

Will didn't know quite why he hurled himself at the man again. Perhaps he was simply trying to impress Antonia, who sat in the seventh row, watching him with her mouth agape and her eyes wide. Perhaps he was remembering that the Khmer Rouge who'd tortured him had also spoken a language he couldn't understand. Whatever the reason, he threw himself into the air again just as the man released his grip on the handbag's straps. The Israeli tried to deflect the missile coming at him, raising the violin by its slender neck, simultaneously stepping aside to his right.

In that instant, Will landed on the man's back.

In the next instant, the bag exploded.

13.

New Year's Eve dawned bright and clear and piercingly cold. Something had gone wrong with Hoch Memorial's heating system during the night, and while technicians fiddled with thermostats and nozzles and valves, nurses ran around wearing sweaters or even coats over their starched white uniforms.

A multitude of people had drifted into Will's room at all hours of the night, there to take his temperature or his blood pressure, to change the dressings on his face and his hands, to offer him medication and the sort of tender loving care a wounded individual deserved. When he heard voices outside the door to his room, he thought it might be more nurses coming in to change the sheets or the dressings or the bags hanging by the bed, but instead it was just someone asking a nurse if it was okay for him to go in and talk to the patient.

The man who entered his room looked a lot like Detective Stephen Louis Carella.

"Hey, hi," Will said. "What're *you* doing here?"

Carella had just supervised the orderly discharge

MONEY, MONEY, MONEY   371

and transfer of one Anna DiPalumbo—which
turned out to be the blond shooter's true and honorable name—from Hoch Memorial to the hospital
wing at the Women's House of Detention downtown, but he didn't offer this information to Will because discussing an informant with a person who
was a known felon was simply stupid and might
come back to haunt him later on. If Halloway's
threats were at all realistic, the arraignment later
this morning might be sent south even without any
further help, but it didn't hurt to err on the side of
caution, as the sage once remarked.

"I had some business here," Carella said, which
was true enough. "How are you doing?"

"Well, okay, I guess," Will said. "A lot better than
some of the others, that's for sure."

The newspapers this morning had reported that
the Israeli violinist, Svi Cohen, had been killed in
what was cautiously being called "a supposed terrorist bombing" at Clarendon Hall. Six musicians
in the string section had also been killed. Plus eight
concert-goers sitting in the first two rows. Plus the
unidentified bomber himself. Carella didn't think
Halloway's case would be helped by the fact that the
person who'd tried to stop the bomber was a professional burglar and not one of W&D's own elite band
of brothers, as he'd called them, or sisters if you included Anna DiPalumbo, who was now on her way
downtown in an ambulance, and whom Carella
never cared to meet again on any snow-covered
street anywhere in the world, thank you. But where

were you when we needed you, Mr. Halloway?
When push came to shove last night, where were all
your knights in shining armor? The only hero last
night had been little ole Wilbur Struthers here, sitting up in bed now and grinning like a kid on
Christmas Day.

"Your picture's on the front page of two newspapers, did you know that?" Carella said.

"Yeah, I saw them. I was on TV, too, early this
morning. They came here to my hospital room, can
you believe it? I guess it was because of the book
deal."

"What book deal?" Carella asked.

"Man from a publisher here in the city came to
see me, offered me a whole bunch of money for my
life story. Not as much as they gave Hillary, but a
goodly sum of money anyhow. I figured I ought to
take it."

"Are you free to say how *much* money?" Carella
asked.

"A million-five," Will said.

"That's a goodly sum of money, all right," Carella
said.

"I guess there's more than one way to make a
killing, after all, huh?"

"I guess so," Carella said.

He stopped at his mother's house on the way home.

The front walk had been shoveled clean, he wondered who had shoveled it for her. He rang the door-

bell, and heard chimes sounding inside, and then her voice calling, "Just a minute." He waited.

When she opened the door, he almost burst into tears.

He had seen her only two days ago, but she seemed so suddenly old all at once.

He took her in his arms.

They hugged.

"Are you okay, son?" his mother asked.

"I'm fine, Mom."

"I love you, Steve," she said.

"I love you, too, Mom."

They sat at the kitchen table the way they used to when he was a boy eating breakfast before heading off to school, sat there now drinking coffee, and he told her he'd just come from an arraignment on what was going to shape up as a very difficult case, but at least they'd got past the first two hurdles. It was a miracle they'd managed to get the guy arraigned at all, and whereas they were hoping at best for bail in the millions, the judge had denied bail altogether, which was very good for their side. He told her all this sitting at the kitchen table, the way he used to sit there after school when he was a kid, drinking his milk and telling her everything that had happened that day.

She asked him what he and Teddy would be doing tonight, and he told her they'd be staying home with the kids, before you knew it Mark and April would be old enough to go to New Year's Eve parties on their own, might as well enjoy the few years they still had left with them. His mother asked him if Teddy would be making lentils for the new year, it was good luck to serve cold lentils when the clock struck twelve, and he told her he remembered how she used to do that when he was a boy . . .

"Well, I still do it," his mother said.

"I know, Mom. I'll tell Teddy."

"Tell her," his mother said. "It's good luck, really."

They both fell suddenly silent.

He could hear the clock ticking in the living room.

He remembered his father winding that clock every Sunday night.

"Well," he said, and there was nothing left to say except that he was sorry.

"I love you, Mom," he said. "If you want to get married, I'll lead you down the aisle. Angela, too, I love you both, I'm sorry I behaved like a shit. I think maybe it was the lion, I think Ange was right, I think that lion scrambled my brains. But there are no more lions now, I'm okay now, I promise you. I'm cool with it, really. I love you both, I'm sorry, life's too damn short, I love you."

They hugged again.

At the front door, she reminded him that the lentils had to be served at midnight, not before.

"For luck in the new year," she said.

"I'll remember," he said.

"Good luck with your case," she said.

"Thanks, Mom."

He was starting for the car when he turned to her and said, "Mom?"

She was just about to close the door.

"Mom?" he said again.

"Yes, son?"

"Say hello to . . . uh . . . Luigi for me, okay?"

"Yes, son," she said. "I'll say hello."

"Don't forget now, okay?"

"I won't forget."

"Happy New Year, Mom."

"Happy New Year, Steve."

He waved, and nodded, and then turned and walked swiftly to where he'd parked the car.

Bad Money
a novel by
Oliver Wendell Weeks

It was a dark and stormy night.

Detective/First Grade Oswald Wesley Watts wasn't overly fond of this section of the city because a lot of Negroes lived here, and they could infrequently be dangerous. On the other hand, "Big Ozzie Watts" as he was affectionately known to the residents of Rubytown,

was here on an errand of
mercy.

An evil individual was
using government funds to
enslave these oppressed
folk, just the way the
British had done in Japan,
turning the entire
populace into a nation of
junkies before the Opium
War put an end to <u>that</u>
little gambit. Someone in
this building was involved
in the purchase and
recycling of narcotics
like cocaine. In police
work, this illicit drug
was called a "controlled
substance." It was sold in
what was known as "keys,"
which was an underworld
expression for
"kilograms." A kilogram
was 2.2 pounds. "Big
Ozzie" knew all this
valuable information
because he had been a
highly decorated (for
bravery) law enforcement
officer for a good many
years now.

Tall and handsome, broad of shoulder and wide of chest, slender of waist and fleet of foot, Detective "Big Ozzie" Watts, pistol in hand (a nine-millimeter semi-automatic Glock, by the way), boldly climbed the steps to the fourth floor of the reeking tenement and knocked on the door to apartment 4C. The sound of music came from somewhere inside the apartment. Its noisome beat filled the hallway tremblingly. He heard the stammering click of high-heeled shoes approaching the door.

The woman who opened the door was a very gorgeous twenty-seven-year-old blonde, thirty-six, twenty-two, thirty-four, wearing a long green gown slit up the side to show her extremely curvaceous thigh. Leaning against the door jamb, the gown's quite low neckline exposed

fulsome white creamy
breasts. She smiled
dazzlingly out into the
hall.

"Hello, Detective
Watts," she exclaimed.

"So, Mother," he
retorted. "We meet again."

ED McBAIN is the only American ever to receive the Diamond Dagger, the British Crime Writers Association's highest award. He also holds the Mystery Writers of America's prestigious Grand Master Award. His most recent 87th Precinct novel was **The Last Dance.** Under his own name—Evan Hunter—his writing career has spanned almost five decades, from his first novel, **The Blackboard Jungle,** in 1954, to the screenplay for Alfred Hitchcock's **The Birds,** to **Candyland,** his most recent novel, written in tandem with his alter ego, Ed McBain.

Damage Noted *Stains*